THE SOUL KEEPER'S ASSISTANT

Tawnya Torres

For Jon, Remi, and Randy. The most
beautiful souls.
I hope to see you in the next life.

CHAPTER ONE

IT ALL STARTED WITH A PROMISE

Mia's mother married my father last year. I don't know why. He's an asshole. My dad makes good money at the law firm, though. That's the only reason I can think of that explains why a sweet woman like Koharu would marry someone like Joseph. She is a kind person and lets my dad boss her around. He ignores Mia. Of course, he takes his anger out on me.

We live in a pleasant neighborhood. It's lined with tulips. All the houses are big and shades of gray or white. Our house is two stories with a hot tub. On the outside, we're the perfect family. But we're not. It's horrible having dinner together every night. It's worse on weekends when we have to eat breakfast together, too. The entire experience is tense. My father spends the hour screaming into his phone. He doesn't even bother to acknowledge his new wife or stepdaughter during our meals most of the time.

I turned fifteen this month. Mia is thirteen. We go to the same middle school a couple of blocks away. She's very small. Barely five feet tall. A petite girl with wavy black hair that hangs down her back. There's so much of it. Shiny bangs cover her face. She hides in it. The wind picks up and black strands wrap around her like a sweater. My dad thinks it's gross for how long it is, but I like it.

My stepsister is an artist. She listens to soft indie instrumental music. Loud rock bands and rappers are what I like to listen to. I'm tall and athletic. I play basketball. It's my saving grace. My father and I both have ash blond hair. He keeps his short, almost buzzed, like an office drone. Mine is shaggy. His eyes are Chartreuse green. The color of envy. They have pronounced crow's feet accenting them.

Mia has dark brown eyes like her mom. They both have heart-shaped faces with round noses and thick eyebrows. Koharu keeps her hair to her shoulders because my dad tells her to. I wonder if she would prefer for it to be her shroud like Mia's. My eyes are a peculiar shade of bluish purple. Neither my mom or grandparents have eyes this color. They all have gray eyes with yellow around the pupil.

I hate looking in the mirror because I share so much with my dad. We have angular features, strong jawlines, and bumps on the bridge of our noses. His face is hardened. My face appears older than I am. Probably from trying to act more grown up. Mia and I are walking home from school. She is a sad girl. Never smiles and keeps her head down.

"How was your day?" I ask her.

My stepsister shrugs.

"It was okay."

Her voice is mousy. Everything she says is really soft. I almost have to lean down to hear her.

"What's the matter?"

"Nothing," she says.

"I'm your big brother. You can tell me."

I am fixated on twirling my basketball on one finger but give her a side glance.

"You're not really my brother, Ryon."

"Okay, stepbrother. C'mon, talk to me. We've lived in the same house for over a year, and you never tell me anything," I say.

Mia stops walking and looks up at me with sad eyes that have thick bottom eyelashes. Koharu told me once that Mia has distichiasis, which makes her sensitive to light and results in double lashes. My stepsister has a doll face.

"Do you care?" she asks.

Mia isn't angry, but her question is abrasive to my ears.

"I do. We're family now."

"You really think of me as your sister?" she asks.

Her dark brown eyes are shiny. I think I said something wrong.

"To be honest, no. You're like a stranger to me, but I would like us to be friends. We are technically family, and I will be there for you if you need me," I say. Suddenly, skinny arms are around my neck and she's hanging on me. I drop my basketball and it bounces down the street. "Mia, what are you doing?"

"You said you would be my friend."

She's crying and soaking the collar of my school uniform.

"I am your friend. I'm your brother, your family. Please, don't cry."

"I don't have any friends," she says.

Mia lets me go and we continue walking home.

"You have to have at least one friend." She nods her head "no." Now that I think about it, I've never seen her sit with anyone at lunch or hang out with anyone. Ever. "Why don't you hang out with me?"

"You would let me?"

"Yes. Why wouldn't I?" I ask.

"Because you're popular. I'm just the weird girl."

I'm put off by my stepsister's observation. Sure, I play sports and have a lot of friends, but I wouldn't consider myself popular. Mia is timid, but that doesn't blind anyone to the fact she is super pretty. I think her shyness is sweet, but a lot of people find her odd.

"You're not a weird girl. You're you, okay?"

"What does that mean?" she asks.

Mia and I are approaching the house. My dad's car is gone. I'm relieved to be free of him for a few more hours.

"You're different, but not in a bad way. You're just you. There's no one else like you."

I smile at my stepsister, hoping to make her feel better, but she looks confused. We walk in and her mom greets us.

"Mia, Ryon, how was school?" asks Koharu.

"It was good. I got an A on my test," I say.

"It was okay," says Mia.

She shrugs off her backpack and takes quiet steps up to her room. Koharu and I make eye contact, but she doesn't say anything. She already knows. I go upstairs to my room, which is right next to Mia's. My homework is almost done. No one has texted me back yet. I decide to knock on Mia's door.

"What?" she asks.

"Can I come in?"

"Sure," she lets me in and I sit down on the chair next to the window.

She lays in her bed and covers her eyes with her arm.

"Mia, why won't you tell me what's bothering you?" I ask.

"It's hard to explain."

"Try. For me, please."

"My father died. Then my mom married your dad two years later. I never had a chance to process it. My life at school is a living hell. I have no friends. Everyone hates me," she says.

Mia cries, and I am quick on my feet to comfort her. I've never had a sibling, but I try my best to be a good brother.

My stepsister is mysterious. There is something about her. Black waves shut me out but lure me in. I'm curious about what goes on in her porcelain skull. It wasn't until recently I felt the urge to reach out to her. As strange as it sounds, it was like I woke up one day and realized I wanted Mia and me to be close the way real siblings would be.

"That sucks. I'm sorry my dad and I came into your life suddenly. It hasn't been easy for you. But you're lying when you say everyone hates you and you have no friends," I say.

"The girls are so mean to me at school. The boys aren't much better."

"What do they do?" I ask.

"The girls make fun of me. Everything I do is entertaining to them. My long hair, my voice, my art. It's amusing for them to torture me."

"Girls can be mean, but they are probably just jealous because you're really pretty."

I kneel down by her bed and brush her tangled hair out of her face. She looks surprised. I guess I am being invasive, but I want to help her.

"You think I'm pretty?" she asks.

Mia sits up to inspect my sincerity.

"Yes. I'm gonna have to beat up a lot of guys," I joke.

This makes her blush and I worry I am making my stepsister uncomfortable.

"The boys say nasty stuff to me and pull my hair. An older boy grabbed my chest in the library today," she says.

Mia keeps her head down. Now I'm pissed. This is why she's upset.

"Mia, why didn't you tell me?"

I hold her shoulders and try to get her to look at me.

"I didn't think you'd care."

"Well, I do. Who was it?"

"No one," she says.

"C'mon, please tell me."

I want to find this dude and punch him in the gut. Mia is cute, but she's just a kid. What a piece of shit.

"It doesn't matter," she sighs.

Sitting next to her, I see how the tears have streaked her fair skin.

"It matters. You matter to me." I take her hand in mine. She refuses to look up at me. "I'm your family. You're always going to matter to me. Even if my dad and your mom split up, I'll still be there for you."

"Do you mean it?" she asks.

"I mean it," I say.

Mia has tears in her doll lashes as she embraces me. This is the first time me and my stepsister have been close.

CHAPTER TWO

A GOOD BIG BROTHER

"Ryon!"

"I'm coming," I say. My dad is calling my name. Not good.

"Ryon! Get down here right now!" he bellows.

"What is it?" I'm running down the stairs.

"I heard you got into a fight with Akito at school. The principal just called me. What has gotten into you?" he asks.

"He was picking on Mia! I saw him rip out a chunk of her hair in the hallway!"

"So you were Mister Tough Guy and beat him up. Is that right? You are so goddamn stupid, Ryon! I'm a fucking lawyer. Do you know how this makes me look?"

"How you look? Is that all you care about?" I ask.

"Appearances are important, son. You don't understand now, but you will someday."

He snarls the words like a dog.

"Would it be better for me to let Mia get treated like shit, then?"

"Absolutely not! Just stop being impulsive. You need to learn to control yourself."

My father is about to rage on me more, but Koharu and Mia unlock the front door. They come in with bags of groceries. Koharu has dark circles under her eyes, hidden by expensive makeup. My father and I put away bok choy and peaches without a word. Mia preps for dinner and Koharu pulls my father into the living room to talk.

"Hey," I say.

My stepsister prepares the salmon and rice while I chop cucumbers.

"Hey," she whispers.

Mia won't look at me.

"So you probably heard I got in trouble at school."

"Yeah, I did."

She drizzles olive oil over the pink skin of the fish and layers it with seasoning.

"I don't think Akito will bother you anymore."

"Thank you," she says.

Mia turns on the oven and rice cooker. I sit down at the kitchen table and gesture for her to sit with me. My father and Koharu are arguing in the other room. I can feel the tension. She can, too. They've barely been married fourteen months and Joseph is making every week more and more dreadful. We are well off, but it's not enough. Koharu does all the housework and takes care of me and Mia, but he feels he is too burnt out from domestics to do a good job at work. He's so full of shit.

"Do you want to do something fun tomorrow?" I ask her.

She is reluctant to join me, but she does. Her hair rests on the tops of her arms, spills onto the table, and falls over the back of the chair. She reminds me of a doll. Her movements are almost mechanical and measured. The way she sits is very proper. Mia is out of place. Like she's not in the right time period. She is old-fashioned.

"Like what?"

"Let's go to the movies. My treat."

I rest my chin in my hand and wait for her reply. My stepsister is hard to gauge.

"You don't mind being seen with me?"

She holds her arm nervously and won't meet my gaze. Her tiny hand on her skinny arm makes me want to reach out and soften her sharp edges.

"Of course not. I don't care if anyone sees us together."

I put my hands up. The sleeves of my hoodie are too long, but it's comfortable. I love not wearing my school uniform. It's nice to be me. Mia is wearing a lacey turquoise dress with a white cardigan. Doll clothes.

"Okay," she says.

"What do you want to go see?"

"I don't care. You pick."

"What's your favorite candy?" I ask.

"I don't really like candy."

"What? Who doesn't like candy?"

"I like popcorn better," says Mia.

She slides the fish into the oven and starts the salad. I get up to set the table. Koharu is drinking a glass of wine on the porch. She's wearing white shorts and a dark red blouse. She's smoking, too. My father has that kind of effect on people. I can hear him screaming into the phone down the hall. He's going to reek of scotch when he comes out.

"Popcorn is good. And soda," I say. She gives me a smile. "I look forward to it. We'll have fun."

"Yeah. I've never been to the movies with anyone other than my mom and dad."

Her admission shocks me.

"Wait, really?" I ask. I stop setting down plates to look at my stepsister. She nods her head "yes." I don't believe her. "You're telling me you've never gone to the movies with a friend? What about karaoke? Or the zoo?"

"I've had no one to do those things with," she says.

"You do now," I say.

I hug my stepsister right as my dad walks in and I feel him eye me suspiciously.

***

It's Sunday morning, which means Sunday brunch. Koharu tries to be sweet and make us pancakes, bacon, and eggs right at 11am. She says that's what traditional brunch is but I think brunch just means eating whatever you want whenever you want on the weekend. I don't mind waking up and reading to the smell of butter and bacon, though.

"Mia! Ryon! Brunch is ready!" Koharu calls us downstairs.

I exit my room right as Mia is leaving hers. I'm wearing my clothes. Not that stupid tie and button-up shirt. I'm comfortable in my black joggers, white tee shirt, and gray zip-up. Mia is wearing a green dress with purple flowers on it. Her chunky sweater is tan.

"Good morning," I say. The sun is coming through the window in the hallway and it reflects off of her dark hair.

"Good morning," she says it like she might greet me wrong.

We walk downstairs and take our seats. My father looks smug, but isn't on his phone.

"Thank you, Koharu," I say.

"Thanks mom."

Mia and her mother exchange a glance and turn up the corners of their mouths. Mia's father died of cancer. Koharu was looking for someone to dull the pain and found Joseph. I wish she found someone else, but I'm happy to know Mia.

"How is my son?" asks my father.

He butters his pancakes with annoyance.

"Good. How are you, dad?"

I try to sound polite.

"I got called in on my day off. I was going to say 'no', but we have a lot of bills and I want my family to have everything. Isn't that right, darling?" He eyes Koharu.

Her job is to suck his dick and massage his ego. I feel bad for this poor woman. My mom ran off on him. I was only five, but I don't blame her. He is a difficult person to be with.

"Yes. I appreciate how hard you work. We all do," says Koharu.

She smiles with her teeth that are stained with fear and coffee.

"Thank you," says Mia.

Her voice is so quiet it's almost a whisper.

"What was that, dear?"

My father is cutting at his pancakes and staring down my stepsister with those ruthless green eyes.

His observant nature is disturbing. It's like we are all prey. We sit at the table and pretend to be a family, but we are Joseph's prisoners. This house is his hunting ground. Koharu is his slave. That's how he treats her. I am his punching bag. Mostly, he doesn't acknowledge Mia. I don't like it when he does.

"Oh, I just was saying thank you..." her voice is too soft.

She doesn't want him to yell at her, but her hesitance is his opening.

"You should speak up. A young lady needs to learn to use her voice," he says.

"Okay. I will," she says, a bit louder this time.

"What time do you have to go?" I ask.

I try not to sound as though I want to get rid of him, but I do.

"In an hour. Plenty of time to have brunch with my beautiful family."

He opens his arms to gesture a grand hug. It makes me want to roll my eyes, but I don't.

"I hope you have a good day at work," I say and shove a piece of bacon into my mouth so I don't have to tell anymore lies.

"Just another day in paradise," he says.

We eat in silence and wait for my dad to go so we can finally breathe. As soon as his black car pulls out of the driveway, I feel my shoulders relax. I put on my headphones and finish the last bit of my studying. Once I'm done, I knock on Mia's door.

"Hey, ready to go to the movies?" I ask.

"Yeah," she says.

Mia closes her door, and we step out into the bright day together. Our house is close to town, so we walk the couple of blocks to the movies. The sidewalk is full of people with dogs, couples, and families. I keep my arm around Mia and guide her through the crowd, since I can tell she is nervous.

"Hey Ryon!"

It's my friend Sora. He, Teo, and Ben have bubble teas in their hands.

"Hey guys!"

I wave to them and feel Mia shrink in my other arm. The boys approach us and eye my stepsister.

"What are you guys up to?" asks Teo.

"We're going to go to the movies," I say.

"Cool. You guys have fun on your date!" taunts Ben.

"It's not a date," I say.

I roll my eyes and shove Ben away from me.

"Oh, c'mon. I think it's sweet he's taking his stepsister to the movies," says Sora.

He is the most mature even though he is the shortest. They all have cropped black hair and brown eyes. Teo has a wide nose and square jaw. Sora has ears that stick out. Ben has a permanent smirk and sly eyes. He wears skinny jeans and rock band tees. Ben has a wild personality that is both fun and frightening. Sora and Teo could be brothers because they have the same jaw and dress similarly. The three of us wear joggers, basketball shorts, and zip-ups. Teo has thick square glasses.

"Call me later!" says Teo.

He and the other boys run off.

"Don't make out in the movies too much!" says Ben as he wraps his arms around himself and makes loud grunting and kissing noises at us.

"Don't listen to Ben. He's a jerk," I say and put my arm back around her.

We walk the rest of the way to the theater without seeing any more people from school.

"Why do they think we are on a date?" she asks as we are waiting in line.

There's two couples in front of us and a family with two kids behind us.

"Boys are always just saying dumb stuff like that. Don't take it personally," I say and pay for our tickets.

We look at the exaggerated characters and posters on the wall. The smell of popcorn and dim lighting eases me. I love the movies. We get to the concession counter and I order for both of us. I hand Mia her popcorn and she lights up. We both have soda and I choose a box of sour candy.

"Thank you for taking me out. This is nice," she says in her hushed way.

"No problem."

"Can we do more fun stuff?" she asks.

The previews are starting, but Mia is staring up at me.

"Yeah. We can do whatever you want."

The movie begins to play, and we share our snacks. My stepsister is happy and I feel like a good big brother.

CHAPTER THREE

BIRDS THAT DO NOT FLY

School is boring as usual. I am waiting for Mia, so we can walk home together. She hasn't come out though. It's been twenty minutes since school ended, so I go back inside. There's a girl in her grade at a locker and I tap her shoulder. She looks at me with watery blue eyes.

"Hey! Have you seen my stepsister, Mia?" I ask.

The girl nods her head 'no' and slams her locker shut. I keep walking down the hall and see a boy in her grade named Ayumi.

"Hey Ayumi, have you seen Mia?"

"Oh, I think she's still in there."

He points to the girl's locker room. I hear static. Something happened.

"Why is she in there? Her physical education class was this morning."

"I heard the girls did something bad to her," he says and keeps his head down.

Ayumi is a nice boy but not the person to break up a fight or stop a bully.

"What did they do?"

"Fumika told me she was in the showers crying with gum in her hair."

I rush past Ayumi and into the girl's locker room, not caring if I get in trouble. I'm already known as 'the crazy white boy.' Mia's sobbing is soft, but I can hear it.

"Mia?"

"Ryon?" she squeaks.

I turn the corner and find her in the showers with sopping wet clothes and damp hair that has pieces of chewed gum in it. I kneel and pull her next to me.

"Are you okay?" I ask.

"Am I going to have to cut my hair?" she sobs into my arms, and I diagnose the damage. There are only five pieces of gum. I think I can cover it with oil and comb it out.

"No, I'll fix it when we get home."

"You promise?" she asks.

"I promise. Let's go."

I help her up, and she takes shaky steps with me out of the locker room. Not many students are in the hall and only a few stragglers see our bizarre exit. Mia doesn't say a word on our walk. Both cars are gone. We're home alone tonight. I don't mind since my dad would probably freak out if he knew I went into the girl's locker room. Try as she might, Koharu would probably just make it worse with her drinking and smoking.

"What are you going to do, Ryon?" she asks.

I have her sit on the bathroom sink as I put vegetable oil over the pieces of gum.

"I read online that this will work," I say.

"Thank you."

Her face is red, and her eyes are sad. I wish my stepsister didn't have such shitty luck.

"Who did this?"

"No one," she says

"Please tell me. I won't beat them up. They're girls, so I can't, anyway."

"It was Biora and Kim. They're the ones who are always really mean to me."

"Why did they do this?"

I begin to gently comb out the first piece of gum. It sticks a bit and strands of hair break. I attempt to be more careful.

"I don't know. They said my long hair was gross, and that I was weird."

Her voice is grown up when she doesn't mumble or whisper. It's right in my ear and I can hear it clearly.

"I think it's because you're beautiful," I say.

I don't want to appear creepy, but I want to cheer up my stepsister. And I'm not lying. She is beautiful. Mia flinches and more hair breaks in the wide-tooth comb.

"Mia, sit still! I don't want to mess up your hair."

I continue to brush out the gum as best as I can without hurting her.

"Biora and Kim said I don't deserve to have you as a brother," she says.

"What do they know?" I scoff at her remark.

Those girls are mean little queens. They both have shoulder length black hair. Biora has green eyes like my dad. They are envious of Mia, that's for sure. She has a round face with no edges. It's almost childlike, but she is too much of a bitch to be innocent. Kim has an oval face with gray eyes and freckles on her nose that's really pointy. They both look stuck up. Neither one of them is ugly, but I find them to be unattractive because of how they treat my stepsister.

"Do you wish you had someone else as your sister?"

"What? No!" I say.

There's only one more piece of gum left in her hair. The oil has soaked in, so it comes out the easiest.

"There! See, your hair is just fine."

She hops off the sink and turns around. Her long hair has suffered minimal damage. Mia runs her fingers through it and smiles in the mirror.

"Wow. Thank you, Ryon."

The oil is dripping down and landing on the floor in small yellow pools.

"Let's wash the vegetable oil out," I say.

We kneel at the bathtub since she has too much hair to wash in the sink. I lather in the ginger and coconut shampoo we all use. The bubbles make rainbow designs. I rinse her hair and put in the matching conditioner. There's a lot of hair but I think I used too much conditioner. Oh, well. I towel her off as we sit on the bathroom floor together.

"Thank you," she says.

Mia puts her skinny arms around my neck. I hug her back and realize she is still in her wet uniform. Biora and Kim not only put gum in her hair but they threw her in the showers, too. If only I could sock them in the face the way I did to Akito.

"I would do anything for you," I say.

She is nuzzled in my neck right as my dad opens the door.

"What's going on here?" he bellows at me.

Mia recoils from my arms.

"Some girls put gum in Mia's hair. I was helping her get it out."

"Get up. The bathroom is no place to hang out," he says.

We both stand. Mia reminds me of a fawn that's learning how to walk. Her legs are shaky under her weight.

"Sorry," whispers Mia as she darts out of the bathroom and up the stairs.

"Is something going on here I should know about, son?" he asks.

My father stares at me with his snake eyes. They don't trust me. I definitely don't trust him.

"No. I was just trying to help her with her hair."

"You shouldn't be so intimate with your stepsister. People might start talking."

"I only washed her hair. What's so weird about that?" I ask.

"I know you mean well, Ryon. But people see something slightly strange and they make up stories. Then half the town is in our business. We don't want that, right?" Joseph puts his hand on my shoulder and squeezes with his meaty fist.

It's like being crushed by concrete blocks. I almost yelp but refuse to give in to my father.

"I understand."

I grit my teeth to keep in the things I want to say.

"Good."

His footsteps echo on the hardwood floor. I hide in my room the rest of the night. He is venomous with his words. A vicious viper. The way he is doesn't surprise me anymore, but the bites are infectious and rot my insides. Mia is crying, but I don't dare knock on her door. I resort to placing my hand on the wall that we share.

***

It's nice out and the guys want to play basketball in the park. I throw on my blue zip-up and black shorts. Mia is home, so I knock on her door. She seems surprised to see me.

"Hey, wanna come to the park with me?" I ask.

"I'm reading," she says.

Mia holds a book to her chest and looks down.

"You can come read at the park. I'm going to play basketball. C'mon, you shouldn't be in your room all day when it's sunny."

"I don't know…"

Mia is probably worried someone is going to be mean to her.

"Don't worry, I'll be there. Nothing bad is going to happen if I'm with you," I assure her.

She grabs her notebook and pen. The book she is reading looks old and boring, but it makes her appear more mature. I think that's why the girls in her grade pick on her. Mia is wearing a lilac colored dress and short black ankle boots. Her hair is messy despite her constant brushing. She has books from the turn of the century and a diary that holds her private thoughts.

"You don't mind being seen with me?" she asks as we walk down to the park with the basketball court.

"I already told you I don't care about that."

I put my arm around her, and we weave through the other people enjoying their Saturday afternoon. There's a vendor selling popcorn and I buy her a bag. She looks at me like it's a trick.

"C'mon, take it. I got it for you," I say.

"Thank you," she doesn't mumble as much around me anymore, but her voice is hardly above a whisper.

I find myself sitting too close or leaning down to hear her better. I see Teo and Sora waiting for me. Ben doesn't play sports. He does more rowdy things like blow up beer cans and chase after girls. Koga and Kirin are with them. They are the twins we play sports with. The twins are almost as tall as me, but not quite. I am the tallest and

17

fastest in our group. Koga and Kirin both have dark brown hair that they keep in buns and gray eyes. The only way to tell them apart is Koga has a round nose and Kirin has a pointed nose.

"Hey guys!" I say and wave to my friends.

My stepsister shrinks behind me.

"Hey Ryon! Hi Mia," says Sora.

He can tell she is nervous and is trying to be nice. Sora is a friend to all.

"Hi," she whispers.

Teo and Sora look over at the twins and me.

"Do you want to play, Mia?" asks Teo.

He bounces the ball a few times.

"No, thank you."

She grips her books as a shield and hides in her disheveled hair.

"You guys start and I'll play next!" I say and walk Mia over to the bench in the sunlight.

It has a fountain in front of it and maple trees to the left. I think it's a nice spot for her to read and I can see her when I play.

"I'll be back to check on you, okay?" I say.

"Okay," she says.

Mia opens her old book with too many pages and turns her attention to the world between scratched hardcovers with no pictures. I survey the park and see that no one else our age is here. It's mostly couples in their twenties and some older women. No one should bother her while I play.

Teo bounces the ball out of bounds and it's my turn. Koga and Kirin are quick, but not as quick as me. Sora and I weave through them and use our power to communicate on the court without words. Kirin steals the ball from me, but I distract him and Sora takes it. He is able to outmaneuver Koga and pass the ball to me and I dunk it.

"Yeah! In your face!" I shout as I drop from the hoop.

"Damn, Ryon. You got mad skill," says Kirin as he takes the ball out of my hand and shoots.

"That was crazy, man. You white guys can play ball," jokes Koga.

No one else points out my otherness anymore, but I don't mind. I've lived in Japan since I was eight. Koga likes to poke fun at my ethnicity and says it's why I act crazy. It's all in good fun. I know Koga isn't being hateful.

"Thanks. I'm gonna go check on Mia," I say.

As I turn to leave, I hear Kirin making an "ooh" noise.

"What?" I ask.

"Your stepsister is hot, dude. No one wants to say it, but I'm gonna say it," says Kirin.

He gets a punch in the arm from Koga, who is shaking his head at him.

"She's just a kid. Leave her alone, you perv," says his twin brother.

"Couldn't you have said it in a nicer way, Kirin? Like maybe you could have said 'Hey Ryon, your stepsister is really pretty' instead of being a creep?" says Sora.

He is the one who scolds the group when they are being out of line. We all respect him, so we let him.

"Yeah. She's cute, but why is she so quiet and standoffish all the time? Is she like that at home, too?" asks Teo.

"She's a shy person," I say as I walk away.

The guys' comments piss me off. I know Kirin is the only one in the wrong, so I keep it to myself. It's probably because I'm the crazy white boy. Mia is writing something in her yellow diary. As I near her, she slams it shut and hides it under her thigh.

"Hey," I say and sit down next to her.

"You're really good at basketball," she states.

"You were watching," I say.

I smile at her, and it makes her look down.

"Sorry."

"What? No! Don't be sorry. I don't care if you watch me play."

"You don't think it's weird?" she asks.

"No, why would I think that?"

"Everyone seems to think everything I do is weird."

"That's because you're pretty and shy. No one can read you," I say.

She has long pieces of hair that fall in her eyes and obscure her face. I push them out of the way so I can see her doll eyes. They are always sad. I wish I knew how to change her perspective.

"Is that a bad thing?" she asks.

"It's just part of being you. I like that you're different," I say.

"Why?"

"Because I've never had a sister. I've never been around anyone like you, either. Now I have both."

I hug Mia, hoping to make her happy, but I think I just make her feel uncomfortable.

CHAPTER FOUR

LONG SLEEVES AND BROKEN TEETH

I'm sitting with Sora and Teo on the grass. We decide to have lunch outside, since it's sunny. I love the hot weather. Many people don't, but I do. My dad and I are from southern California where it's hot all the time. Koga has joined us, but Kirin is somewhere else. He's been avoiding me.

"I think I bombed that test," moans Teo.

"I have a low grade in social studies. My mom is going to freak," sighs Sora.

"My dad is on my case about what I'm going to do with my life," groans Koga.

The boys go on like this for a while, but I'm not really paying attention. I watch the clouds pass over us and space out.

"How are things with your dad, Ryon?" asks Sora.

Everyone knows what he means.

"They're okay. Tense as always," I say with a shrug.

"How do Mia and him get along?" asks Teo.

He takes a bite of rice and keeps his head down. My dad is known to be a scary asshole.

"He barely acknowledges her."

"That's good though, right? I mean, at least then he's not yelling at her," says Sora.

He tries to be wise. He is kind with his words.

"Yeah, I make sure he yells at me and leaves her alone."

"It's sweet watching you two," says Koga.

It surprises me and I almost spit out my soda.

"What do you mean?" I ask.

"I don't know. It's just nice to see how you are with her is all," he says.

"She doesn't have any friends. The girls are really mean to her. I want to be a good brother."

"The girls all hate her because Nero asked her out, and she turned him down," says Teo.

How does he know this and I don't? I'm not much of a gossip, but apparently my friend is. Nero is the popular rich boy in her grade. His dad makes more money than my dad. They live in a bigger house and drive a nicer car. He isn't a bad guy, but he has an air of arrogance that irritates me. His shaggy black hair smells like hairspray because he styles it for an hour every morning. Nero is the kind of guy to have perfect nails, perfect teeth, and wear expensive watches. He is one of the taller boys in his grade, about 5' 6". His face reminds me of a celebrity's, chiseled and fake. I shouldn't be, but I'm pissed she didn't tell me.

"Really?" I ask.

"Yeah. My sister told me. Nero has asked her out three times. She always says 'no.' All the girls are jealous of her. They're jealous because you're her stepbrother, too."

Teo's sister Fumika is in Mia's grade. This must be how he knows. Teo and his sister are close.

"Why would they be jealous that I'm her stepbrother?"

"Don't play dumb, dude. They all think you guys sleep in each other's beds and make out every day," laughs Koga.

Sora smacks the back of his head, but not hard.

"Ugh! Why does everyone think that about us?" I ask.

"If you were Japanese, they probably wouldn't say anything," says Koga.

He rubs the back of his head and eyes Sora as he tells me this. I don't want to admit it, but he's probably right. If I wasn't the crazy white boy, everyone would just assume we were regular boring old step-siblings.

"Maybe," I sigh and scan the yard. Mia is sitting by herself under an oak tree. She is reading one of her old books. "Later, guys." I pick up my bag and walk over to her.

Mia looks up at me with a bewildered expression.

"Hi," she greets me first this time.

"Hey. I wanted to come sit with you."

I put down my bag and join her in the shade.

"Why?"

"Because you're my stepsister and I want to see how you are today," I say.

I smile at her, but she doesn't smile back.

"I'm okay," she says.

Mia is looking over my shoulder. I turn around to see Biora and Kim walk by with smug expressions. It's an impulse, but I grab Mia and pull her closer to me and glare at them. The girls open their mouths to say something but decide against it. They know I'm older and more popular than them, so they let me win this time. School has a fucked up system of hierarchy, but I will use my popularity to help Mia.

"Have those girls been mean to you again?" I ask.

"No."

"I heard about Nero."

I don't want to sound angry, but it's jagged as it comes out of my mouth.

"I don't know why everyone is so mad at me for declining."

She crosses her arms and looks away from me. I realize I still have my arm around her and let go.

"It's because they're jealous," I say.

"Why? I'm not anybody. I didn't ask for anyone to like me."

"You're pretty and mysterious. It's no wonder all the boys like you."

I pull the long strands of black hair from her face.

"Only Nero has asked me out," she says.

"That doesn't mean more boys don't like you."

"They should like someone else."

"I don't think it works that way," I say. The bell rings and we pick up our bags. "I'll wait for you at the usual spot after school."

"Okay."

She walks in the opposite direction. I steal a glance over my shoulder to see Nero stick to her hip as she heads to class and I want to break his pretty boy teeth.

***

My dad is in an extra shitty mood tonight. Work was long, Koharu doesn't do enough, and I'm a horrible son. He's drunk on scotch and slurring his words. It's only 6:18pm but he's wasted. He punches me in the stomach and shoves me into the wall. Nothing I can't handle. He's done worse. One time he broke my nose, but we told everyone I broke it playing basketball. I let him berate me until he falls asleep in his chair. I take the bottle out of his hand and put it to my lips. It's top shelf, so it doesn't burn as badly, but it still bites. I take two more swigs and slam it down on the table.

As I walk up the stairs, I feel my vision blur slightly and my legs wobble. It's warm in my stomach and the heat moves through my veins. I don't get drunk very often, but sometimes it's nice to forget. I want to listen to music and space out. Joseph will get up in the middle of the night and shake me awake with his half drunk rage. He always does. I contemplate grabbing the bottle and getting wasted myself, but I hear Mia crying in her room.

Koharu made dinner early and left to go see a friend. She hasn't come back yet. That probably means she's drunk, too. We have little parental guidance at home. I want to protect Mia from the chaos of our house, but I can't. We are trapped here together. I run up the stairs and throw open the door. I know it's rude but I'm worried. Mia is sitting on her floor with a razor in her hand. Her left wrist has cuts up and down it. Some are scars and then there's the new one. I knock the blade out of her hand.

"Mia! What are you doing?" I ask.

I wish I didn't take those other two pulls because I cannot process this. I should take care of her, but here I am getting drunk and goofing off.

"I'm sorry," she says.

Mia recoils and hides her scarred arm in her gray cable-knit sweater.

"I'm not mad. Why are you doing this?"

I hold her arm and roll up her sleeve. The left arm has scars that go up halfway to her elbow. Now that I think about it, I've never seen Mia not wearing a sweater or long sleeves. It makes sense now. I've been blind to my stepsister. How could I be so thoughtless?

"I don't want to hurt anymore."

"So you hurt yourself?" I ask.

"It makes me feel better," she says.

"You have to stop. Please, promise me you'll stop."

I can't sleep at night knowing this is what she's doing in her room. Mia is a sensitive person. A precocious girl. I want to help her. My stepsister is too pretty and sweet to be cutting herself. I'm really worried about her.

"I don't know if I can."

"What?" I ask.

"I've been doing this since my dad died," she says.

My stepsister's admission drops a rock on my heart. I don't know what to do or say, so I hug her. Sometimes I think she finds my embrace creepy, and other times I sense she is comforted by it. She never tells me to stop and maybe I should, but I want my stepsister to know that she is cared about.

"Please stop. I don't want you to hurt yourself," I say into her messy hair.

The ginger coconut shampoo mixes with her scent, creating a unique fragrance unlike anything I've smelled before. She smells like violets and sadness. It reminds me of the beach.

"Okay," she says.

Mia puts her arms around me. I hold her to my chest and analyze the razor on the hardwood floor in front of me. How it is stained with blood. I examine the shiny steel. The white and blue rug has tiny droplets of blood on it. No one could notice unless they were sitting on the floor like we are. She's stopped crying, but her face is wet. The salt sticks to my neck. I move and rearrange the long locks around her shoulders. Making Mia happy is my new goal.

* * *

***

"Hey Ryon!" It's Koga and Kirin.

"Hey guys. What's up?"

"You wanna play ball at the park after school?" asks Koga.

"Yeah, I'll meet you guys there. I gotta walk Mia home first," I say.

"Oh, c'mon. She can walk the short distance by herself," groans Kirin.

Koga gives him the side eye but doesn't say anything.

"I want to walk her home." I slam my locker shut.

Now I'm irritated. I don't know why, but lately I've been really agitated.

"That's cool, man. See you there," says Koga as he shoves his brother down the hall.

He knows I'm still mad at Kirin for what he said the last time we played basketball together. I grab my books and head to class. It's biology with Mr. Tanaka. Not my favorite, but not the worst. I sit down and open my books, but my mind is elsewhere. Mia should be in her art class. I hope she's having a good day.

"Hey."

The girl that sits in front of me turns around. Her name is Setsuna. All the guys have a crush on her. She has wavy brown hair that she keeps in a long, high ponytail. No one else would say it, but she has a perfect hairline. It's not crooked or uneven, doesn't sit too high or too low. Her eyes are blue green and full of life. I didn't notice until now, but she has a beauty mark on her top lip. Setsuna has a vibrant demeanor. She is a bubbly person.

"Hey Setsuna," I say.

She brings me back to the present.

"What are you doing this weekend?"

"I'm not sure. Why?" I ask.

"Do you want to do something?" she asks.

"Like what?"

"I don't know. The movies? Or we could go to the beach," she says.

Setsuna beams at me. I see her every day in class, but have never really talked to Setsuna for more than two minutes.

"Um, sure."

I have a lot of friends, but girls rarely ask me out. The bell rings and class begins.

"Great! Let's meet up at 3pm on Saturday," she says and hands me a piece of paper with her name and phone number on it. "Call me!" she says and turns back to face our teacher.

I stare at her ponytail and try to figure out what's going on in her head. Does she want to be my friend or does she like me? Girls can want both or nothing. Sometimes they don't know what they want. Girls flirt with me but never attempt to hang out with me.

Once class is over, I wait for Mia outside. Tiny girls with black hair in uniforms bounce past me, but none of them is her. It's nearly twenty minutes after school is over when I head back inside. Ayumi is in the hall and I stop him.

"Where's Mia?" I ask.

He grimaces. I don't like this.

"She's in the art room."

"What's she still doing in there?"

I rush past Ayumi and half run to the art room.

"Ryon! Wait!"

Ayumi calls for me, but I am too busy worrying about Mia. I turn the corner and rush into the room with high ceilings that smells of acrylic paint. Mia is hiding in between the shelves that hold everyone's work. She's leaning against a shelf and crying in her hands.

"Mia!"

She doesn't acknowledge me. I sit down with her and try to get her to look at me.

"Mia, what happened?"

My stepsister is pretty even when she cries. Tears drip from her doll eyelashes. She reaches for a painting on a shelf with her name on it. Her head is down as she holds out a portrait of me.

Mia can paint just as good as any of the greats in a museum. It's very realistic. Almost like a photo. The elegant brush strokes and accuracy of my face in paint shock me. There's three large streaks of black paint through my eyes, mouth, and shoulder. Someone vandalized it, but it's still amazing. I didn't know she was so talented.

"This is beautiful."

I smile and find myself crying as well.

My stepsister cares about me, too. Mia touches the tears on my face like they're going to hurt her. She rubs the liquid between her fingers to make sure they're real.

"You don't think it's weird?" she asks.

"No, of course not. You're really good at painting," I say.

"I wish it didn't get ruined. I told you everyone hates me," she sobs again and I feel at a loss for what to do.

I can't fix this.

"They only ruined it because they're jealous."

"You always say that," she says.

"Because it's true."

"Why are they jealous of me?"

My stepsister is pretty but doesn't know it. She is smart but doesn't think so. Her art is beautiful, but she doesn't believe it.

"They're jealous you can paint better than anyone in this school."

"You really think so?"

"Mia, this is incredible. I didn't know you could paint like this," I say.

"Thank you."

I take her hand and help her up.

"Let's go home," I say.

She puts the painting back on the shelf and we exit the school. I'm relieved to be in the sun. It makes me feel calm. The wind picks up and lifts Mia's hair. It swirls around her shoulders and neck. I don't know why anyone says it's gross. I know I told the guys I'd play basketball, but I want to be with Mia. She's sad, and it's my job to cheer her up. My dad's car is gone, but Koharu is home.

"Mia, Ryon, how was your day?"

She is folding laundry with despair. Her cardigan reeks of cigarettes. Her breath is boozy. I can smell it from here.

"It was good," I say.

My stepmom is nice. She tries her best to keep up with our family's demands. Everything would be great if my dad didn't run her ragged.

"It was okay," says Mia.

She and her mom talk with their eyes, and I am left out.

"Mia and I are going to watch a movie in my room," I announce.

Mia seems surprised, but Koharu turns up the corners of her mouth and folds one of my dad's shirts.

"That sounds nice. I'll bring you two a snack in a little bit," says my stepmom.

"Thank you, Koharu."

I head upstairs, and Mia follows. My room is spacious. I have a couch and a recliner across from my bed. The TV is a fancy present my dad got me after he beat me up last year. It's mounted on the wall as my trophy.

"What do you want to watch?" I ask.

"Whatever you want."

"Okay," I shrug and put on a movie I've seen a hundred times.

We sit on the couch in silence. I'm leaning on the arm. She's curled up on the other side. The space between us is measurable this time.

"Thank you, Ryon. For everything." She speaks into her knees, but I can hear her.

"You don't have to thank me," I say and loosen my tie.

My school uniform is stiff and makes me feel like someone else.

"You're the only one who acts like they care about me besides my mom," she says.

"I do care. I care about you a lot."

Mia's skinny arms are clinging to me again. She hides her face in the collar of my shirt. I hold her until Koharu comes up with tea and the biscuits Mia likes. Her mother doesn't say anything, but I feel her watch the way I touch my stepsister.

CHAPTER FIVE

THE CRAZY WHITE BOY

I try to be less affectionate towards Mia. Everyone has been making me feel really weird about it. In movies, it seems like siblings always hug or sit next to each other. My father thinks anything I do to her is inappropriate. The way I touch her hair or ask her how her day was, it all has ulterior motives with him. I care about Mia, and I want us to be close the way real siblings are, but I worry that maybe I'm being creepy.

Koharu thinks it's nice that I've taken an interest in Mia. She's happy to hear that I want to go to the movies and take her to the park. She probably enjoys seeing Mia have a friend. I wish she had other people to hang out with, but now that I've noticed her, I see the way people treat her. She does nothing to deserve it. Everyone's such a dick to her. I try to protect Mia as much as I can. She hides things from me, though. I thought about opening up her diary but I couldn't bring myself to do it.

Sora and Teo think our relationship is sweet, but Koga, Kirin, and Ben all make me feel awkward. Koga doesn't say the stuff Kirin and Ben say, but I can tell he thinks something is going on between us. Since Teo's sister is in Mia's grade, I find myself gossiping. I try to act cool about it, but I ask about Nero and bring up how bitchy the girls are.

"Biora and Kim think they're hot shit because they got their periods before everyone else," jokes Ben.

His comments tend to be offhanded and gross.

"Ew dude," I say and roll my eyes at him.

Something about Ben puts me off. He's in my friend group, but I don't connect with him the way I do with Sora or Teo.

"Nero told all his friends that Mia and him made out in his pool," announces Teo.

My anger is making my hair stand up, but I try to be casual.

"What?" I ask.

"Yeah. Fumika told me that last night," says Teo.

He keeps his head down but gives me the eye. I think he assumes I'm pissed off at him, but really, I want to kick Nero's teeth down his throat.

"What an asshole. I wish I could beat him up."

I start eating even though I'm not hungry, so I don't say anymore stupid shit.

"You could," shrugs Kirin.

"I don't feel right fighting someone younger than me," I say.

"You could confront him. Not every fight has to be physical," offers Koga.

His idea isn't half bad, but I don't like the thought of intimidating Nero either. I just want to punch him in the mouth. That's what makes me feel better. Like when I shoved Akito into the lockers and socked him in the face three times. That's the kind of release I need from this anger.

"I guess I could."

"Don't do it, Ryon. You should talk to Mia. Fuck all those other people, she's the person who matters," says Sora.

My friend's maturity impresses me. I wish I could think like him.

"Yeah. You're right," is all I say. I should try to control myself. "See you guys later."

I pick up my bag and head back inside.

It's not that I'm mad at my friends, but I'm mad at everyone. Why did Nero have to say that? Because he's a guy. I hear stories like this all the time, but never bothered to care. Now it's about Mia and knowing his pretty boy face is smug as he tells his friends makes me clench my fist.

Classes will be boring. I'll space out for half of it and then I can leave. I tell myself to keep it together for a few more hours. I need to get a grip. Maybe Koga is right. I am the crazy white boy. When I first moved here, people stared. I was taller than everyone by the time I was twelve. My hair is blonde, my eyes are a strange shade of blue, and my stepsister is sweet but is the target of constant bullying. What do I do? I am rounding the corner to see something that brings out the psycho in me.

"Oh, c'mon! You made out with Nero. Why won't you kiss me?"

"I didn't kiss him," cries my stepsister.

"That's not what everyone else is saying."

"They're lying."

"I heard you sleep with your stepbrother, too." A boy in my grade named Fuyuhisa has his arms around her. He has spiky black hair and brown eyes that aren't warm or kind. They are cold like shark eyes. She's squirming out of his grasp, but he keeps tugging on her. She shrieks, and he laughs. His front tooth has a chip in it. Neither of them have noticed me yet. My blood is fiery hot and I lose it as he sticks his hand up her skirt.

"Fuyuhisa!"

I shout his name and throw down my books. He looks up at me with dead shark eyes. To enrage me more, he puts his hand in the shirt of her school uniform. I lunge at him and rip Mia out of his arms. Then I tackle him and smack his head into the floor. He attempts to choke me, but I grab his wrist and squeeze. My hand is much bigger than his. Fuyuhisa groans but continues to fight me. I punch him in the face and enjoy the sick smacking sound it makes.

"Ryon!"

One of the teachers is grabbing me and pulling me off Fuyuhisa.

"Let me go!" I shout.

"Calm down, Ryon," says the teacher.

"No! That sick perv just put his hand in my stepsister's shirt," I snarl.

Now that I'm aware, I see the student body has gathered around me. They all look down at Fuyuhisa, who has blood dripping down the back of his neck. It's staining the collar of his shirt. He coughs up red spit onto the floor. Then they turn to me. The crazy white boy.

***

My father is pissed at me. I tried to explain to him I was protecting Mia from Fuyuhisa, but he thinks I am bloodthirsty. Like him. Maybe I am. It made me feel good to see Fuyuhisa bleed into his crisp school uniform. Joseph doesn't ground me or take things away. He punishes me with his fist. I don't care anymore. He beats me up less now that Koharu and Mia live with us, but it still happens.

I have a giant purple bruise on my stomach. There's one on my chest as well. I lift my shirt in front of the full-length mirror in my room and examine the damage. My dad makes sure to not hit me in the face anymore. He targets my torso and avoids my face, arms, and legs. No use having a son if he can't play sports. People were suspicious when my nose was broken, but my dad is too scary for anyone to question.

He's done worse to me. I think the worst is the time he threw me down the stairs right before he married Koharu. We were fighting about nothing, as usual. He was drunk and accused me of being the reason my mom left. Sometimes I think he's right, but I was five when she left, so I still remember her. I know she loved me.

My mom was much younger than my dad. I think he took advantage of her youth. She had blonde hair and gray eyes. Her name is Holly. She wore red lipstick and high heels every day. After she married my dad, she got to have all the fancy stuff she could never afford. I think that's why she married him. Joseph has little to offer besides money.

He didn't start beating me up until I turned thirteen. It all started with one test I didn't get a perfect score on. My dad shredded it up in front of me while he shouted every awful thing someone could say to their son. I knew my father wasn't a loving person, but that day shook me to my core. I saw him for who he really was. He was waiting for me to be old enough to kick the shit out of.

The purple and green contusions will heal fine, but my body aches. I played basketball and pretended nothing was wrong, like I always do. It hurts to do most of the stuff I do. I try to act like I'm confident and happy, so other people believe that about me. I'm still studying my injuries and have my hand to the one on my stomach as Mia walks in my room. She cringes at the sight. I put down my gray tee shirt and look away because I'm embarrassed. Mia knows my dad beats me up, but never witnesses it or sees the marks.

"I'm sorry, Ryon."

She's wearing a pink sweater. I look at the long sleeves and hate myself.

"It's not your fault," I say.

"Yes, it is. If it weren't for me, you wouldn't have gotten into a fight with Fuyuhisa," she says.

Mia takes timid steps towards me.

"Fuyuhisa was touching you. I couldn't let him get away with it."

"Why do you care so much about what happens to me?"

She stares up at me with her sad doll face. How can someone so cute and innocent have such shitty luck?

"Because I love you," I say.

Mia recoils at my words like I said something bad. Maybe I did. I think about how my dad and friends perceive our relationship, but it's true. I don't love her the way I would a real sister, but I still love her.

"You do?" she asks.

"Yeah. I do." I shrug, hoping to tone down the tension, but Mia just keeps staring at me. "What?" I ask.

"I didn't think anyone loved me except my mom." To my surprise, it's my stepsister who closes the gap between us and hugs me. She is careful not to touch my bruises. Mia is tiny and only comes up to my chest. I wrap my arms around her and pull her messy hair out of her face. "I didn't make out with Nero," she says.

"I know."

"Why does everyone think I kissed you, too?"

Mia pulls back and waits for my answer. I don't have one.

"I don't know. Might be because I'm white," I tease, and she turns up the corners of her mouth.

"Do you have a girlfriend?" she asks.

Her question makes me laugh.

"No," I say.

"Why not?"

"I don't know. I'm supposed to hang out with this girl on Saturday."

I sit down on my couch and Mia joins me, but not too close.

"What's her name?" she asks.

"Setsuna," I say.

"She's really pretty. And nice. She stood up for me once."

Mia touches her heart. Setsuna must be a good person if my stepsister thinks so.

"I'm glad to hear someone was there for you," I reach out and put my hand on her shoulder.

"You're always there for me now."

"I am. No matter what," I say.

***

Setsuna wants to go to the beach. We meet at the bubble tea place where everyone hangs out. Her hair is down. She is wearing a red shirt and white capri pants. I buy her peach tea and I get a lychee one. We make small talk with our classmates that are there. Setsuna is nice to everybody, and this puts me at ease. She's not like Biora or Kim.

As we walk to the beach, we pass people our age with humongous headphones and barking dogs. Setsuna makes kissy noises at them. She thinks everything is cute. Old people, babies, kids, and dogs. Making sure I don't miss any cuteness, she points it all out to me. It's nice to be around someone who sees things this way. I act confident and casual, but most of the time, I'm a mess. We get to the beach and take off our shoes. Setsuna is jumping around and chasing the wind.

"It's such a nice day!" she sings.

Her arms are open, and she attempts to fly like a bird.

"I love sunny weather. I'm from California. It's hot there all the time," I say.

"I've never been to the United States. What's it like?"

"I can't really remember it anymore."

"Do you enjoy living here in Japan?" she asks.

"I love it. It feels like home," I say.

Setsuna takes my hand and starts guiding me down the beach. We walk along the waves and let them pass over our feet. As long as the beach is near, I am at home. I don't think I could live somewhere without an ocean nearby.

"Thanks for joining me at the beach. It's always better with a friend," she smiles at me.

I can't tell if Setsuna likes me or just wants to hang out.

"Thanks for inviting me, Setsuna."

We continue meandering the shoreline. Other people are enjoying the beach. I see some families taking pictures and a few couples. A little kid is flying a dragon kite. His dad stands behind him to make sure his son doesn't lose his toy. I wonder if my dad and I ever had moments like that. We must have. I don't remember them though.

Setsuna grabs my shoulder and takes a picture of us. She giggles as she posts it online. Girls always want to take pictures and show everybody. It's kind of weird but also nice to see Setsuna be so happy over a goofy photo of us. There's a couple sitting quietly, admiring the ocean. They stand out to me. They're in their twenties. Both of them are Japanese. The woman is wearing a white sundress, and the man is dressed in all black. They are opposites, but together.

"I've always lived in Japan. Someday I want to live in Paris, or Greece, or maybe California!" she teases.

The wind is picking up and blowing her wavy hair all over the place. It's not as long as Mia's.

"I've never been to Paris or Greece."

"Neither have I."

"What makes you want to live there?" I ask.

"They're both so different from here. I like experiencing new things and traveling. I want to see everything," she says.

Setsuna is full of life. The kind of girl who is happy just being alive. I think of what Mia said. That she was nice, and that she stood up for her.

"That's really cool," I say.

"You think so?"

"Yeah. Most people want stuff to stay the same."

"I guess that's true. Not me though. I could go somewhere new every day!" she cheers.

"What do you plan to do after school?" I ask.

There's a full seashell by my foot. I almost step on it but notice it in time. It's pink and white. I hand it to Setsuna, and she jumps with glee.

"I want to be a teacher or a nurse. A job where I can help people," she says.

Setsuna is serious this time. She isn't giggling or smiling.

"I like that."

"What do you want to do, Ryon?"

"I'm not sure yet," I say.

"You're fantastic at basketball."

"Yeah, but I don't want it to be my job. It's just for fun. I think I want to help people, too. I'm not sure how, though."

"You'll figure it out." She is back to being all smiles.

"I hope so."

"What does Mia want to do after she graduates?" she asks.

I'm surprised Setsuna brought up my stepsister. I avoid talking about her because I don't want people getting ideas.

"I don't know. She is a talented artist," I say.

"I've seen her paintings. They're superb."

CHAPTER SIX

BIT BY A SNAKE

I've been agitated. It's like there's something ugly growing inside me. I find myself angry with everyone about everything. Kirin, Koga, and Ben haven't talked to me much. Sora and Teo are still cool. They don't say weird stuff about me and my stepsister. I get annoyed by the stuff Teo tells me, though. It's not his fault, but knowing what's happening to Mia makes me grind my teeth. There are times he doesn't want to tell me what Fumika says, but I pry it out of him. It's my fault I'm irritated all the time.

I never cared about gossip before. There was nothing interesting about it to me. Now I hear ridiculous stories about my stepsister that makes my blood boil. She hardly speaks and never does anything to warrant attention, but all eyes are on her. Nero has convinced everyone she makes out with him but is too shy to admit it. Half of the school thinks she sleeps in my bed with me. The girls tear up her drawings and read her poems in front of everyone. The boys are worse. They have convinced themselves she's a slut. I want to punch them all in the face.

Since everyone saw what I did to Fuyuhisa; no one tries to touch her anymore. The girls still whisper and the boys will be boys, but at least no one is shoving their hand up her skirt or fucking with her hair. I hate when people say it's gross. It pisses me off that Biora and

Kim wanted to mess up her hair so she'd have to cut it. They are truly twisted and wicked mean queens. Mia's hair is important to her. I don't know why, but it makes it important to me. If someone tries to take scissors to it, I'd have to kill them.

Koharu has mixed feelings about our relationship. She wants so badly for Mia to have someone, but I don't think she wants it to be me. I wonder what I do that makes everyone question my motives. I try to be a nice guy, but apparently I'm the dude who sneaks out of his room to kiss his stepsister at night. Maybe if I were Japanese, it wouldn't be a big deal. I am an outsider even though I am one of the more popular ninth graders.

I am waiting for Mia on the steps. In a few months, I'll be going to high school. I don't want to leave Mia here by herself. Ayumi is on his phone walking by. It's an impulse, but I grab his shoulder. He is startled, but I smile at him and he relaxes.

"Hey Ryon. What's up?"

Ayumi is small like Mia, but a little taller. He isn't popular or unpopular. Ayumi has a group of friends but they keep to themselves. He shaves his head on the sides but keeps it long at the top. On his wrist is a watch that's not cheap but not expensive. I think I can trust him. Taking his phone, he looks upset, but I hand it right back.

"I put my number in your phone. If you see anyone bullying Mia, will you call me, please?"

"Of course," he says.

Ayumi has warm hazel eyes. They are lively, unlike Fuyuhisa's dead shark eyes.

"I'm worried about what's going to happen to her when I go to high school," I admit.

Ayumi and I don't talk a lot, but I sense I can be honest with him.

"I'll keep an eye on her," he says.

Ayumi nods and takes on a stoic posture.

"Thank you."

"I'm glad you're her stepbrother."

Ayumi doesn't walk away like I thought he would.

"Why's that?" I ask.

"Because she has someone strong to protect her now," he says.

As he smiles at me, his hazel eyes brighten. Ayumi has probably seen Mia get tortured for years.

"Thank you. A lot of people think it's weird," I say.

"It's because they don't understand what it's like to care about someone. We go to school with some heartless bastards."

Ayumi's words stun me. I didn't think he'd curse, let alone be so insightful. I laugh to myself.

"You're really smart, Ayumi."

"Thanks! I gotta get going. I'll watch over Mia for you."

With that, he bounces down the steps.

I am more relaxed now knowing someone understands how I feel. Ayumi doesn't think I'm creepy or weird. Waiting for Mia gives me anxiety because I get worried she will not walk out. It's only ten minutes past the end of class, but I am fidgeting. Thankfully, Mia takes tiny steps out of the school into the bright day. Her hair is the blackest black and super shiny. She isn't looking at the ground this time.

"Hey Mia," we start down the steps together, "how was your day?" I ask.

"It was good. No one did anything bad to me today."

"Good. Hey, do you want to do something fun?"

"Like what?" she asks.

Mia perks up at this.

She is still shy around me, but I think she enjoys the time we spend together.

"I thought we could go to one of those art museums."

"You like that kind of stuff?"

She pushes her hair back and looks up at me.

"I don't know. I've never tried it."

It's hot out, but Mia keeps her blazer on. I wish I could take an eraser to her wrist. We walk the couple blocks to the nearest one and I pay. My dad gave me a ton of money after he beat me up last time. I call it "hush money." He leaves it on my coffee table.

I'm not an artsy person, but I try to understand it from Mia's point of view. Some paintings are good, a few are terrible in my opinion, and most are just weird to me. I like all the animal and ocean ones. The sculptures and mixed medium pieces are interesting. Mia guides me around to look at this and that. She stops at one. It has her attention. This piece takes up the entire wall. It's a beach scene. Dozens of boats are on the water. They are heading towards the shore where a geisha is standing.

"Why do you like this one?" I ask her.

"I don't know. It makes me feel something."

She doesn't mumble or whisper.

"What do you mean?"

I try to look again but I don't get it. It's a nice painting, but I'm not sure what Mia is saying.

"Art isn't about making a pretty picture. It's about capturing a feeling," she says.

"What's the feeling of this one?"

I take in the face of the men on their boats. They are all on the geisha. Her eyes are looking into the forest. She doesn't notice the men. Her umbrella and kimono are red. She has black hair adorned with flowers.

"Longing."

Mia keeps her eyes on the painting for a while before walking into the next part of the museum. I stop in the doorway and look at the geisha over my shoulder.

***

My dad shouts into his phone during dinner, as usual. It's tense and awkward. He doesn't care, though. Joseph enjoys making things uncomfortable for everyone. Koharu looks at me and then at Mia. We talk with our eyes. Mia is especially frightened of my father. He barely acknowledges her, but she flinches when he gets up. She keeps her head down as he walks behind her to the sink. I see the way she hides her face from him. He comments on her hair being too long. One time, he ran his fingers through it and she shuddered.

I don't like my dad touching her, but he is the one person I lose to. There is no fighting Joseph and winning. We are both tall and athletic. He's only a couple inches taller than me, but his hairy arms bulge in his button-up shirt. His fists are meaty and hard as concrete. I've never lost a fight at school, but my dad is stronger than me. I don't even struggle anymore. It's over more quickly if I just let him hit me.

I used to block him or cower. Not anymore. I have resigned to sitting there as he wails on me. Fear made him more bloodthirsty. I keep my face neutral as he shoves me into walls, throws me downstairs, and hits me in places no one can see. It's difficult, but I've gotten good at holding in my anguished screams.

Once dinner is over, I go into my room and Mia goes into hers. I want to hang out with her, but I don't. If my dad is home, I avoid her. Not that I am trying to be mean, but it is better for both of us this way. I think Mia understands. After my dad caught me helping her with her hair, I know he thinks something is going on. I'm laying in bed listening to music with my headphones and my dad walks in. I stop the song and sit up.

"Hey dad."

I try to be nice to my father even though our relationship is less than ideal. He is still my dad.

"Son," he draws out the word. Joseph is drunk.

"What's up?" I ask.

"I was going to ask you the same thing."

He leans in my doorway. I know Mia can hear him.

"Huh?"

"Don't play dumb," he says.

My dad lunges at me and grabs my hoodie. Designer headphones fall off and hit the floor. He gets in my face. I smell the familiar scent of scotch and cigarettes.

"Dad, please don't do this," I plead.

I want to like my dad, but he makes it impossible. Why can't he just leave me alone?

"Are you fucking your stepsister?" he asks.

"No," I choke out the word as he squeezes my collar tighter.

"Don't lie to me, son."

His knuckles are huge and in my face. I wonder if he is going to lose it and give me a black eye.

"I'm not! I swear," I say.

"Do you want to fuck her?"

"Ew, dad. Please stop."

Joseph's nostrils flare, and he hits me in the ribs. I breathe in fire and it spreads all down my left side.

"Tell me the truth," he growls.

"I am telling you the truth!"

He socks me in the shoulder. As he walks out, he leaves a trail of boozy air and stale smoke. I put my hand to my new injuries. The other ones are completely healed, but I am broken inside. I lay back down, defeated. It's Friday so I don't set an alarm. I don't care when I wake up.

I hope my dad gets called into work. Somehow I fall asleep even though the blood is leaking out of the vessels and bruising under the skin. It stings, so I sleep on my right side, which is facing the wall I share with Mia. I fall asleep wondering what she's doing.

"Ryon?"

Mia is whispering my name behind me. I look at my clock. It's 4:03 am.

"Mia, what are you doing?" I ask.

"I wanted to make sure you're okay."

My stepsister is kneeling next to my bed in her lavender pajamas. They have long sleeves as well. She takes my hand and holds my wrist.

"Yeah. I'm okay."

"I'm sorry," she says.

"My dad is an asshole."

I grimace as I move and feel my injuries.

She looks down. I don't think my stepsister can bring herself to say mean things even if they are about horrible people. We both hear someone walking around downstairs. Her dark eyes are full of fear and she gets up to leave.

"I love you," she whispers as she darts out of my room.

I lay back down and face the wall. Mia's words touch me and I hurt less knowing she loves me, too.

***

I smile a lot. Even though I don't want to. It makes me feel in control. Like I can trick people into believing I'm confident. I have so many friends but feel alone. My grades are perfect but I lack understanding. Everyone thinks I'm cool for the most part. I probably would be if my dad wasn't around. Sometimes I wish he'd just leave in the night and never come back.

Today is cloudy, and the trees are bright red against the gray sky. It's fall. I enjoy watching the leaves change. It's cooler in the mornings and at night. I miss the heat of summer. The day starts out orange and turns light blue with the sunrise. All seasons are fun, but summer is my favorite. It reminds me of California.

Teo and Sora are waiting for me at the park. We play on the court for a while. I'm having fun shooting the ball. I make it every time. Sora takes it from me and jokingly attempts to dunk it but can't reach. He's funny like that. Teo shoots the ball a couple of times. He misses, and it bounces off the hoop. It makes a ringing noise.

The three of us decide to walk around the park and check out the red leaves. There are other people doing the same thing. A man with a large black dog and sunglasses is enjoying the changing season as well. There's girls our age taking pictures of each other and laughing. They're all wearing pilot jackets and boots.

"How are things at home, Ryon?" asks Sora.

Everyone knows my dad is scary, but only Sora and Teo know about the beatings. I don't talk about it around Ben or Koga and Kirin. They've seen mine and my dad's tense conversations but aren't aware of how fucked up my home life is. My father covers me in bruises, school bores me, and everyone thinks it's weird how I feel about Mia.

"They're okay," I say.

"You can talk to us," says Teo.

I can't keep it in and the words tumble out of my mouth.

"My dad thinks something is going on between me and Mia," I admit.

Sora and Teo look at each other and don't talk until we pass a group of people our age. None of us trust other teenagers. We are cold-hearted monsters.

"But there's not, right?" asks Sora.

He isn't being judgmental, just asking.

"No. I love her like a sister."

"How does Mia feel?" asks Teo.

I don't feel awkward talking about my stepsister with Sora or Teo. If Ben or Kirin were around, I'd keep these things to myself.

"She loves me, but not like that. Mia's never had a friend or brother."

"Fumika heard Nero say that the only reason she won't choose him is because she loves you," says Teo.

His face is serious. He thinks I'm going to be pissed off at him.

"She'd never choose him," I say.

I roll my eyes and the guys laugh.

"You never think about her like that?" asks Sora.

If Koga asked this question, I'd tell him to fuck off but I can talk to Sora. He doesn't bait me to make me act foolish the way Koga does sometimes.

"No. I don't see her that way."

"What made your dad suspicious?" asks Teo.

We pass two couples and wait until they're out of earshot.

"Biora and Kim put gum in her hair and I fixed it for her. My dad caught me washing her hair and hugging her. Now he keeps his eyes on me when I touch her. Koharu watches the way Mia clings to me. I think it bothers her," I say.

Scanning the park, I wonder what it's like to be a normal person.

"I'm sorry, Ryon," says Teo.

"I think Koga is right. If I was Japanese, no one would look twice at us," I say.

"We live in a messed up society," says Sora.

We sit on a bench. People pass us wearing chunky sweaters, coats, and scarves.

"Do you guys think it's wrong the way I feel about Mia?" I ask.

"No. I think it's nice," says Teo.

"It's pure. There's nothing wrong with it. People just don't understand," says Sora.

Wise as always.

"I get worried there must be something wrong with me for everyone not to trust me around her."

"It's because you're a boy," says Teo as he stretches his arms. "If you were a girl, you'd have the same problem, but it'd be different."

"What do you mean?" I ask.

"Fumika tells me that no one trusts Mia, either. They think she is the temptress which makes you the victim. The other scenario is that you are preying on her. Neither are true, but you and her suffer from society's double-edged sword."

Teo is also wise. I like my friends.

"We love each other, but not the way people think," I say.

"Don't care what other people think," says Sora.

"I don't. I just wish I could talk to her when my dad is home. We avoid each other if he's around."

"Someday you won't have to live with him. Maybe you and Mia can move somewhere together," says Teo.

"That sounds nice," I say and I smile, because I want to.

CHAPTER SEVEN
POEMS FOR THE DISPOSSESSED

"Hey Mia. Want to hang out?"

My dad got called into work on a Saturday. He'll probably get drunk and throw me around later. As long as he's gone, Mia and I can talk and hang out freely. I still make Koharu nervous, but she never says anything about Mia being in my room or stops us from leaving together.

"Yeah. What do you want to do?" she asks.

Mia seems happier. Her face isn't as sad, and she brightens when my dad isn't around. She's wearing a gray dress with long sleeves. I haven't looked at her arms in a while, but I don't think she cuts herself anymore. Sometimes I get the urge to roll up her sleeves when she's sleeping, but I stop myself. It might scare her.

"Whatever you want to do," I say and we walk downstairs and I grab her white coat for her.

I throw on my black zip-up and red sneakers. Mia decides on her boots.

"Koharu, Mia and I are going to go into town!"

"Have fun! Be safe," she replies from somewhere in our big house.

"Bye mom," says Mia but not loud enough for Koharu to hear.

We step outside and make our way down the street. It's cool out but not bad. Mia is bundled up in her long jacket, but her legs are bare. She never wears knee-high socks except for school.

"What do you want to do?" I ask.

She is looking at the maple trees that line the neighborhood. They are dark red. The elm trees turn golden yellow this time of year. We crunch leaves under our feet. The concrete and sky are the same shade of gray. I'm happy me and my stepsister can hang out. I feel bad about avoiding her at home.

"Can we go to the bookstore?" she asks.

Mia keeps her eyes on the different colored leaves.

"Yeah, we can do whatever you want to do."

This makes her smile and I feel like a good brother. The neighborhood is pristine. It has a sterile and perfect vibe to it. The lawns are green and flawless. Every house is lavish and the gardens are immaculate. The driveways are full of fancy cars.

A house that's bigger than the others has a chestnut tree in front. The path up to the sliding door is lined with roses. It's nicer than ours, and I wonder if it pisses my dad off to drive past this one. He is that kind of person. I wonder if the family that lives there is like us or if they are normal. Mia pulls her hair to one side and I can see her better. Her bottom eyelashes and white coat really make her look like a doll.

As we near town, we see people we go to school with. Some of them whisper, a few of them snicker, and all of them stare. I glare them all down as we pass by. Mia has averted her gaze. She's anxious and I'm irritated that everything we do is under observation.

I don't care if they talk about me, but I wish they'd leave her alone. No one has touched her, but the girls are as cruel as ever. I don't know how to take care of mean queen bullies. Boys settle things with their fist but girls are vicious with their words. I try my best to block Mia from their view as we walk into the bookstore.

Mia relaxes and starts looking around. The paper has an unidentifiable scent that's comforting. She picks up all sorts of books. Old ones with hardcovers, new novels with paperbacks, and ones filled with poetry. Mia is reading a poem, and it makes her smile.

"What are you reading?" I ask. She closes the book and looks embarrassed. "It's okay, I'm not judging you."

I want my stepsister to share more with me. She is a lonely girl.

Mia doesn't whisper as much, but she doesn't tell me anything unless I ask her. Even then, she keeps things from me. She lies, but I try not to take it personally.

"I don't think you'd be interested," she says.

The book is clutched to her chest.

"I am though."

I'm trying to show my stepsister my sincerity, but I understand why she is hesitant. Everyone is such a dick to her. She opens the book and hands it to me with her head down.

> *To love*
> *Is to know*
> *The truth*
> *Inside somebody's soul*

"Do you like it?" she asks.

Her dark eyes are pretty and secretive. Mia has a world inside her I know nothing about. I am so curious about what goes on in her mind. It makes me happy she shared this with me.

"I really like this poem, Mia."

My stepsister lights up. She looks less like a doll and more real when she smiles.

"You don't think it's weird?"

"No. Not at all," I say.

We walk around the bookstore, and she shows me more poems and interesting series. It's not normally my thing to hang out in a bookstore or read poetry, but I want to know Mia. She picks the first poetry book we read, an old novel with a blue hardcover, and two popular light novels. I buy them for her. My dad left my cash on my coffee table after he accused me of screwing Mia. I'm happy to be free of my dad and have time with my stepsister.

I'm too distracted by how happy she is to notice Nero and his friend Yusa. They both have shaggy hair that reeks of hairspray. Their watches gleam on their wrists. Nero looks Mia up and down, which is his first mistake. It makes me want to yank out all his girly hair. He turns his attention to me and gives his friend a look.

I'm almost a foot taller than Nero and I stare him down. His friend

Yusa is anxious and backs up from me. I pull Mia close and usher her down the street. It probably looks bad, but it's an impulse. I didn't hate Nero until I heard him lie about my stepsister. Why can't he just find someone else and leave her alone?

"Nero tells everyone we make out, but it's a lie," says Mia under her breath.

I stop and make Mia look at me.

"I know."

"Are you mad at me?" she asks.

"No, why would I be mad at you?"

"Everyone says I won't go out with him because you're my boyfriend."

Mia hides in her messy hair that is disheveled but stylish. I push it out of her eyes.

"I don't care what they say."

"You don't?"

"No. You and I both know the truth," I say.

We continue walking home, but take our time. There are cracks in the sidewalk and I fantasize about breaking Nero's teeth.

***

It's the middle of the night and I can hear my dad and Koharu fucking. I'm downstairs getting some water. They're both wasted and being really loud. I'm sure Mia is awake. It's 3:32 am and even though the house is spacious, the sound travels all the way upstairs. I'm grossed out and go back to my room to put in my earbuds. I bet Mia is super uncomfortable.

I'm listening to rap and hip-hop to drown out the disgusting noise. My dad and Koharu's relationship is stereotypically depressing. He works, she takes care of us and our home; he yells at her, she drinks, she cries, he guilts her and then she's forced to fuck him. I feel horrible for her. My mom was smart and got away from him. I don't resent her for it. She would have taken me with her, but she was afraid he would come looking for me.

I don't think my father really wanted me. He just needed something to anchor his wife to him. It's a sad truth, but I think he messed with her birth control. She loved me, but she was distant. My father is a sick bastard. I'm sure he charmed Koharu into marrying him so he would have a personal slave. That's how he treats her.

Koharu and I get along but I catch her looking at me like, "Why didn't you warn me?" But how can I tell anybody the truth about Joseph? He is too powerful to deny or expose. No one knows the real him except us. Everyone at work thinks he's a saint because he works long hours, but he is just in it for the money. The neighbors find him funny and charming because he only talks to them for two seconds. He does favors for them and they treat him like he's such a good guy. I don't think my dad is capable of doing anything nice for someone unless it benefits him.

My eyes are closed and I let the music blare through the earbuds. The bass rattles my insides, but in a good way. Music doesn't hurt when it's hitting me. I let the beat and the lyrics take me somewhere else. Then there's a small hand on mine. I open my eyes to Mia.

"What are you doing?" I whisper.

Now that the song is paused, I can hear the gross noises again.

"I can't sleep."

She grimaces. I know what she means. Her pajamas are pink with red flowers. The long sleeves are loose and I find myself hoping for them to accidentally get pushed up. I don't want to make her feel bad, so I ignore the urge to roll up her sleeve.

"Here."

I offer her one of my earbuds.

She seems put off by my taste in music, but I can tell she is also interested in what goes on in my head. Mia and I listen to a few songs together. I don't know if she likes them, but she doesn't complain.

She sits with me on my bed while I lay down. I stare up at the ceiling. Mia is looking out the window at the night sky. It is the blackest black, like her hair. The stars aren't visible tonight. She holds my left hand with both of hers. They are tiny and soft.

"Thank you," she says.

Mia hands me back the earbuds. I sit up so I can talk to my stepsister.

"I wish we could hang out more."

"You do?"

"Yes. My dad doesn't trust me around you. I don't mean to avoid you, but I don't want to give him any reason to bother us," I say.

"I know."

"I love you."

I move her hair to one side and admire the length of it.

"I love you," she whispers.

Mia hugs me. The house is silent again. We both notice it and she darts out of my room. I'm happy Mia and I have each other. We have a few more months at school together, but I lay in bed and worry about when I go to high school. How will I protect her? Ayumi said he would watch over her but I'll be a fifteen minute drive from her school. I plan on applying for my motorcycle license in three months.

I will always be there for Mia. If she needs me, I want to get to her as fast as I can. My heart races thinking about all the boys who will think they can touch her when I'm gone. I won't let any more bad things happen to her. There're jagged rocks in my stomach knowing that Biora and Kim will terrorize her, thinking I'm not paying attention but I am. I'll smash all their porcelain faces.

***

The elm and oak trees at school are deep red and gold. I'm watching the wind rustle the different shaped leaves. My friends are talking, but I'm not really listening. The past two weeks have been stressful. My dad's extra shifts are making him angrier than usual. He could not pick up the phone for once, but he tortures himself so he can use it as an excuse to take it out on me and Koharu. I make sure he ignores Mia. If he's wasted, I tell her to stay in her room and I hang out downstairs as his moving target until he goes to sleep.

I heard him walking up the stairs with his heavy feet last night. They thud extra loud when he's been drinking. I was worried he was going to bother Mia, so I met him in the hall. He didn't say a word to me, but he grabbed my shirt and tossed me into the painting of a red spider lily Koharu bought. The frame broke, the glass was smashed into pieces, and shards of glass stuck in my arm.

"Were you thinking about going into her room, son?" Joseph slurred his words.

The scotch made him smell sweet and sickly. His shirt was covered in cigarette smoke.

"No," I choked.

There were six small pieces of glass in my arm. I watched droplets of blood build where the shards were sticking out.

"What are you doing up?" he snarled.

"Seeing what you're doing up here," I said.

I'm not scared of him like I used to be. Now I talk back to him. I learned it doesn't matter. I get beat up just the same. Mia could hear everything, and I'm sure she cowered under her turquoise blanket.

"Whatever I want," he said flatly as he grabbed my neck.

"Why do you do this?" I coughed.

"Shut up. You're such a pussy," he slammed my head into the wall.

Warm blood pooled down my neck. It's a familiar feeling. My blood is all over our house. It's been on his hands and his shoes. There are stains of it on the walls and certain parts of the floor. The stairs he walked up crushed half my ribs on my way down when he threw me that one time. Our house holds a tragic story written in broken bones, bruises, and blood.

"Dad," I couldn't finish my sentence because he punched me in the stomach.

"You better not be going in her room at night, Ryon."

He got up and stomped down the stairs. As soon as he was gone, Mia came running out. She kneeled at my side and cried. My father scares her and seeing what he does to me hurts her more than it hurts me. She helped me up, and she used tweezers to pull out the pieces of glass and cleaned my cuts. My stepsister taking care of me made it feel less horrible, but I'm still sore. I keep it in around the guys. Sora and Teo can tell something is wrong, but don't bring it up in front of Ben or Koga and Kirin.

"Hey Ryon, you alright?" asks Koga.

I stop spacing out and try to pay attention to my friends.

"I'm okay. I didn't sleep good though," I say.

I smirk and try to conceal the pain behind my navel where my dad hit me. Mia wrapped my arm after she cleaned it. The broken glass will be gone when I get home. Koharu always cleans up Joseph's messes.

He'll leave me cash and she'll make me a bunch of food, or make a point to distract my dad. Nothing distracts him from abusing me for long. Not her love, body, or mind are enough to stop his fury. He says it's because he misses my mom, but I don't think my dad is capable of such a deep emotion.

"Why don't you ask Mia to join us?" says Sora.

He nods towards Mia, who is by herself. I wave at her to come over, but she freezes.

"I'll be right back." I get up and head towards her. "Want to come sit with me and my friends?"

"It's okay, you don't have to invite me everywhere," she says.

"I want you to hang out with me. C'mon, please."

I give her my exaggerated smile, and she follows me back towards the guys.

"Hi Mia," says Teo.

"Hey Mia. How are you?" asks Sora.

He tries to make her feel comfortable.

"I'm okay."

She sits in the grass with me. I can tell she is nervous.

"You have beautiful eyes," says Kirin.

He's trying to flirt with her nicely, but I don't like it. Her doll face turns pink, and she hides in her shroud of blackest black.

"Thank you," she whispers.

I want to tell Kirin to piss off, but no one else seems upset, so I keep it in.

"Why's your hair so long?" asks Ben.

He reaches out and picks up a handful of it. I wanted to make Mia feel like part of the group, but I think I made a mistake. Boys are boys even if they are my friends. I gently push his hand away. Ben gets the hint and laughs.

"Sorry," he says and puts his hands up.

"What are you reading?" asks Teo.

He points to her book. It's the one with the poem she showed me.

"Just a book of poems," she says.

"Can I see?" asks Koga.

My stepsister grips her book like it's the most important thing in the world. I don't want Koga to see inside her mind, but there's technically nothing wrong with him being curious. Why am I getting mad at my friends? Reluctantly, Mia hands over the pages filled with poetry about love, hope, and despair. Stuff that Koga wouldn't get. He skims over a couple of poems. His expression changes. It's mischievous and his eyes scan the pages, looking for secrets.

"I like it," he says and hands it back.

Mia seems surprised. She probably thought he was going to rip it up or make fun of her.

"You do?" she asks in her hushed voice.

"Yeah."

Koga nods.

I'm not sure what he's thinking, but it's putting me on edge. Kirin seems jealous that Koga is having a connection with Mia. The bell rings and I help my stepsister to her feet.

"I'll walk you to class," I say.

Once we are far enough away, I apologize for my friends' behavior.

"I'm sorry if Ben or Koga and Kirin made you uncomfortable."

"They seemed nice," she says.

"Ben and Kirin like you."

"Why?" she stops walking to look up at me.

"Because you're really pretty and sweet," I say.

"They don't even know me, though."

She seems annoyed as we approach her classroom.

Nero and Biora give me the side eye as they pass. I'm higher on the food chain, so they keep their mouths shut as I walk with my stepsister.

"There's something about you. Boys just like you. I'm going to have to beat up my friends," I joke.

I get her to grin before she goes into class. As I'm walking to mine, I lock eyes with Fuyuhisa and Akito. Both of them have hardened features. They have a look I can't describe until I recall the painting that captured my stepsister's attention at the museum. The boys watch her with longing.

CHAPTER EIGHT

WORTH A THOUSAND WORDS

Mia is painting in her room. I'm downstairs helping Koharu around the house. She is grateful, but I know she doesn't trust me. I'm not sure what my dad has told her or if it's her own intuition. We are folding laundry together. Even though it's just the four of us, there seems to be a mountain.

"Thank you, Ryon. I appreciate the help," says Koharu.

A strand of hair falls in her face as she picks up a sock and I see how much Mia resembles her.

"You're welcome."

I smile at my stepmom and she gives me a small grin but doesn't show her teeth.

"Mia has become quite fond of you."

"I'm fond of her as well," I say.

I want to be polite but don't want to come off creepy.

"I've never seen her open up to anyone. Her father was sick most of her childhood. I think it made her grow up too quickly," she says.

Koharu holds one of Mia's dresses, the lilac one, and sighs.

"I'm glad she chose me. It makes me feel special," I say.

I keep folding button up shirts and slacks hoping to ease Koharu's suspicions of me. My clothes are completely done and so are Mia's.

"I'll take these upstairs."

Our house is big. When it was just the two of us, it seemed empty. Now it feels fuller, but spaces in the living room and kitchen echo. Maybe it's because I perceive it as hollow. Everything is white and gray. My dad doesn't like bright colors, a lot of decoration, or anything anyone would call "kitschy" or "cute." We have mirrors that take up the bare walls because Joseph would rather look at himself than a piece of art.

Koharu has some paintings that he has allowed her to put up in the dining room. One of them is a koi fish done in watercolors. The other is the tail of a mermaid under ocean waves. Mia painted this one. I admire the shades of blue and green. How can someone so young be able to paint with such maturity? Mia's mind amazes me.

Upstairs has two mirrors in the hallway. There is no longer the painting of the red spider lilies. The mess is cleaned up, but I know my blood stains the wooden floor and slate walls. I hear Mia listening to something slow and electronic, but it makes my heart beat faster. She knows how to find music that reacts inside the soul like a chemistry project. I knock on her door.

"Come in," she says.

I lean in the doorway with her clothes. She's painting a black and white bird sitting in someone's hands. It's not finished, but I can tell it's going to be great.

"I have your clothes," I say as I set them down on her bed.

Mia's room is full of canvases, paints, books, paper, and pens. Instead of a couch and TV like my room, she has a small art studio with a table and chair. There's a light that hangs from the ceiling. She places her easel there. There's a shelf full of different brushes, tubes of acrylic paint, and loose leaf paper with her handwriting.

"Thank you."

She turns down her music and gets up to put her stuff away. Mia is the kind of person to do everything right then and not wait. I sit down on her turquoise and white bed to admire her art projects. Besides the painting of a bird, I see she has a few in the making sitting on the floor. There's an owl with a girl's face, a fox peering out from ferns, and a yellow snake with green eyes. It looks angry and venomous.

"I like your paintings," I say.

I smile at my stepsister and she gives me a full smile, which makes her look like a real girl.

"Do you want to hang out in a little bit?" I ask.

She nods her head "yes" and I go back downstairs to help Koharu. She's doing the dishes, so I decide to vacuum. Our house is clean, but it feels dirty. There are secrets here that can't be washed out with soap.

I wonder how Koharu handles being at my father's mercy. Even though I take all the beatings, our interactions are short and inconsistent. I can go a week without talking to him, but she has to be his doting wife.

"Thank you, Ryon. You didn't have to do that," she says.

"I wanted to."

"You're a sweet boy."

She touches her heart and again I am reminded of Mia. Koharu is wearing black capri pants and a red blouse. My stepmom is a decade younger than my dad and too pretty for him.

"Thank you, Koharu. Can I help you with anything else?" I ask.

"No, I'm fine."

She rubs the back of her neck. I'm sure she is sore from being uncomfortable all the time. Koharu used to work in a bank but has been a housewife since marrying Joseph. He likes to eliminate any independence a woman might have.

I go back upstairs and ask Mia to come watch a movie with me. She picks an old classic one I've never seen before. I don't watch this sort of stuff, but I do it for Mia. She has taught me to enjoy deeper things. My life consisted of school, sports, and friends. Now I'm learning about depth, emotions, and how it all connects to art.

"I'm glad you're my stepbrother," announces Mia.

She's sitting next to me, but not too close. I'm leaning back with my head on the back of the couch.

"Me too."

I say and reach for her hand right as Koharu walks in.

I have terrible timing.

"I brought you two something to drink," says Koharu as she sets down milky teas.

"Thanks mom," says Mia.

She grabs hers and doesn't seem embarrassed or concerned about

Koharu seeing me hold her hand.

"Thank you, Koharu."

I sit up and out of the corner of my eye I see Koharu pause an extra second in my doorway as she leaves.

***

I meet Sora and Teo at the park to play basketball. Mia has joined me. She's wearing her white coat and black boots that make her look like a doll. I'm happy she smiles more, but her eyes are still sad. They keep secrets from me. I thought about opening up that yellow diary again, but I never have the nerve. It doesn't feel right.

The sky is blue with misty clouds. The red and gold leaves stand out against the bright day. Fall can be white and gray like our home. I like it better when it's all the colors. The amber, orange, and brown leaves litter the ground and make satisfying crunching noises under our feet. It smells like it's about to rain. That grassy aquatic scent around the park is cool and refreshing.

There's a bench in the sun that's near to the court. She has the book of poems and her journal with her. I kind of hope for it to fall open just for a second. There's something about her long hair that shrouds her mysterious mind that makes me curious past the point of acceptance. Not wanting to make my stepsister uncomfortable, I let her tell me things at her own pace. She's become more trusting of me and I don't want to ruin that.

"Will you be okay here for a little bit?" I ask.

"Yeah. I'll be fine," she says.

Mia nods her head at me and her doll eyelashes flutter. Something about her doesn't seem real. I think this is why all the boys are obsessed with her. I walk over to the guys and we shoot some hoops with no real game or goal in mind. We just bullshit and hang out.

"How's Mia doing?" asks Sora.

He jumps to shoot and scores. Teo and I clap for him and he gives us a bow. We all laugh and he throws me the ball. I barely have to do anything to make it. Teo and Sora shake their heads at me and laugh.

"She's good. I think she's happier. People don't bully her so much anymore," I say and pass the ball to Teo. He bounces it but doesn't shoot.

"Yeah, man. You're scary when you're mad. Watching you almost murder Fuyuhisa was a sight to see," says Sora.

"He shouldn't have put his hand in her shirt or up her skirt. I saw him do both," I say.

I'm furrowing my eyebrows and getting pissed just thinking about it.

"Too bad you can't do that to Biora or Kim," says Teo.

He bounces the ball and shoots but doesn't make it.

"I know. Those girls are fucking mean. They put gum in her hair and threw her in the showers. Can you believe that?"

I shouldn't even talk about it because it's making the psycho in me come out.

"At least you stopped all the boys from bothering her. Nero won't go near her anymore," says Teo.

"Really?"

I laugh as I get the ball and dunk it.

"Yeah! Fumika told me Nero saw you and her at the bookstore and that you looked at him like you were going to go full crazy white boy," says Teo with a grin.

"I was," I admit.

Sora puts his hand on my elbow and looks up at me.

"Don't let them bring out the worst in you, Ryon. If you have to fight, be sure to always do it with Mia in mind," says Sora, who is always thoughtful and wise.

"I'm going to go check on her."

I pass the ball to Teo and walk over to the bench she's on. She's reading a poem and smiling to herself. "What are you reading?" I ask as I sit down next to her.

Mia pulls her hair out of her face and reads to me right away this time.

Two birds
One sky
Never parting
When they fly

My stepsister looks up at me to read my expression. She thinks I don't get the things she likes, and she's right, but in some ways I understand her completely.

"That's a wonderful poem," I say.

She closes the book and scans the park.

"I really like that one."

Mia's voice seems stronger. It was never shaky, but it was so soft it was like everything she said was a secret. I see her looking at the swings.

"Do you want to go over there?" I ask.

"I'm too old to swing," she says.

This makes me laugh, and she has a hurt look on her face.

"No, you're not. C'mon. I know you want to."

I take her hand and pick up her books. We walk over to the swings. I gesture for her to sit down and she nods her head "no" at me.

"C'mon, I know you want to," I say.

She gives in and I push her on the swings, but not too hard. I don't want to scare her.

"Why do you do this?" she asks.

"Do what?"

"Always try to make me happy."

I grab the swing as it comes back and stop it.

"Because I want you to be happy," I say.

"This is the happiest I've been in a really long time. Thank you, Ryon." I continue to push her a few more times.

She and I go back over to the bench and I meet Teo and Sora on the court.

"Hey guys."

I wave at them, and they approach me.

"Don't freak out, but Akito and Fuyuhisa are here," says Sora with a stern look on his face.

"Where?" I ask.

"Over there."

Teo nods his head but doesn't look. The two of them are walking by with smug expressions. I could deck them both in the face right now. They stare at me but it's when their gaze is fixated behind me, on Mia, is when I start to get really pissed. I go over to confront them, but

Sora grabs my gray hoodie.

"Don't," he says.

Sora is being very serious.

"They're being creeps," I grumble.

Akito and Fuyuhisa are out of sight, and I relax my shoulders. Sora lets go of my jacket.

"They didn't do anything. Let it go," says Sora.

"Okay."

I sigh and grab the back of my head with both hands.

"Want to play ball a little bit?" asks Teo, wanting to diffuse the situation.

"Yeah," I say. Sora agrees.

We play for an unknown amount of time. I'm here, but not here. There's the nagging thought of the boys staring at Mia with longing. Dissociated and agitated, I bounce the ball and shoot with no conviction but still make it. It rains as I look over my shoulder to make sure Mia is safe. No one is bothering her and I see her smiling as she writes something in her yellow diary.

***

The girl that sits next to me in math keeps staring at me. Her name is Chisaki. She has short hair, almost boy short, but it looks good on her. As weird as it is to say, she has a nicely shaped head. She wears sparkly earrings.

"Hey Ryon, what are you doing after school?" she asks.

Her voice is deeper than most girls. Chisaki has a lot of freckles and big lips. They are full with no discernible corners.

"Nothing, why?" I ask.

"I need to take some pictures for the Photography Club. Do you want to join me at the east end park?"

She has soft brown eyes with orange around the pupil. They remind me of a deer. Her question catches me off guard, but I feel like I should give her a chance.

"Sure. I need to walk my stepsister home first, though."

"She can come with. Mia, right?"

"Yeah."

"Okay, I'll meet you guys on the steps!" she exclaims.

"Sounds good, Chisaki."

I'm surprised Chisaki invited me somewhere, let alone Mia. I wonder if this is a trick. She has never done anything mean to anyone. As far as I know, Chisaki has been known as the girl with no friend group. She has many people to hang out with but all from different cliques. Her popular friends don't include bitchy people like Biora, but it makes me question her motives. Maybe she likes me. Girls are unreadable.

The bell rings and I wait for Mia. It's overcast and cold. I think about loosening my tie as soon as I walk off these steps. I hate the way I feel like someone else. Chisaki is out first and she waves at me as she runs over. Her neck is adorned with a bulky camera. She has a backpack with a bunch of clip-on stuffed animals and glittery things. Her smile is warm, and she doesn't appear to have a suspicious air to her. Analyzing her further, I notice she is missing a canine tooth. I think Mia will be safe around her.

"Thanks for joining me!" she chimes.

"No problem. Thanks for inviting us," I say.

I feel awkward but Setsuna turned out to be a nice girl, so maybe Chisaki will be, too. Mia exits the school and looks at me and then Chisaki.

"Hey, Mia. We're going to go to the park and take some pictures before we head home, okay?"

"Okay," she says.

Mia seems unsure, but she trusts me, so she and I follow Chisaki to the park, where she wants to take the photos. Chisaki points out different parts of the neighborhoods and talks about contrasting and illuminating. I don't really know what she is saying, but I try to listen because photos are art and art is important to Mia. We arrive at the east end park where there are tons of oaks, elms, and chestnut trees. The leaves get redder as the season goes on. The yellows are tinged brown. Winter is almost here.

The grass at this park is plush, and my shoes sink into the soft earth. There aren't too many people out today. Several couples, a few teenagers like us, and young families stroll around and enjoy the multicolored leaves. It's quiet and everything seems muffled by the gray atmosphere. The roses have dark green stems, black thorns, and bright red flowers.

I catch Mia admiring the dangerous looking roses. They are deceitful, inviting, but not. I get nervous she is going to reach out and grab one, but she doesn't. The idea of her squeezing a thorn into her palm to make herself bleed is a disturbing and intrusive thought. I have them more often. The long sleeves she wears make me paranoid.

Chisaki snaps photos in rapid succession. She guides us over a small bridge and closer to the giant oak. The girl with the camera makes a million clicking noises as she spins around. She kneels down to get a better picture of a rose. I notice Mia isn't next to me anymore. She's still on the steel bridge that goes over a small stream. The different shaped leaves fall into the water and race in teams.

"What are you looking at?" I ask her.

"Watching the leaves," she says.

"Are you okay?"

"Yeah. I'm good. No one's done anything bad to me. I was just thinking about that."

She gives me a small smile but quickly returns her gaze to the racing leaves.

"Good, I'm glad."

I put my arm around her, and we watch the red and gold play their game. Red wins. I let her go and search for Chisaki. She is taking mine and Mia's picture. The girl with short hair and big lips comes running at me out of breath.

"This is an amazing photo!" she says.

"Can I see?" I ask.

She hands me the camera. It's Mia and me with my arm around her. She has her tiny hands on the railing of the bridge and we're both looking down. Mia's sweater is dark blue. The background is shades of slate, white, and indigo, but the fall leaves add a nice splash of color.

"Do you like it?" asks Chisaki.

I know she is being sincere. She is an artist, too. I wonder if Mia and she have an unspoken bond over such things. The emotion captured in this picture is lost to me, but I feel it deeply.

"I love it."

CHAPTER NINE

ALL THE BOYS HAVE BAD INTENTIONS

Winter is here. I'm spacing out and watching snowflakes float past the window. I should get back to my test, but I'm distracted. Chisaki got an award for her photo of Mia and I. It's not that I'm upset that she won, but it feels like she stole a moment from me and now everyone is a part of it. She is a nice girl, though. I shouldn't hold it against her.

She thought it was beautiful, and it is. Her perspective is unique and interesting. I wonder if that is why she invited us to the park. Chisaki knew it would captivate, unlike our other classmate's work. A white guy and a Japanese girl watching leaves race down the stream. That's not what the girl with the camera titled it. She put it under the name "Divergent."

The Photography Club put out a magazine with the best photos. Ours was on page six. There are a lot of other good photos, but that one made everyone pause, even the teachers. Chisaki brightened every time someone gawked at it. She took no offense. I saw her take in everyone's emotions as they skimmed the book's pictures. Hers made people in every grade take an extra glance.

Of course, the rumors are back in full swing, but I don't care. Chisaki didn't take that photo to hurt us. I know that was not her intent. Mia told me she admired Chisaki's photos. Apparently, she is a talented violinist as well. I am learning all sorts of things about people and the things that make them tick. Mia showed Koharu the picture happily and I saw a dark shadow come over her mother's eyes. It lasted only a second, but I noticed it. She definitely thinks something is going on between us. I'm at my locker when Akito approaches me.

"What do you want?" I snarl.

"I get why you're so protective of her."

"Fuck off, dude."

"I think you two are in love. It all makes sense now," he laughs.

Akito has a big forehead that is accentuated by a buzzed haircut and a pig nose. I want to break it. His eyes are bottle green and devoid of any light. The malicious stare of a predator. I think about him tugging on Mia's hair and I want to rip his face off.

"Yeah? So what if I am? I bet you're jealous," I say.

I give him my smuggest smile and his jaw drops.

"You're really sick, man."

"You're the sick one. Stay away from her."

I snap as I slam my locker shut.

"She's all yours. I wouldn't want to take away the crazy white boy's girlfriend," he says.

Akito backs up and cackles like the psychos in movies do. I don't care what people say. If the worst they can come up with is I'm her boyfriend, then I can take it. I know it's worse for her. Girls are a particular kind of vicious. If Mia's my girlfriend, then I'm a stud, but no matter what, Mia is a slut.

I'm walking to class and see Mia at her locker. She got a haircut, but it's still long. Koharu insisted on her fixing it up so now it comes to the middle of her back. It's messy despite all the brushing. I like it though. It captures a wilder spirit that I'd like to see Mia have.

"Hey Mia. How's your day going?" I ask.

"It's okay. Everyone's saying you're my boyfriend because of Chisaki's picture though," she says.

"Don't be mad at Chisaki. I think she liked that photo of us."

"I'm not. It's a really good picture. I just wish people didn't have to judge everything we do," says Mia, as she grabs a notebook out of her locker.

"Me too. But I don't care what they say. You shouldn't either."

I smile at my stepsister, hoping to make her smile and it works this time.

"The boys won't go near me, but all the girls have been extra mean," she admits.

I knew this was happening, but was waiting for her to tell me.

"What are they doing?" I ask.

"They ask me gross questions like what it's like to sleep in your bed and how often we make out."

She grimaces and seems embarrassed.

"I know you don't believe me, but they're just jealous that all the boys like you," I say.

"They took the poetry book you bought me and ripped it up. They said it was wrong to read gushy love poems while thinking about my stepbrother."

Mia's voice is more grown up. She's not as afraid to use it anymore. I'm pissed that those girls ruined her book, but I feel powerless against them. I wish I knew what to do against the mean queens.

"I'll buy you a new one," I offer.

We're nearing Mia's class. I don't walk her to all of them, but I make my presence known.

"It's okay. I don't need it. But it makes me sad they destroyed it," says my stepsister, and I want to hug her but don't dare do anything to draw attention.

"They destroyed it because they'll never have anyone care about them the way I care about you." I meant to make her feel better, but Mia seems frightened of me. "I'm sorry. Was it something I said?" I ask.

"I didn't know you felt so strongly about me."

"Well, I do. I'll always be here for you," I say.

Mia goes into class, and I feel hundreds of eyes on me as I walk to mine.

***

Koharu and my dad are passed out at 8:24 pm on Christmas eve, which is fine by me. We had our tense dinner and opened gifts. I gave Mia an expensive teal dress with long sleeves in front of Koharu and my dad, but I have another present for her. Mia painted the basketball court me and my friends go to. It's very realistic. I can't believe how talented she is.

My dad got me a new basketball, designer sneakers, and a sweatband. They all reek of fancy department stores. Koharu gave me three silk button ups in hues of olive green, black, and maroon. Not my typical style, but they're really nice. I was put off by my dad's gifts for the girls. He got Koharu a pair of super extravagant earrings and a matching bracelet. They glittered under our chandelier and I wondered what my dad did to her this time to make him feel the need to buy her something flashy. Something that says "I'm sorry."

He gave Mia a charm bracelet with a dozen diamond trinkets on it. Sparkly rabbits, koi fish, and hearts dangled from a gold band. It's uncomfortable how lavish it is. Maybe it's just the paranoia but I wonder what he's up to. Did he do something to Mia? Is he buying her off for his future destruction? I try to put those thoughts out of my head.

My dad isn't good at discerning what's acceptable when it comes to family matters. Maybe he just didn't know what to get her. The thing that won't leave me alone is the look on her face after she opened it. She seemed shocked but also like she knew something. Another secret. Everything about her is private and everyday I grow closer to tearing through her yellow diary.

It's a relief hearing the loud snoring coming from down the hall as I walk downstairs. I grab a bottle of aloe green tea and stand by the window in the living room. Our curtains are slate, just like our rugs and furniture. A black coffee table with neatly stacked books sits in the middle. There are four parlor palms, one in each corner, but the living room doesn't feel alive at all. No one ever sits in here. I don't think we have ever watched anything or sat together as a family in this room.

The snow is coming down in thin ribbons. It's dark but the Christmas lights in the neighborhood illuminate everything red, green, purple, and blue. No one is out. Now is the perfect time to ask Mia to go on a walk with me. Even though my dad is asleep, I still want to give her this gift somewhere else. Something about his presence makes me feel like I'm doing something wrong. I go back upstairs and knock on Mia's door.

"Do you want to go for a walk and look at Christmas lights with me?" I ask.

"Okay," she says.

Mia grabs her light pink jacket with the fur. She is wearing a white dress and tan boots. Her legs are bare. Mia doesn't put on leggings in the winter.

"Aren't you going to be cold?" I ask.

"I like the freezing air. It's my favorite time of year because of the cold."

Mia's answers sometime leave me in a daze. I don't know anyone who likes the cold, but I'm from California. What do I know? My stepsister is odd, but I find her more and more intriguing.

I lock the door and we start down the street and admire the Christmas decorations. They are sterile and perfectly lined up in this neighborhood. It almost feels like we're walking through a movie set. Mia's hair shines orange under the streetlights. She takes tiny breaths that leave her mouth in clouds of white mist.

One house has all pink and white lights. It reminds me of springtime when the cherry blossom trees come back to life. Mia has stopped to look at this one as well. An orange cat slithers across the yard and into the garden. There's no one but us on the street and all the curtains are closed.

"Mia, I have something for you."

I pull the small gift out of my red bomber jacket. It's in silver wrapping paper with a turquoise ribbon. When I think of Mia, I think of the color blue. Not just because she is sad, but also because she is deep, like the ocean.

"But you already gave me a present," she says as she holds the tiny package in her hands.

"I know, but I got you another one," I say.

Mia studies me for a moment before carefully opening her gift. She lights up when she sees it.

"Ryon, this is too nice. I can't accept this," she says as she holds the silver chain of the necklace I got her.

It has a snowflake pendant with sky blue topaz. I spent a long time looking for something that reflected her personality. Her birthday is in winter. She likes the cold, her aura is blue.

"Yes, you can."

I kneel down and take the necklace from her so I can put it around her neck.

"Thank you."

"Do you like it?" I ask.

"I love it," she says and puts her skinny arms around me.

I'm glad Mia and I have each other. Sora and Teo are my best friends, but Mia and I have a closeness that's different than with the guys. Mia opens my eyes to things I never bothered to look at. She gives me a purpose. I won't let her be sad the way she used to be. It's my goal to make Mia a real girl.

***

There is snow on the ground, but not very much. It will be gone by tomorrow. The guys and I are hanging out at the ramen place where all the teenagers go. Teo and Sora are happily slurping away at their noodles. Kirin and Koga are texting. They've been detached from the rest of the group. Or maybe that is just the way I perceive it. I think I made things awkward. Not really paying attention, sipping on my tea, I'm zoned out when Setsuna comes over to talk to me.

"Hey Ryon!" she beams at me.

The guys all go slack jaw and I hear Teo gulp. Setsuna has her hair up and is wearing a burnt orange coat. It brings out her blue-green eyes.

"Hey Setsuna. What's up?" I ask.

"Can I sit with you guys?"

"Sure," I say and scoot over.

All the guys look at each other and then me as Setsuna sits next to me.

"What are you guys talking about?" she asks.

"Not much," I say.

"Yeah, just sort of out of it. The tests today were brutal," says Sora.

"I think my brain is done for," jokes Teo.

Koga and Kirin stare at Setsuna but don't say anything. They're the biggest talkers when it comes to girls, but as soon as one sits down with us, they're dead silent.

"Yeah, today was rough. Nothing like ramen and tea to take the edge off," she says in her bubbly voice.

I can feel the guys' hearts pulsing in their necks.

"For sure," I agree.

Setsuna is nice to everyone and I can't tell if she's just my friend or if she likes me. We talk at school but haven't hung out again. Chisaki comes up to me in the halls to show me her latest work, but we haven't hung out much either.

Girls are confusing. They're nice to be around, though. I love my friends, but girls are way more interesting. Not in the typical way boys are attracted to girls, either. They have these deep feelings that are only describable with a song lyric, a painting, a photo, or a poem. Their hair is shiny and they have big smiles for no reason a lot of the time. There's something alluring about them.

"I bet you all did great," says Setsuna as she takes a sip of her peach bubble tea.

She is the person to always see the bright side.

"Thank you. I hope so," says Sora.

"Are you guys excited about high school?" she asks.

I get a lump in my throat. Sora and Teo know I don't want to leave Mia. Kirin and Koga nod their heads "yes" but don't say anything. I avoid answering the question.

"It seems like it all went by so fast," says Teo.

He's stopped eating. His glasses fog up and he takes them off to clean them.

"Yeah, but also like it took a million years!" laughs Sora.

"What about you, Ryon?" asks Setsuna.

"I figure school's all the same, right?" I say.

Everyone nods to agree, but I think the guys feel the tension in my voice.

"I suppose. It's an experience though," sighs Setsuna.

She is thinking about this in a way I'm not familiar with. She is saying it's going to be fun because it will be different.

"That's true," I say.

Setsuna gets up to leave.

"I gotta go. Nice to talk to you guys! Bye!"

She waves at us and we watch her long ponytail sway through

the window as she walks down the street. Once she's out of sight, I hear the guys all take a breath.

"Damn, Ryon. All the girls like you," says Kirin.

I roll my eyes at him.

"Setsuna is just my friend," I say.

"What about Chisaki? I see her come up to you in the halls and flirt with you," says Koga.

Great, now they're chatty.

"She doesn't flirt with me."

I'm getting pissed.

"What's up with you guys? You seem really talkative now that Setsuna is gone. Maybe you should be like Ryon and actually try talking to a girl," says Sora as he throws a look at Koga and Kirin.

The twins accept being chastised and keep their mouths shut.

"Ryon is smart and nice. It makes sense why all the girls want to talk to him," says Teo.

He's returned to his ramen now that it's just us guys. I feel weird having my friends analyze me and the girls I talk to.

"I barely talk to any girls." I say and go back to my lychee bubble tea so I don't grind my teeth.

"Bullshit," says Kirin.

"What are you going off on me for?"

"It's not just Setsuna and Chisaki. Naomi is always trying to get your attention in social studies. She wants you to ask her out but you don't seem to notice," says Kirin.

He's making a face like I disgust him.

"Yeah. Mayu has been in love with you since seventh grade. I heard her tell Airi that," says Koga with a smug expression.

What the fuck?

"So what if they like me? You guys got a problem with that?" I ask.

Sora and Teo look over at me to see what I'm going to do next. We lower our voices so people from school don't stare.

"I do, actually," says Kirin.

This shocks me.

"What?" I ask.

"You don't notice them because your eyes are on Mia. It's not fair!

Save some pussy for the rest of us," says Kirin.

"Whatever," I say and grab my bag.

Koga and Kirin remain seated, but Sora and Teo follow me out into the cold. I zip up my red parka and let the snowflakes cool me down. The crazy burns me from the inside.

"Don't listen to those guys," says Sora.

He pats my back like a brother would. Teo is on my other side and he nods to agree.

"I can't believe how they think. Like it's your fault the girls don't talk to them. Look at them, they didn't even say two words to Setsuna," says Teo, who gestures a lot with his hands.

Sora and I laugh, and it makes me feel better.

"You don't think they're right, though, do you?" I ask.

My friends stop in the middle of the sidewalk. No one else is out and we collect snow in our hair.

"They both have a crush on Mia. It's obvious they think something is going on and they're jealous. We know there's not, Ryon," says Sora.

"You really care about her. They're just making it weird," offers Teo and we keep walking.

"All I want is to make her happy and everyone treats me like I'm doing something wrong," I say.

"It's because they have bad intentions," says Sora.

The three of us part ways and head home. I walk up to my house and think about the bracelet my dad gave Mia. The way Koga skimmed through her poetry book. The rumors about her and Nero causes a headache behind the eyes. It churns in my skull as I recall what Fuyuhisa did to her. I replay the way Ben touched her hair and what Akito said to me. There's a reason no one trusts boys. It's because they all have bad intentions.

CHAPTER TEN

BLOOD AND LACE

I've been good and haven't gotten into any fights even though I want
to. Mia told me no one has tried to touch her, but the girls still gossip. I
am powerless against the mean queens. They have shiny hair that
reeks of name brand products and chew gum aggressively. Their lips
are light pink and spread lies. I wish it was acceptable to choke them
out. Turning their faces blue invades my thoughts, but I push them
out of my mind.

"Are there any girls that are your friend?" I ask.

We're standing at the window downstairs, admiring the quiet of
the neighborhood. There isn't a lot of snow but the thin white blanket
quiets everything. It's peaceful. My dad and Koharu are out and we
can be next to each other.

"Not really. I try to talk to the artistic girls, but they snub me. The
smart kids don't think I'm smart enough. The popular girls hate me
even though I've never done anything to them. I don't fit in," she says.

"I like that you don't fit in," I say.

"You do?"

"Yeah."

"I'm glad you're my friend. I don't need anybody else," says Mia.

She smiles with her teeth. It looks good on her. She's wearing a light pink dress and a fuzzy black cardigan. More doll clothes. I like the way she dresses, but it perplexes me. She never wears tights or socks except for school, even in the coldest months. Her coats are vintage. Mia likes textured sweaters, floral dresses, and long sleeves.

"Are you happy?" I ask.

She reaches up and holds the snowflake pendant in her tiny hand. Her reflection in the window is content.

"I am," she says.

I put my arm around her.

"Good."

"I'm going to miss you when you go to high school."

She lets go of her necklace and crosses her arms. I can tell it makes her anxious thinking about me not being there.

"We still have three months together. And guess what?"

"What?" she asks.

"I'm getting my motorcycle license so I can get to you wherever you are as fast as I can," I say.

"Really?" she asks.

My stepsister's eyes are wide with surprise.

"Of course. I want to always be there for you if you need me."

I kneel down to take in Mia's shocked but happy face. Every day, I think she looks more real. I wonder if she felt hollow, like a porcelain doll. Right now, her eyes are shiny, her eyebrows are expressive, and her raspberry mouth is smiling.

"You're the best," she says.

Mia puts her arms around my neck, and I hug her waist. She feels so small in my arms. I'm reminded of her painting. The one with the little bird in the palm of someone's hands. I wonder if this is the feeling she was conveying in that piece. Mia makes me wonder about all sorts of things. We go back to taking in the snow kissed streets. I feel better knowing Mia is happy. For once, everything might be okay. Right then, Koharu and my dad walk in. I'm glad Mia and I aren't hugging anymore.

"Hey son," says my dad.

His voice booms, even if he's talking at a normal level. It contrasts with Koharu's voice, which is soft but not as quiet as Mia's.

"Hi kids," says my stepmom.

Her face is pretty, but there are dark circles under her eyes. I'm sure Joseph is on her about something. He's never satisfied.

"Hey dad," I say.

"Hi," says Mia.

She gives them both a small wave.

"Ryon, can I talk to you for a second?" asks my dad.

Shit, what now?

"Yeah," I say and follow him to his study.

This room has an ominous energy to it. I feel the hair on the back of my neck stand up. I'm cold even though I have on a hoodie. "What's up, dad?" I ask.

"You're going to be a man soon. I can't believe how grown up you are," he says.

I'm confused by my dad's strange behavior. It usually means something bad is going to happen soon. He pours himself a glass of scotch in a rocks glass. So it begins. "You're going to be turning sixteen and entering high school."

"I know. I'm excited," I lie, but try to seem enthused.

My dad leans on his desk and sips his scotch.

"I got you a present, son."

"You didn't have to do that," I say.

His gifts make me uneasy.

"But I did," he grins and ushers me out to the garage where he keeps his fat black car.

The door makes a rattling metal sound as it opens. In the middle of the brightly lit room is an all black motorcycle and matching black helmet.

"Wow, dad! Thank you!"

I say as I run up to inspect my gift.

It's a small bike, but it's undoubtedly expensive. My dad wouldn't skimp on a bribe.

"Do you like it?" he asks, the rocks glass still in his meaty hand.

"I love it. Thank you! This is great," I say.

I walk around the bike and study the frame, the tires, and the black on black. Everything about it is sleek and glinting. The chrome stands out against all the black. I can't wait to ride this thing.

"I know you don't get your license for another two months, but I wanted to show you I care," he says.

This is odd. My dad's words seep in with a sting. It's hard to tell if he loves me or not. Our relationship wasn't always bad. When I was a kid, I didn't know any better, but we had some good times. There were days we went to the park, or he helped me with homework and I remember things being relatively normal until I turned thirteen. I know he hits me because he is a sad and shitty person, but I often wonder if he really loves me the way a normal dad loves his son.

***

I wake up excited because it's sunny and it's Mia's birthday. Looking out the window, I see that it's clear with no snow on the ground. I throw on my clothes and run my hands through my shaggy hair. My dad says I should get a haircut, but every time he says that, it makes me put it off longer. I look in the mirror and see someone different from him with my hair like this, so I keep it.

After I get ready for the day, I check on Mia's gifts. I got her a stuffed red panda. It's almost as big as her. I thought it was cute like her and I know other girls like this stuff, so I figured she would enjoy it. Then I got her a new set of paint. I bought the one that looked the nicest. The guy at the store said these were what more "experienced" painters like. There's a chunky white sweater I got from one of the places all the girls in my grade talk about. I also got her a new diary. It's teal with gold snowflakes on it. I thought she could keep a happier journal now that I'm in her life.

I go downstairs and scope the place out. My dad is gone. I can hear Koharu taking a shower. I'm happy my dad got me that motorcycle, but he still makes me nervous. Being around him is a rollercoaster. A wild ride that leaves me black and blue. It's early, but not too early. I knock on Mia's door.

"Hey," she says.

"Happy birthday," I say and hand her the giant red panda.

She takes it in her skinny arms and hugs it.

"Thank you."

"Wait, I got you other stuff."

"You get me too much stuff," she says.

"You deserve all of it," I say, and I grab her other gifts out of my room.

She stands in the doorway in astonishment. I hand her the sky blue bag with sparkly tissue paper. Mia lifts up each item with care and her eyes fill up and tears spill out. I kneel down to comfort her.

"What's wrong?" I ask.

"Nothing. You're just so nice to me," she says.

"Don't be sad about it," I tease as I wipe away her tears.

"I'm not sad."

"Then why are you crying?" I ask.

Girls are confusing, but Mia is something else. There is so much that goes on in her head that I'm not privileged to.

"Sometimes it happens when I feel something deeply. Right now I'm really happy," she says.

I think I get it, but I'm not sure, so I just nod my head.

"So you like your presents?"

"Yes. Thank you," she says.

"What do you want to do for your birthday?"

"I don't know. What should we do?" she asks.

Mia is the kind of person to disregard herself even on her own birthday.

"I want to do whatever you want to do," I say.

"Can we go to the movies?" she asks.

"Of course."

"Then can we go to the bookstore?" she asks.

Now she seems excited.

"You want to go to the bookstore again?" I tease.

"We don't have to."

"I'm just joking. Yeah, I'll take you to the bookstore. I'll take you anywhere."

We tell Koharu goodbye and set out on Mia's birthday adventure. She puts the white sweater I got her over her dark blue dress with daisies on it. They compliment her snowflake necklace. My stepsister is pretty and I think about how she is only going to get prettier and I think of all the guys I'm gonna have to beat up.

Mia picks out a drama. Normally I don't like these kinds of movies but it's her birthday and I want her to choose. I buy her popcorn and catch glimpses of her during the film. She reminds me of a rabbit the way she nibbles her popcorn. It's cute but I would never say anything because it might embarrass her. The movie isn't bad and I try to be deeper than I am. It's kind of entertaining perceiving things differently.

We're walking to the bookstore. Mia reaches for her necklace and I watch her hold it and the way it guards her heart. I wonder what boy is good enough for her. Who is holding her heart? I don't ask her. She wouldn't tell me, anyway. Mia seems like the girl to focus on her studies instead of chasing boys. There's some people from school in the store. I make awkward eye contact with Naomi and look down. She's a sassy girl with curly brown hair and dark eyes. Her left cheek has a dimple in it. Usually I'd smile at her, but I feel weird. Kirin and Koga made me feel like I can't look at a girl without there being something there.

As we walk past shelves full of astrology, physics, and psychology books, I see Chisaki. She appears to be lost in a book about the history of photography. It lasts only a second, but she looks up at me and smiles but doesn't come up to me. I wonder if she and Setsuna have crushes on me or if they talk to me because I actually talk, unlike Koga and Kirin.

I'm irritated to see Fuyuhisa and an older boy hanging out by the manga section. Fuyuhisa gives me a shit-eating grin. They're both wearing windbreakers and ripped up jeans. The older boy has shoulder length hair that's completely straight. It covers his eyes and obscures his face. I can tell he's older from the lines around his mouth and the way he holds himself. He's definitely not a teenager.

Mia doesn't notice them, but their eyes roam over her body that's covered by her sweater and hair. But I feel the rage build up in me. It starts in my stomach and runs up my spine until it enters my skull and burns me up like a fever. I hear static. I'm in my pool of anger until Mia tugs at my sleeve. She holds open a book and points to a poem.

If I could fly

Away

It would be

No use

I can't

Escape
Myself

"What do you think?" she asks.

Her bottom eyelashes curl dramatically and I take in her doll features as she stares up at me.

"You have good taste in poetry."

"You think so?"

"I like everything you show me," I say.

She takes the book from me, and we continue browsing. I let her pick out whatever she wants. Mia decides on another poetry book. This one is heavy and bound in red leather. She grabs two light novels. On our way out, she picks up a pocket sized poetry book. It's gray with purple and yellow flowers on it. As we stand in line, I study the cover. The title is written in hunter green: "Stepping on Broken Stemmed Violets." Fuyuhisa and his friend come up behind us. I instinctively put my arm around Mia.

"Hey Ryon," says Fuyuhisa in an exaggerated, friendly way.

"Piss off," I say over my shoulder.

Mia is looking down, clutching her books. I pull her closer to me and keep my eyes on Fuyuhisa.

"I was just being polite," he says.

His dead shark eyes have a glossy sheen to them. They are dangerous and unpredictable. I see them scan Mia and I resist the urge to punch him in the quiet bookstore. We step closer to the register and I try to cool my fevered head.

"Is she your girlfriend? She's pretty cute," says the older boy.

He flips his hair and I see his face. There's defined lines around his dark blue eyes. He has a five o'clock shadow. His hair is sleek like he uses a lot of product on it. I embrace Mia and glare at him. This guy has to be in his twenties.

"She is. And she's too young for you. Stop looking at her," I snap.

The man puts his hands up and laughs. Fuyuhisa and he exchange a glance. They're both on the taller side, probably around 5' 8", but I tower over them at 6' 2".

"You look way older than her," says the man.

"I'm only two years older than her. What are you? Twenty?"

"I'm twenty-one and I like 'em young," he sticks his tongue out at me.

I'm glad we're next in line because I'm going to freak out. Mia sets her books down. I pay for them quickly and I keep my eyes on those two until we're out of the store.

"I'm sorry," I say.

"It's not your fault. It's mine. Everywhere I go, I draw attention. I don't know why," she says.

"It's because you're so pretty."

"You always say that."

"It's true," I say.

Mia clutches her books and smiles.

"I heard Biora has a crush on you. Everyone sees how nice you are to me. That's why she treats me the way she does," says Mia.

"Ugh. Like I'd ever kiss that mean little green-eyed snake."

I make a face at Mia and we both laugh.

"A lot of girls in my grade like you."

"A lot of boys in my grade like you," I say.

"Fuyuhisa is going to tell everyone you're my boyfriend."

"I don't care what that piece of garbage thinks or does."

"Me neither," she says.

We walk home in the sunshine and I feel good about making my stepsister's birthday a happy one.

***

I'm sitting in class looking out the window. It's sunny with some creamy clouds. The shadows pass over the schoolyard. I feel my phone buzz but ignore it. I'll answer it after class. It's faint and I'm spacing out, but I hear everyone else's phone buzz as well. One after the other. The teacher doesn't notice. We all stare in false engagement. I see a girl across the room look at her phone and gasp.

The boy in front of me holds out his phone to sneak a glance. The teacher is oblivious. They keep writing on the chalkboard and talking too fast. The boy in front of me has hair that's buzzed in the back and sides and is long on top. His bangs shake when he flinches. What is everyone looking at?

There is a warm pulse starting at my temple. I feel anxious and clench my fist. Somehow, just somehow, I know this is linked to Mia. I have that sick sense of knowing. The girl to my right opens her phone and giggles. She covers her mouth and everything. I know it must be bad because she turns to look at me. Her expression is hard for me to gauge. It's not mean but not sympathetic either. I think her name is Risa. She has a short black ponytail and rosy cheeks. Her eyes are dark like Mia's and difficult to read.

As soon as class is over, I unlock my phone. I almost don't want to click on it, but I have to. To my horror, it's a picture of Mia. It looks like she's in the shower in the girl's locker room. Her hand is up and she is trying to cover herself, but her nipples and navel are still visible. Her long hair covers up half of her, but there is too much revealed. I look up to see everyone staring at me.

I call Mia. No answer. I weave through the crowds of people and call her again. Still no answer. I text her. Please, Mia. Just call me back. I run up the stairs and pass groups of girls giggling. They all hair medium length black hair and dark eyes that share something sinister. I brush past a boy looking at his phone. He turns bright red and puts it in his pocket as I pass him.

I call her another ten times. The bell is about to ring, but I'm not going to class. I need to find her. There is no way she is okay. I'm rounding the corner and bump into Kim. She looks me up and down. Her nose is a snobby beak. I grab her sparkly pink phone out of her hand.

"Hey!" she shrieks.

I look through her "sent" text. No picture of Mia. It must have been Biora.

"Where's Biora?" I ask.

"I don't know. She's not attached to my hip," she says.

"Tell me where she is right now."

"I think she has classic literature next," she grumbles and crosses her arms.

I fast walk down the hall towards that class. I'm pleased to see Biora. Before she walks through the door, I grab her arm.

"Hey!" she huffs.

I take her lemon yellow phone and search through her "sent." She attempts to grab it from me, but she is too short and I can keep her at arm's length. I find Mia's picture sent to half the school.

"Give it back!" she screams.

"No," I say and crush her dainty phone in my hand.

The metal and glass cut up my palm, but not much. I barely feel it. Biora cowers and runs into her class. I run back down to the first floor and try to find Mia. She won't take my calls. I think of where she would go. It hits me: the library. I slow my pace and meander through the books at a leisurely pace. If I attract too much attention, I'll never find her. I'm supposed to be in class, but I know I won't be able to concentrate until I see her.

There's a boy in my grade wearing headphones looking at books in the sociology section. His name is Jin. I tap on his shoulder. He seems surprised, but I smile at him and he relaxes. Jin steps back from me.

"Hey Ryon," he says.

"Hey Jin, have you seen Mia?" I whisper.

"No, sorry."

"Thanks."

"I feel terrible for her. It's messed up what the girls do," says Jin.

"I broke Biora's phone," I admit.

Jin makes a thoughtful face and puts his headphones back on.

"She was addicted to that thing," he says and shakes his head.

I go down every section in search of Mia. My chest hurts from how hard my heart is pumping. I think my blood is going to ignite inside me. It's so hot. I'm pulling at my tie as I turn down the historical fiction section and see Mia leaning against the shelf with her knees to her chest. Her head is buried in her hands. I don't want to scare her, so I reach for her and whisper her name.

"Mia."

"Ryon," she looks up at me with her sad doll face.

"It's okay. I'm here now," I say.

"Did you see?" she asks.

I frown and tell the truth.

"Yeah. I saw."

Mia sobs quietly but violently in my arms. I don't know how to help her. All the boys want her and the girls want to be her. She's beautiful, and it calls a lot of attention from people with bad intentions.

"I don't want to be here," she cries.

"We don't have to be here," I say.

She stands up on shaky legs and we walk as nonchalantly as possible out of the school and head towards our neighborhood. Mia is stumbling over herself. I can't tell if she can't see from her crying or if it's because she is distressed. She stops in the middle of the sidewalk and covers her sobbing face. I pick her up and carry her the rest of the way home. A few people look at us, but I don't care.

As we approach our house, I see neither car is here. I'm glad we are home alone. I don't know how to explain this. Thinking about it, I should probably delete that picture. If my dad goes through my phone, he'll really freak out. I unlock the door and we hurry inside like we just robbed a bank. We go up to my room and she sits on my bed. I sit next to her and let her cry on me.

"Everyone's seen me naked. I really am a slut," she sobs.

I am furious, but not at her. I hate Biora and Nero for making her feel this way.

"No. You're not. Don't say that."

"What am I going to do?" she asks.

"I don't know. I wish I could break all their teeth," I say.

Mia is shivering, so I put my blanket over her. I get up to go downstairs, but Mia grabs my hand.

"Please don't leave me alone."

Poor Mia. She looks so sad with her tears soaking her thick bottom lashes. I lay next to her and try to cheer her up with stories about my friends and basketball. It hits me like a bus and I fall asleep, not realizing how tired I am.

CHAPTER ELEVEN

THE WRATH OF A VIPER

I'm awake, but not really. Mia is pressed up against me. My hand is in her hair that's fanned out across my white sheets. Her violet and seashell fragrance coats my pillowcase. She's holding me and I am relaxed. The feeling is nice until I notice an ominous presence. It's the lurking sensation of being watched. I know it's him and I don't want to open my eyes, but I do. It's my dad. He has his snake eyes on me, examining my palm that's gripping a handful of hair.

Mia and I are fully clothed, but that's not going to stop him. She has her arms around my shoulders and I'm sure my dad is filling in the blanks with his sick story. The one that everyone else tells about us, too. I brace myself.

"I knew it," he says in his deep and horrifying voice.

"Dad—"

I can't finish my sentence because he's grabbed me by the collar and is ripping me out of bed. Mia opens her eyes and sits up. My dad stares my stepsister down but doesn't say anything. He holds my collar and bashes my head into the hardwood floor.

"I thought you were sneaking into her room. Turns out she's been coming in here," he hisses.

My dad reminds me of a viper. The way he watches me, his slithering footsteps, and venomous words.

"We didn't do anything—"

I start, but my dad hits me in the stomach.

"You're a teenage boy. I don't believe you."

My dad stands up and brings me up with him. My feet are off the ground. He is the only person taller than me standing at 6' 7".

"She just wanted me to be with me. I didn't do anything wrong," I say.

He throws me into my dresser. All my trophies come raining down. Metal makes a hollow clunking noise as it hits the ground. Out of the corner of my eye, I see Mia cover her mouth to keep in her scream. I'm worried my dad is going to turn his attention to her.

"Stop lying to me, son."

My dad hits me in the ribs three times and shakes me by the collar. I still have my tie on. It's amazing he doesn't use it as a noose to choke me out.

"I'm not lying," I say.

My voice is hoarse from him, restricting my breathing.

"I was young once, Ryon. I know what it's like," he says.

My dad pushes me back into the floor and glares at me with his mean snake eyes. They are the same as Biora's. He doesn't make Mia leave. Instead, he takes slow, heavy, methodical footsteps downstairs. If I'm fucking her, it's already happened, and he doesn't care. He just wanted to beat me up.

I lay on my side that he didn't brutalize. He can be a ruthless dick. I cough and squeak as I try to inhale. Mia rushes to my side. She has tears running down her face. I feel horrible she had to witness that. My dad put a good show for her. He probably got hard making her watch him throw me around.

"Ryon! I'm so sorry," she says.

Her hair falls over me as she gives me a gentle hug.

"It's not your fault. My dad is a bad person."

Mia helps me onto the couch. I cough up blood onto the sleeve of my white button up and Mia cries even more.

"Are you okay?" she asks.

"I'm fine. He's done worse to me."

"I love you," she says.

"I love you, too."

I fall asleep in her lap and have dreams about ticking clocks, buzzing phones, and books being stacked on my chest until I can't breathe. I wake to Mia's tiny hand on my stomach. She lifts my shirt. I hear Koharu's voice. She makes a sharp noise with her breath.

"Does Ryon need to go to the hospital?" cries Mia.

I feel bad that she's so upset. My eyes are closed and I should open them, but I'm too tired. My step-mom's hand touches my injured ribs and bruises that are forming around my navel.

"I think he'll be okay. Ryon is a healthy boy," says Koharu.

I hear her get up. She pulls the red and blue blanket from my bed and puts it on me. She tucks it in around my shoulders. Mia has her hand on my heart. I know she's worried it's going to stop beating.

"I'm really scared," says Mia.

"I'm going to make dinner and I'll come right back. If his breathing becomes shallow or changes, come get me, okay?" says Koharu.

My stepmom tries to be strong, but I know Joseph scares the shit out of her. She's forced to make him his after work meal and take care of his damaged son.

"Okay," says Mia in her small but sweet voice.

I hear Koharu's light steps as she walks downstairs. It's impossible to move and too hard to talk so I stay laying down. I should say something to Mia, but I can't. It's painful just being awake. As fucked up as it is, I feel loved and I think that's what makes this hurt bearable.

***

My curtains are slightly open, and the light is coming through. Looking at my clock, I see it's 10:14 a.m. Mia shifts in my arms and I realize she's sleeping with me. I try to sit up but regret it immediately. Everything is sore. Mia's arm is around me, and it makes me feel a little better. Her hair is covering my whole pillow. She has on the white sweater I got her for her birthday and leggings. I'm still in my uniform, but my neck is free of my tie.

"Ryon?" my stepmom enters my room.

She looks like a sad doll, too.

"Hey Koharu," I say.

My voice is quiet. My lungs dig into my battered ribs and make it hard to speak.

"How are you feeling?" she asks.

"I'm okay."

"I called you both out of school today."

"Thank you," I say.

Koharu picks up her daughter's hair and moves it to one side. She's braiding it loosely. It's sweet to see the way Mia's mom loves her. She doesn't seem upset about Mia embracing me or my arm around her.

"I'm so sorry, Ryon," says my stepmom.

"It's not your fault. I'm sorry I didn't tell you about my dad."

"You're the child. I'm the adult. I should have paid better attention to all the signs. Now I feel like there's nothing I can do to protect you," she says.

Koharu puts her hand on my shoulder and gives me a serious look.

"I'll be fine. I worry about Mia though," I admit.

Koharu hangs her head and sighs.

"Your father hardly says a word to her."

"Good. It's bad if he pays attention to someone," I say, and we make intense eye contact.

She knows what I mean. Joseph has a way of making a woman feel special. He lures them into his money fueled world and pretends to be a nice guy. Then once it's too late, the real him comes out.

"I'll make you breakfast and bring it up here. How does that sound?" she asks.

"That sounds nice. Thank you."

My stepmom stands up and opens the curtain more. She has her hair up in a messy bun with long black strands framing her face. The light illuminates her eyes and I see what she would look like if Joseph didn't have his grasp on her.

She is small like Mia, maybe two or three inches taller. Her hands are manicured and pretty. My stepmom always has white tipped nails. They match her white and pink striped shirt and black capri pants. She reminds me of someone in an old French movie. Koharu has a grace about her. I see where Mia inherits her quiet and captivating nature.

Koharu gives me a warm look as she exits my room. I don't feel bad about her seeing me and Mia together. She could just feel bad for me, but I hope this means she trusts me. I unbraid Mia's hair to distract myself from how much my body aches. It stings in places. My neck has red marks from my shirt being pulled on. There's an awful pain around my navel. My back hurts from hitting the dresser.

I look over to see Koharu has already cleaned up the scene of the crime. My trophies are standing up. My floor is mopped and free of any blood. I can't see it, but I'm sure my stepmom had to scrub my blood out of the couch. The back of my head hurts and I remember my dad slamming me into the floor. I wonder if I bled all over Mia's school uniform.

"Ryon?" says Mia.

Her eyes are still closed, but she reaches for my face.

"Yeah?"

"You're alive," she whispers.

I laugh but stop myself because it hurts too much.

"Yeah, I'm alive."

"I was worried you were going to die."

"Don't worry. I'm fine," I say.

"You can't die until I die."

"Hey! Stop acting like I'm going to die," I tease.

Mia looks at my arm and I see her eyeing the blood I coughed up.

"I should probably shower and change."

I get out of bed and grab a white tee shirt and my basketball shorts. My bathroom has a fancy marble counter. All my towels are white, gray, and dark blue. My dad designs our house to look like a psycho lives here. I guess two of them do.

The shower feels good and bad. The warm water reduces some of the pain but causes a pressure I can hardly stand on my ribs and around my navel. My dad really did a number on me this time. Now that I'm looking at my injuries, I see why Mia and my stepmom were so worried. My ribs are purple and black. All down my right side is bruised. My stomach has patches of yellow and green mixed with the dark purple blood pooling in places.

I get out of the shower and examine my back. There's red marks where I hit the knobs of the dresser drawers. The back of my head has a bump that's tender to the touch. My shoulders and lower back have purple and green splotches. Tiny scrapes cover my shoulder blades where my dad dragged and pushed me into the floor. Once I put my shirt on, it looks like nothing's wrong. That's the kind of dark magic my father has.

CHAPTER TWELVE

PLAYWRIGHTS AND PYTHONS

I turned sixteen a couple of weeks ago. It took me two tries, but I got my motorcycle license. I can't take Mia on it for a year, but I don't care. This allows me freedom and the ability to reach her as fast as possible. I never want anything to stop me from being there for her. The bike makes a satisfying roar as it starts. It purrs as I ride through the streets. I'm not allowed on the highways until I'm twenty, but that's okay.

Mia is really excited for me. She enjoys watching me put on my helmet and take off down the road. It's cute to see my stepsister so happy about my recent accomplishment. She knows it's for her and I'm having fun. My dad left me another pile of money on my coffee table after his last beating. The lower ribs on my right side are still tender to the touch.

I start high school in less than a week. Mia is nervous about being without me, but I have made my presence known to her peers. It doesn't bother me if they think I'm her boyfriend. Guarding her, protecting her, is my job. It's been my goal to make sure Mia is never sad the way she used to be. She lights up all the time now.

If anybody touches or hurts her, I'll have to kill them. Mia's happiness is that important to me. It's actually kind of messed up the impulses I get. I think about breaking teeth, smashing skulls, and punching people out. It must be the crazy in me. Rubbing the back of my head, I try to massage away the tension. I'm waiting for Mia on the steps. Soon I won't be able to walk her home. I plan on getting up early and walking her to school, at least for a little bit. Ayumi is moving past me and I grab his shoulder.

"Hey Ryon, what's up?" he asks.

"Can I ask you a favor, Ayumi?"

"Sure. What is it?"

"Can you walk Mia home when I go to high school? At least for a month or two. Please," I say.

I reach into my pocket and hand him a large portion of the money my dad gave me. Ayumi looks at the wad of cash with wide eyes. He runs his hand through his hair and sighs.

"You don't have to pay me. I'll take care of her," he says.

Ayumi's hazel eyes are serious.

"Thank you. You're a good person."

"I try. I don't want to be like everybody else," he says.

"I know what you mean."

"I gotta go. I'll make sure Mia is okay," he says.

"Bye."

"Bye."

He waves at me before bounding down the steps.

I feel a weight lift from my chest. Knowing someone like Ayumi is watching over Mia is comforting. As I wait for her, I notice fifty eyes on me. Scanning the yard, the steps, and sidewalk, I catch glimpses of people whispering to each other and looking in my direction. The way I care about Mia disturbs them.

I've never loved anyone the way I love Mia. She's not my actual sister, but I have the need to watch over her. I don't know what it's like to have a sibling. Maybe it's wrong how I feel. But how can I let anything bad happen to someone so sweet and innocent? I think about her scarred wrist and hate myself. Never again. Mia won't be alone anymore.

It's spring and the cherry blossom trees rain pink and white petals everywhere. The breeze carries the scent of fresh cut grass and flowers. Summer is my favorite, but spring wakes everything up. I see Mia walk out of the school. She smiles at me right away.

"Hey Mia. How was your day?" I ask.

"It was good."

"Good."

My stepsister and I walk home. We don't talk much this time. I feel like she's hiding something from me, but she's smiling. Mia lies to me, but I try not to pry. I think she will shut down completely if I pester her too much.

"I'm going to miss you when you go to high school," she says.

"I know. But we still live together and I have my bike now. I can get to you super fast."

"Yeah," she says.

Mia doesn't seem upset, but I have a lingering suspicion. We get home and Mia goes into the kitchen to talk to her mom and I head up to my room. My dad hasn't spoken to me. I know he's in his study. I can hear him shuffling paperwork and the annoying scratchy noises his pen makes.

Once I'm in my room, I peel out of my uniform and throw on a tee shirt and joggers. I do the last of my homework and stare out the window. The sky is bright with a splash of clouds. I lay in bed with my headphones on and think. Sora and Teo have remained loyal friends, but I've been distant from Ben, Koga, and Kirin. Ever since Kirin freaked out on me, it hasn't been the same. I daydream about moving somewhere with Mia and not living with my dad anymore. The thought makes me happy and lulls me into a brief nap. I wake up to the smell of Koharu cooking dinner.

I knock on Mia's door. No answer. My dad hasn't bothered me about Mia being in my room or us hanging out. He figures I've already done the worst to her. I cringe thinking about how he perceives our relationship. I crack the door and whisper her name.

"Mia?" I say as I peek into her blue everything room.

She's asleep on her bed, still in her school uniform. It's horrible, but I use the opportunity to go through her things. I look for that yellow diary on her bookshelf, her art supplies, and under the bed. She rolls to her side and I freeze. Mia resumes sleeping and I keep snooping through her things. My stepsister deserves privacy but the psycho in me leaves me unable to stop until I find it in the bottom drawer of her dresser wrapped in a teal sweater.

The yellow diary shakes in my hands. I look at my stepsister and contemplate putting it back. But I don't. I tell myself I'm trying to help her, but I don't really know what I'm doing. All I know is I need to see what goes on in her head. It probably looks bad, but I touch her hair all the time, trying to get closer to her mysterious thoughts. I open to the first page.

My dad is gone and my stepfather treats me like I don't exist. It was lonely when it was just me and mom but somehow this big house makes me feel more alone.

I can't stop and I open to the middle.

An older boy in the library grabbed me and called me a "tease." I don't understand how existing elicits such a response?

My stepsister is beautiful, but incredibly sad. I wish I had paid attention to her sooner. It seemed like no big deal to me until one day I woke up and realized I wanted to be close to Mia the way a real brother would be. Unable to resist, I skip towards the end and find a poem she wrote.

He is an army
On his own
Because of him
I am never alone

It touches me in a way that makes me want to cry. I'm surprised I feel so strongly about this. Art never used to speak to me, but hers does. Everything about Mia is deep and meaningful. It makes me feel special that she trusts me. I'm being nosy, and I return her yellow diary to its resting place in the bottom drawer. I slink back into my room to process these emotions. I'm not ashamed to cry, but I am confused how four lines written by my stepsister could invoke such a reaction from me.

***

* * *

High school isn't much different from middle school. Classes are boring, the teachers are strict, and everyone attempts to be cool. I park my motorcycle and take off my helmet. My hair is getting long. I thought about cutting it, but Mia said it looked nice, so I kept it. Girls always want to touch it, so she must be right.

Ever since Kirin said I was taking up more than my fair share of pussy, I've felt weird about the attention girls give me. Are they my friend? Do you they want to fuck me? I don't know how to read them. Naomi took notes for me the days I stayed home after my dad destroyed me. Setsuna photocopied her notes and gave them to me, too. Chisaki thought I had a cold or something, so she made me a "get well soon" card with one of her photos. It's a picture of a rose growing out of the snow covered ground.

I walk through the halls and tower over everyone. Sora and Teo are standing by their lockers and wave me over. I'm glad things haven't changed between us. Ben hasn't said anything to me in weeks. I'm not sure, but I think I saw him hanging out with Fuyuhisa and Akito downtown.

"Hey Ryon," says Sora.

"Hey guys," I say.

"How's the first couple weeks of high school going for you?" asks Teo.

"It's okay," I say.

"How's Mia?" asks Sora.

"She's good. I wake up early to walk her to school and Ayumi has been walking her home."

"Ayumi is a good guy," says Teo.

"I'm glad I found someone who cares about her, too."

The guys nod at my statement and make thoughtful faces as the bell rings. I think the girl in my calculus class has a crush on me. I catch her staring at me a lot. Her name is Nina. She has a straight black bob and wears sticky pink lip gloss. Her eyelashes are coated in mascara. She's pretty, but kind of fake looking. Class ends and she's tapping on my shoulder.

"Hey," she says.

Her voice is really feminine and smooth. It reminds me of a pop singer.

"Hey."

"Do you want to have lunch with me?" she asks.

"Sure," I say.

I'm not sure how to react, but I figure there's nothing wrong with hanging out with her.

"Great! My favorite spot is over by the maple trees on the west side."

"Okay. I'll meet you there," I say.

I go to my next class and space out for half of it. Why can't I focus? It's probably because Mia is too far away from me. I check my phone. No calls or text from her. Ayumi hasn't called either. Everything must be okay. After social studies is my lunch break. I go to the west side of the school to meet Nina.

"Hey," she says.

Her face is slender and almost alienish. She's still pretty, though.

"What's up?" I ask.

"Nothing really. I was just thinking about what I'm going to do after high school."

"What's that?" I ask.

Girls always have more interesting stuff to talk about than boys. I see Sora walk through the yard and wave. He smiles and walks into the school. Kirin and Koga pass me with double glares. It must eat them up inside to see me talk to girls, sit with girls, and live with a girl. I turn my attention back to Nina.

"I want to entertain people. I think I want to be an actress," she says.

"That sounds really cool. What kind of movies?" I ask.

"Dramas."

"My stepsister got me into dramas recently."

"Mia, right?" she asks.

I'm surprised she knows her name. Nina didn't go to my middle school. People have been talking. I wonder why Nina is even interested in me, but she seems okay.

"Yeah."

"I heard you beat up all the boys that look at her," laughs Nina.

Her smile is crooked, but it's cute. Nina's comment surprises me, but I laugh, too.

"I guess. Being a brother is new to me. I feel protective of her," I admit.

I think Nina is going to call me weird, but she doesn't.

"That's really sweet."

"You think so?"

"I wish my older brother cared about me. He moved out three years ago. We haven't talked since," she says.

Nina sips her blueberry tea and looks sad.

"I'm sorry. That sucks," I say.

"It's cool. I still have my sister."

"What's she like?"

"She's like my mom. My parents travel for work and I was left alone a lot until my sister moved back home."

"I'm glad she came back," I say.

"Me too. She's my best friend," says Nina and she brightens.

"What's her name?"

"Kanami. She's a musician."

"What does she play?" I ask.

"Piano."

"I'm not good at any of that stuff," I admit.

"I hear you're great at basketball," she says.

Rumors run rampant in middle school. They spread like wildfire in high school.

"Yeah. It keeps me sane."

"That's how I feel about acting. I'm trying out for the lead role in the school play. The Drama Club is putting on a big show at the end of the semester. You should come see it," says Nina as the bell rings.

"I will," I say.

"It was nice hanging out with you, Ryon. Bye!" she says and runs off towards her class.

I don't understand girls, but I'm fascinated by them. As I make my way to my locker, I pass Fuyuhisa. He smirks, and it makes him look like he's in his twenties. There's something hardened about his face, even though we are the same age.

I wonder who Mia is talking to right now. Ayumi walks her home, but does he sit with her at lunch? Who is it that preoccupies her time now that I'm not there? I wonder if she found a friend yet. Biora and

Kim are envious of her, but I hope someone can put aside their jealousy and see her for who she truly is: an amazing artist, a caring girl, and a beautiful person.

***

I'm zoning out. Staring at the ceiling while I blare rap music where the artist sings so fast I have to really focus to hear what they are saying. I don't want to think right now. Mia says everything has been fine, but I have a sick feeling in my stomach, like something bad is going to happen. I'm right, because my dad walks in. I pull out my earbuds.

"Hey dad," I say.

He looks me up and down with his snake eyes. It's 9:08 p.m., and he's swaying.

"You better be using protection, son," he says with his disgusting venomous voice.

"Ew, dad. I'm not having sex with Mia."

I look him in his eyes and try to show that I'm not lying. He kneels down at my bed and does this thing that reminds me of a cobra where his head goes side to side as he examines me. My dad grabs me by the collar of my shirt and grins. He reeks of scotch and rage.

"I'm not paying for her abortion," he spits.

The sentence hurts me worse than his punch to my chest. My heart skips several beats from the impact. I wonder if he will punch me again and if it would restart.

"I'm not having sex with Mia," I repeat.

"There's something off about the way you are with her," his voice is hoarse from all his yelling into the phone.

"I care about her. What's so wrong with that?" I ask.

He tightens his enormous hand's grip on my shirt. I have red marks that burn all over my neck from his hold on me. I reach up and put my hands on his.

"Please, dad. Let me go."

"Why can't you just tell me the truth?" he slurs.

"I am telling you the truth."

I gasp as he digs his knuckles tighter around the cloth of my shirt.

"If you keep fucking her, Koharu is going to take her and leave us.

98

Just like your mom," his words bite.

The last four especially. I miss my mom and I know she would have taken me with her if it wasn't for this psychotic asshole.

"Koharu wouldn't do that. She likes me," I say, but my dad throws me down and stands up.

"If you get her pregnant, it's your problem, Ryon."

My dad takes well managed footsteps out of my room and I hold my heart where he not only hit me but damaged me so I can't begin to explain. Music is playing through my earbuds. I don't put them back in. There are no words to describe these emotions. Ever since I started spending time with Mia, I get these unexplainable feelings. I used to just zone them out and play basketball with my friends. Now I study them. What test will these be used in? I'm not sure, but it seems important. I realize why it's so painful. It's because everyone thinks I have bad intentions towards my stepsister.

CHAPTER THIRTEEN

CAN'T LET GO

It's windy and the breeze scatters cherry blossom petals all over the schoolyard. My dad would say it's messy, but I like it. I put my hand to my chest. The bruise is fading, but the pain in my heart won't go away. I know my dad says these things to make himself feel better. He wants me to hurt the way he hurts. I go back to taking notes and pretending that I care about this stuff. It's difficult but I can do it while only giving it half of my attention. My phone buzzes. I ignore it. The teacher continues to drone on. Another buzz.

I get the anxiety that something bad is happening to Mia, but I've been getting in trouble for slacking off and daydreaming out the window, so I temporarily resist. Maybe it's one of the girls trying to ask me to sit with them at lunch again. The teacher scrapes chalk against the board in slow motion. I can't concentrate. The room blurs and I panic as I feel my phone vibrate in my pocket. Someone is calling me.

As sneakily as I can, I pull out my phone and, to my horror, it's Ayumi. It's only 2:34 p.m. They should still be in school for another thirty minutes. I get up without asking and the teacher tries to stop me, but I am already running towards the parking lot.

"Ayumi, what's wrong?" I ask.

"It's Fuyuhisa and Akito! They shoved Mia into an older boy's car!" he shouts.

It sounds like he's running, too.

"Why aren't you two in class?"

I ask as I run down the stairs.

"Our teacher let us out early! I was walking her home, and they grabbed her. I'm sorry, Ryon!"

"What kind of car?" I ask.

"A silver Honda Civic. The license plate is 11-798. They went south towards the freeway," he says.

I'm glad Ayumi is the kind of person to pay attention to detail.

"Thank you," I say and hang up.

There's a large rock next to my foot. On impulse, I grab it and put it in my pocket. Who knows, I might need it. I start my bike and take off towards the freeway. I'm not supposed to drive on it, but I don't care. Whatever those boys are planning isn't good, and I have to get to her right now. I drive the speed limit and follow the traffic signs. If I get pulled over, I'll never reach her in time.

My motorcycle is light and fast. As soon as I enter the freeway, I pick up my speed. I look for a silver Honda Civic but that's like every six cars. The license plates aren't 11-798. I've only been driving this thing for two and a half months, but I'm good at it. I felt like I was meant for this. The wind blows my tie around. I should have taken off my tie and jacket, but there's no time for me to mess with my clothes.

I slow down and examine the traffic. All the cars blend together. These cars are headed through the suburbs and countryside where there are lots of back roads and places no one would know where to look for unless they had been shown by someone else. The pulse in my throat is choking me out. I have to find Mia. There are people listening to pop music and other cars blaring rock metal. Some girls in a red car blow kisses at me and shout "Hey sexy! Nice bike!" but I'm not interested. My helmet obscures most of my face. They don't even know what I look like.

Switching lanes, I pass a line of black, green, and white cars. Then I see a silver Honda Civic. It's not the one, though. I'm anxious but I need to keep it together. Panicking isn't going to help me. My anger is also distracting me. It sears me from the inside, right between my eyes and in my shoulder blades. It's that ugly, hateful feeling that reminds me of Joseph.

There's a newer Honda up ahead. Gleaming silver paint job. I hear loud hip hop coming from it. As I cross over, I glance at the license plate. It's the one I'm looking for, 11-798. I speed up but stay two cars behind while I assess the situation. There's an exit coming up that will take us further into the countryside. They take it and I follow their tail. I know what they're planning to do, and I can't let it happen.

I get up to the driver's side and knock on the window. The car swerves to hit me, but I dodge him. All the windows are tinted and loud bass emanates from the speakers. I stay on them as we drive through neighborhoods. He leads me to a road that is the beginning of farmland. The car speeds up and hugs the edges as it maneuvers down a windy back road. I've never driven this kind of terrain, but I keep up with him. My knuckles are white as I weave through gravel and dirt.

The car continues to elude me. Without him knocking me off the road, I can't get up to the driver's side. I'm sure he's going to break check me eventually, but he hasn't yet. I need to get Mia out of there. The idea of them putting their hands on her makes me go full psycho. I don't stop following him. He thinks I'll give up, but I won't. We've been at this for over an hour.

We exit the windy road and come upon a long dirt road that stretches on for miles. He takes off as fast as he can and so do I. I am right behind him and he does as I assumed he would and breaks. I swerve and get ahead of him. Once I am at enough distance where he can't run me over right away but I can make the shot, I take the rock out of my pocket. I never miss. Aiming for the driver's side, I throw the rock as hard as I can. It breaks the window and the car veers off the dirt path and into the grass.

I take off my helmet and approach the vehicle. The air is dusty and my face is covered in dirt. So are my hands. I walk up in a furious daze, but remain collected. Ripping open the back door, I see a sight that simultaneously chills me and burns me out like a fever. The older boy from the bookstore is the driver. His head has a cut on it and he's bleeding down the right side of his face. Good. Fuyuhisa stares at me with blank shark eyes, but I can tell he is afraid of me. The thing that gets me the most is who is in the backseat. I knew Akito would be touching Mia, but it's Ben who has his hands on her arm that shakes all the screws loose in my brain. Both of them drop their hands. I kneel and pull Mia close to my chest. She's sobbing and clinging to me. I get in both of their faces.

"If you go near her again, I'll kill you," I say.

I carry Mia to the motorcycle and put my helmet on her. Passing them, I give them my best crazy white boy look and they cringe. Mia holds onto my waist and I drive home, but not too fast. I don't have another helmet, so I use the back roads and neighborhoods and avoid the freeway as much as possible. It takes twice as long, but we get home without getting pulled over and I park in the garage. My dad's car is gone. I take the helmet off her and bring her into the house. She can't seem to move, so I carry her upstairs to her room. I try to set her down, but she won't let me go. Her bed is messy and unmade, like her hair. I choose to sit down with her as she cries hot tears all over my shoulder.

"It's okay, Mia. I'm here," I say.

My stepsister is so scared I can feel her shivering like it's cold but it's warm in the house.

"You came for me," she cries.

"Of course I did. I would never let anything bad happen to you."

"Thank you."

"Are you alright?" I ask.

She pulls back and looks at me with her sad, shiny doll eyes.

"I am now," she says.

"What did they do?"

"Nothing," she says, but her eyes fill up with tears and I know she is lying.

"Please. I need to know. I'm not mad at you," I say.

"Scared me, mostly."

"Did they touch you?" I ask.

Mia gets uncomfortable and hides from me. She is always hiding things from me. Her thoughts, her face, and the things that people do to her when I'm not around.

"Yes," she squeaks.

I bring Mia closer to me and hold on to her. The painting of the small bird in someone's hand is staring at me. I think I know the feeling she was trying to capture. It's the same one I can't explain as I try to protect her from something that's already happened.

"What did they do, Mia?" I ask, trying to hide my crazy white boy rage.

My stepsister shakes her head and looks away from me, but I force her to face me. I think I'm scaring her, but she's scaring me.

"Please, tell me."

"They put their hands all over me. Akito said it was awesome to have a naked picture of me to jack off to. Fuyuhisa kept showing the boy driving the photo of me in the shower. Ben..."

She stops and starts crying. Looking down, I see bruises resembling hands on her thigh. Now I'm really freaking out.

"What did Ben do?"

"He put his fingers inside me." She grimaces and looks like she wants to throw up.

My stomach churns from the psychotic rage that's creating a hormonal stew. It gives me flashes of murdering them all. The image is satisfyingly real.

"Ryon?" she whispers my name and I realize I'm gripping onto her too tight.

I loosen my grasp and go back to hugging her.

"I'm sorry. I should have got there sooner," I say.

"You came for me. They said you didn't care about me."

"They only said that to mess with your beautiful mind," I say.

She brightens at my words. I can tell she is still upset, but she's not shaking anymore.

"I love you," she says, and she hugs me back.

"I love you," I say.

Mia clings to me for the rest of the night. I smile at her and try to make her feel safe. She and I watch a movie in my room, but I do not know what's going on because I keep thinking about all the different ways to kill someone.

***

Mia has been sleeping with me for the past three nights. I know my dad has seen us. To add insult to injury, he left a giant box of condoms next to my bed. He's such a dick. I know Koharu isn't upset with me, but my dad's words sift around in my mind. What if she really thinks

I'm doing something bad to Mia?

I tried to get her to sleep in her room, but she refuses. The boys have caused her to revert back to her scared and quiet nature. She was making such progress. I thought Mia seemed really happy. It's fucked up, but I think about hurting them.

Images of me choking Ben out pop up throughout the day. Visions of myself sitting on Akito's chest and punching him in the face. I dream about taking that rock and bashing it against the older boy's skull. Today I hunt down Fuyuhisa. Akito and Ben don't go to my high school. I know Kirin won't tell me anything. Ben won't take my calls. Of course he doesn't. I told him I was going to kill him. I find Fuyuhisa leaning against one of the oak trees. Students are walking back and forth, so I am subtle.

"How do I find Ben?" I ask.

Fuyuhisa looks up from his phone and narrows his eyes at me.

"Why would I tell you that?" he smirks.

"Because I'll find him with or without you," I say.

"What did she tell you?" he asks.

I know he's going to try to piss me off.

"Everything you did to her."

"She liked it," he laughs.

I pick him up by his collar the way my dad picks me up. Bringing him off the ground slightly, but not enough for people walking by to notice, I whisper in his ear.

"Don't lie to me."

"Ben will be at Ume Park at five today," he says in a flat tone.

I drop him and walk off without looking back. Going into class and pretending I'm normal is hard, but everyone believes me. I smile at them and they smile back. Everyone thinks I'm a chill, happy, confident guy. If only they knew the dark thoughts that plague me.

When school's over, I head straight for the parking lot. I don't socialize with anyone. It's not that I don't want to talk to my friends, but I'm distracted. Mia is still frightened, and I want to be there for her. Also, I need to check on her before I head for Ume Park. Ben and I are going to have a few words.

The ride home isn't very long. It feels like I'm not even here. Arriving at the house, I think about my drive and how I barely remember it. I tell myself to be more careful and stop spacing out all the time. Mia told me I can't die until she dies. I touch my heart. It's easier for me to process these emotions, but they can stop me in my tracks.

"Hey Ryon," says Mia.

She's in the kitchen with her mom.

"Hey Mia. How was your day?" I ask.

"It was good," she says.

"Good." I smile at her and then her mom.

Koharu watches me, but I can't tell what she's thinking. She doesn't seem disgusted, or angry, or upset. I feel like she is judging my character. Maybe she is just tired.

"I'm going to take a shower," says Mia.

Her footsteps are barely audible as she walks down the hall.

"Hey Koharu, can we talk for a minute?" I ask.

"Of course. What is it?"

"Are you mad at me?" I ask.

"What? No, not at all. Why would you ask me that?"

Koharu takes my hand. Her white tipped nails touch the top of my wrist. The ring Joseph got her has an enormous diamond on it. She has movie star hands.

"My dad said you think I'm having sex with Mia and that you're going to take her away from me."

I let the word fall out of my mouth. Koharu sits back with a grave face.

"We both know what kind of person your dad is. She has been sleeping in your room. I also know what you did for her. I hate to think what would happen to her if you weren't around," she says.

"Mia told you," I say in surprise.

"Yes. I can't believe all you do for her. You are so brave, Ryon."

"So you're not going to leave with her?" I need Koharu to reassure me.

"No. Mia loves you. I would never separate you two," she says.

"Thank you," I say.

I'm losing my voice. Looking at the clock, I see it's almost 4:30 pm. "I have to run an errand. Tell Mia I'll be back in time for dinner."

"Okay. Be safe!" calls my stepmom.

I get back on my motorcycle and head for Ume Park. It's 4:54 p.m. when I get there. I take off my helmet and scan the place for Ben. There's a bench nearby and I take a seat. I have my earbuds in. The rock music's intense guitar riffs and loud drumming soothe me. It's 5:12 p.m. as Ben and Akito walk into the park. They don't notice me until it's too late. I get up and grab Ben's arm.

"Mia told me what you did," I say in a dead tone.

Ben squirms, but I keep my grip on him. Akito runs off, but I don't care about him right now. I'm after Ben at this moment.

"I'm sorry, Ryon. I don't know what came over me—" he starts, but I sock him in the mouth and pull him down to the bench so it looks like we're just two guys talking.

"I thought you were my friend, Ben."

"I am—" he stops talking because I elbow him swiftly in the ribs.

"A friend wouldn't force himself inside my stepsister," I say.

"Oh c'mon. I only fingered her," he says, but regrets it.

I punch him in the gut the way my dad hits me. No one bats an eye. It happens too fast for anyone to notice.

"Why would you do that?" I ask.

I don't expect a genuine answer, but I ask it anyway.

"I don't know. It was stupid. I'm sorry. I don't know what came over me," he spits up blood.

It's foamy and red sitting on the dirt.

"What's the older boy's name?" I ask.

"Shinji."

"Did he touch her?" I ask.

"No, he only drove the car."

"If any of you talk to her, look at her, or go near her, I won't hesitate to kill you all."

I get up to leave, but Ben laughs.

"What?" I snap.

"I always knew you had the hots for her," says Ben.

Blood drips down his face and lands on his green shirt. It mixes into an ugly gray color. I kneel down so I can be eye to eye with someone that used to be my friend.

"I love Mia so much. I'm not only willing to die for her, but I'd kill for her."

I give him a smug smile. He sniffs my neck and a mischievous smile appears on his face. There's blood on his front tooth.

"You smell like her. Like vanilla and violets," he grins and I think about breaking his teeth, but I don't.

"Forget everything about her," I hiss the way my father does.

Ben keeps his head down until I get on my bike and ride off.

CHAPTER FOURTEEN
THE BLOND DEMON

"Hey Ryon!"

It's Sora. I'm staring at the grass not eating my lunch. I haven't been hungry lately.

"Hey," says Teo.

They sit down next to me.

"Hey guys," I say.

Both of them grin at each other. They look at me and I know something is up. What?" I ask.

"You have a new nickname. It's pretty cool," says Sora.

"What?" I ask.

"Yeah. Fuyuhisa told some of the guys that you were a white devil. The Blond Demon," says Teo.

I crack up laughing. The guys join in and I feel lighter. It's been a while since I laughed this hard.

"That's great. I like that name," I say.

"I can't believe you hunted them down and broke Shinji's window. So heroic," says Sora with a pleased expression.

"I had to. I can't let anything bad happen to Mia," I say.

"Ben told everyone you're like a serial killer and threatened him on a bench at the park," says Teo.

"I did," I admit.

The guys laugh and so do I. It feels good to smile for real.

"How is Mia doing?" asks Sora.

"She's okay. The boys terrified her, though. She's by my side every minute that I'm home," I say.

"Does that annoy you?" asks Teo.

He continues eating his lunch. Teo is always hungry.

"No. I like that she wants to be around me."

"I don't think any guy is ever going to live up to you, Ryon," says Sora.

I think he's joking at first, but I see he is being serious. Sora isn't unkind. He is wise and sees what others don't.

"What do you mean?" I ask.

"You have done so much for her. The Blond Demon chases down four guys on a motorcycle and beats up all the bad dudes? She's always going to compare the men in her life to you. I don't think there will ever be much competition," says Sora.

"Mia deserves the best," I say.

"The boys in her grade heard about what you did, too. Fumika said they also call you The Blond Demon. No one bothers her at school," offers Teo.

"I wish I could do something about that picture, though," I say.

"Yeah. That was terrible," says Sora.

"Akito told her he enjoys jacking off to it," I admit.

The guys make disgusted faces but try to be sympathetic.

"It must be hard being a girl. Knowing guys are always trying to fuck you. It must be scary not being able to trust anyone. To feel like everyone is watching you," says Teo.

He has more insight than Sora or me because he is close to his little sister.

"I never thought about stuff like that until I started paying attention to Mia," I confess.

Teo and I make eye contact and he nods.

"My sister has opened my eyes to things I'd never consider," says Teo.

"Girls are way cooler than boys," says Sora.

"Too bad none of us have a girlfriend," jokes Teo.

"Ryon could have like five girlfriends," teases Sora.

"Hey! That's not true," I say.

"Let's see: Naomi, Mayu, Chisaki, Setsuna, Nina..." says Teo.

"Oh, whatever. They're just my friends," I say.

"How come you don't date any of the girls that you hang out with?" asks Sora.

He isn't being rude. Sora is my friend and is curious, but not judgmental.

"I don't know. I guess I'm just not that into them," I admit.

I shrug my shoulders and pluck at the grass. Sora and Teo have their dark eyes focused on me.

"What?" I ask.

"Do you love Mia in a romantic way?" asks Sora.

I have a lump in my throat.

"No. I don't feel that way about Mia. Her happiness is my biggest priority, though. It might not make sense, but I have this need to keep her safe," I say.

The guys accept my answer, but I sense they want to ask more.

"How are things with your dad?" asks Teo, changing the subject.

"Super shitty. He thinks I'm having sex with Mia. I don't see him very often, but it's tense when I do. His beatings are less frequent but getting more violent. Last time Mia and my stepmom thought I was going to die in my sleep."

"Is it true?" asks Sora.

"What?"

"That she's been sleeping in your bed."

"Who told you that?" I ask.

"I heard Fuyuhisa saying dumb stuff in the showers after physical education," says Sora.

"What did he say?" I ask.

I'm not mad at my friends, but I'm angry about this situation. The rumors are already starting. I'm sure they're circulating at the middle school. Why won't she tell me anything?

"He said 'you can tell that Ryon sleeps with his stepsister because he smells like her perfume,'" sighs Sora.

He takes a sip of his aloe green tea and runs his hand through his hair.

"What else did he say?" I ask.

I hope I'm not coming off aggressive to my friends.

"That she smells like violets," he says.

***

Things are more tense than usual at home. My dad has gone out of his way to make everything uncomfortable. I came home from school yesterday to a bone chilling sound. Him and Mia talking in his study. The place where he does his paperwork, drinks scotch, and gets pissed. I set down my things and try to keep my composure as I walk down the dim hall to his large office space. Mia is sitting in his cushy chair at his enormous mahogany desk. He has his giant hand on her shoulder and they appear to be examining something together. I don't like this.

"Hey dad," I say as nonchalantly as I can.

Mia looks up and grins at me.

"Son! Come look at this. Your stepsister has quite an eye," he says.

I feel my heart drop into my stomach as I approach them. On the desk are stacks of business cards. They are neat, black and white, with special fonts, and a rabbit watermark. I pick one up to further study it.

"They look fantastic," I say.

"Mia helped me make them. They're great. I love them," he says and kisses the top of her head.

She makes a face but says nothing. He removes his hand but stands too close to her.

"All the guys at the office are going to love them, too."

To my horror, he runs his massive hand through Mia's long hair and I feel myself losing it.

"I'm glad you like them, Joseph," says Mia.

I know she fears my dad. We all do.

"Honey, call me dad," he says.

I would rather die than hear her call him by that name. Even I don't like calling him 'dad', but it's a habit. There's an awkward pause because he is waiting for her to say it, but I interrupt.

"I got all A's on my tests this week," I say.

"That's fantastic, son."

My dad gets the hint and moves to exit the room. He ruffles my hair and gives me the side eye. I wait until I know he's in his room to talk.

"Are you okay?" I ask Mia.

"Yeah. I'm fine," she says.

Mia gets up and bounces out of the room and up the stairs without saying anything else to me. I feel hurt. Why won't she talk to me? I always find out everything when it's too late and I have to hear it from someone else. Joseph will not tell me anything. He wants me to feel this way. I hate that it's working. I hear Koharu walk through the door. She has groceries in her hands and I take them from her.

"Thank you. How was your day, Ryon?" asks my stepmom.

"It was good. How about you?"

"It was good," she says, but I know she's lying.

Her makeup is done, and her hair is styled, but she has dark circles under her eyes. She's about to head for the kitchen, but I stop her.

"Have you noticed my dad paying attention to Mia?" I ask.

"This morning he said he was going to ask her to help him with his business cards," she says.

"Anything else?" I ask.

She shakes her head and her wavy black hair moves across her small shoulders.

"No. I asked him why he wanted her opinion and he said she's the artist in the family."

Koharu shrugs and makes her way to the kitchen, and we set down the items she just bought. I head upstairs and knock on Mia's door.

"Hey," I say.

"Hey."

"Can I come in?"

"Sure," she says.

I sit in her chair by the window.

"Everything okay?" I ask.

"Yeah. No one does anything bad to me anymore."

Mia lays down on her bed and plays with her necklace. I don't think she ever takes it off. My fists are clenched and my knuckles ache.

I'm fidgeting in the chair. I try to stop my erratic behavior. Hopefully, she doesn't notice.

"How was spending time with my dad?" I ask.

"It was nice, I guess. We don't talk much, but today he really wanted us to spend time together," she says.

Her long hair falls over the side of the bed like a black waterfall. I don't know why but I don't like when other people touch it besides me and Koharu.

"The business cards look amazing," I say, hoping to hide my nosiness.

"Thank you."

"So everything's good?" I ask.

"Everything in my life has been good since you've been around, Ryon."

"Good, I'm happy to hear that."

I get up and go into my room. The shower helps relax me. Looking at myself in the mirror, I have no bruises. My skin is clear of any scrapes, cuts, and abrasions. It feels like forever since I've seen myself like this. Dinner is cooking downstairs, but I am sick to my stomach because I know Mia is hiding something from me and I don't trust my dad. I trust him less than he trusts me.

***

Sora and Teo meet me at the park, so we can play basketball. Koga joins us, but not Kirin. At first it's kind of problematic, but Koga attempts to squash our disagreement.

"Look, I'm really sorry. I got on Kirin's hate train. It was stupid of me," he says.

"Why does Kirin hate me? I never did anything to him," I snap.

I'm still upset.

"Because all the girls like you. It's the simple truth. It's dumb, but that's what it is," says Koga as he bounces the basketball.

It makes a loud but satisfying hollow echoing sound.

"Maybe you guys could try talking to a girl," I tease.

Koga passes the ball to me and laughs.

"I know, I know. I fucking choke," he admits, and the four of us laugh together for the first time in forever.

"So we're cool?" I ask.

"Yeah, we're cool."

"Let's play then," I say.

Sora and I team up against Teo and Koga. Sora weaves past them and passes me the ball. I take the shot and make it. Teo and Koga groan but playfully. We go on like this for an hour. The four of us are sweaty and out of breath. It's been a while since I've focused on nothing but the game. It feels good. The sweat soaking my hair, the sun on my face, and the sound of our sneakers on the concrete. I'm somewhere else.

We sit in the shade of an elm and sip on our water. Teo pushes his hair back and gulps his loudly. Sora lays back and stares up at the passing clouds. Koga and I sit next to each other. He high fives me and it makes me smile. We look down the hill at the other people enjoying the park. Families by the swings, couples walking dogs, and lots of teenagers sitting around like us.

"I missed playing ball with you," says Koga.

"Yeah? Same," I say.

"Now I can tell everyone I played ball against The Blond Demon," says Koga with a smirk.

"Ryon's nickname is so cool," says Teo.

"I think it suits him," jokes Sora.

He sits up and we all laugh. I don't feel bad because we're just messing around. We get up and head back to the court and shoot some hoops. It's like I'm a normal person today. My hair is curling and frizzy from being damp, but I don't care. I'm having a great day.

"Hey Ryon!"

It's Mayu.

She goes to a different high school, but apparently she had the biggest crush on me in middle school. At least that's what all the guys say.

"Hey Mayu," I say.

Mayu is taller than most girls, about 5' 5". Her dark hair is cropped with microbangs. Not as short as Chisaki's. Mayu has a gap in between her two front teeth and big blue eyes. The guys go silent behind me.

"I haven't seen you in a while. How have you been?" she asks.

I toss the ball to Koga, who almost falls over. Sora and Teo turn away to hide their faces. Mayu wears dangly earrings that bounce when she talks.

"Good. How about you?"

"I'm great! I got a solo for the big choir concert," she exclaims.

Mayu has a husky voice that stands out.

"That's awesome. You've always been a talented singer," I say.

"Thank you. I'm really happy I saw you, Ryon. Take care!" she waves to me as she runs off to join her two friends, who are also pretty.

"It was good to see you, bye!" I say.

The three of them giggle as they scurry off and I turn around to face my speechless friends.

"What is wrong with you guys?" I tease.

"Shut up! It's not so easy for the rest of us," says Koga.

He isn't actually mad, but I can tell he is flustered.

"Just be yourself," I say and take the ball from him.

I shoot and score. Sora bounces the ball a few times and attempts to dunk but can't reach. We all die laughing.

"All the artist girls like Ryon," announces Teo as he shoots the ball.

He makes it and punches the air.

"I guess so. Nina is an actress. Chisaki is a photographer. Mayu is a singer," I start, but Koga stops me.

"Mia is a painter and a poet," he says.

I shove him away from me.

"Don't start," I say.

"Sorry. It just seems like you two are together," he says, but doesn't make eye contact with me.

"Well, we're not. She's my stepsister. I don't think of her that way," I say.

"But what if she thought of you that way?" he asks.

"She doesn't."

I snap and shoot the ball. I make it, but just barely. My excessive force causes the ball to roll around the basket more than usual.

"Have you asked her?"

"I just know. Stop talking about her," I sigh.

Koga backs up and looks embarrassed. I decide to let it go this time.

"Sorry," he says.

"It's getting late. I should be getting home," says Teo.

"Me too," says Sora. Koga and I both agree.

The four of us go in separate directions. Walking home, I think about the way Mia holds me when I sleep, but I stop myself from analyzing everything we do, so I don't go crazy.

CHAPTER FIFTEEN

VIOLETS IN A SEA OF GREEN

It's Saturday night. Mia and I spent the day at an art gallery. She pointed out all the ones that stood out to her and why. I am eager to know what makes her tick. There was a painting of a white fox turning into a woman that she had stared at for a long time. I asked her what was special about that one. Mia told me it made her contemplate transformation and the duality of our human side versus our animalistic nature. I thought it was a good painting, but Mia has so much to say about them. I like seeing the world through her eyes.

After the art gallery, we went out to eat. A group of guys my age kept looking at her, so I had her sit with me on my side. I shielded her from their view, and Mia relaxed. Remembering what Teo said, that girls knew everyone was watching them, has me feeling extra protective of her. My dad hasn't had Mia in his study or talked to her much during dinner. I think he just wanted to scare me. It's working, but I try not to show it.

She and I started a movie, but she fell asleep. Mia is leaning on me, so I put my arm around her and let her sleep on me. Her hair covers my arm. Today she's wearing her long sleeve gray dress with buttons down the front. Another outfit that a doll would wear. Her left arm is touching me and I get the urge to lift up her sleeve. I try to watch the movie but I can't.

Mia trusts me, and I keep betraying that trust. I tell myself I'm helping her, but I think I'm doing it for myself. Am I a psycho? I wonder if maybe I am doing something bad to Mia, but I can't finish the thought because I'm gently pulling up her sleeve. I gasp at how many scars there are, but there are no fresh cuts. Long lines, short lines, crooked lines, and x's go up halfway to her elbow. Touching them, I feel their different textures. Some are smooth and others are jagged. They are shiny and translucent purple on her fair skin. I wish I could erase them.

I roll down her sleeve and hug her close to me. It's a bad habit, but I space out and disconnect, as I often do when I get overwhelmed or stressed out. The movie keeps playing, but I'm not following it. Moving pictures distract me, but then I feel Mia stir in my arms and sit up. She yawns and looks up at me with a smile that goes away too soon.

"What's wrong?" she asks.

"What?" I wasn't prepared for her to wake up.

I'm in a daze. Mia reaches up and touches my face. I didn't know until now, but I've been crying. She studies my tears on her hand and looks confused.

"Are you okay, Ryon?"

"Yeah, I'm fine."

I lean back against the couch and pretend to watch the movie. Mia is sensitive and sweet. She lets me cry and doesn't bother me about it. My stepsister holds onto her necklace and we finish the movie but I can't stop glancing at her left arm that's covered in scar bracelets.

I vow to never let Mia hurt herself again. As long as we are together, I'm going to protect her. I will make her happy. No matter the cost, I will do it. Even if it means I have to steal. I would die for her. I'd kill for her. It's horrifying the things I would do to keep my stepsister safe. My dad is right. There is something off about the way I care about Mia. She feels better, so she sleeps in her room again. I pull her light yellow and sky blue comforter over her.

"Goodnight," I say.

"Goodnight."

The giant red panda I got her sits on the bed with her. She keeps her necklace on. Mia's room has tiny sapphire lights that hang around her bed. Everything about her reminds me of the color blue. I go back into my room that's all shades of black and gray. I have red and blue blankets on my bed, but my dad keeps everything sterile.

I lay down and face the wall I share with Mia. The slate color is fit for a prison, but I'm glad Mia is here with me. I know she loves me, but I wonder how much. If someone hurt me, would she plot revenge? Does she have fucked up thoughts like me? No, she's not white.

****

It's pouring rain today. The sky is gray, but it's calming. I decide to hang out in our covered hot tub. Putting on my favorite rap and hip hop playlist, I sit back and space out. I needed this. My thoughts have been angry and my behavior has been aggressive. I need to chill out.

"Hey," says Mia.

I didn't hear her walking up. I turn down my music.

"Hey. Want to join me?" I ask.

"I'm okay."

"Are you sure?"

"Yeah, I'm fine."

Mia is wearing the white sweater I got her and playing with her necklace.

"I won't judge you or anything if that's what you're worried about," I say as I run my hand through my hair.

It sticks up and makes my stepsister laugh, which makes me laugh. Mia looks down and touches her left arm. I frown but am quick to replace it with a smile so she doesn't feel bad.

"Really?" she asks.

"Of course. Have I ever judged you?" I ask.

"No. You're always nice to me."

"Are you going to join me or not?" I joke.

She smiles and runs back into the house. Mia returns shortly with one of our perfectly white towels. Her long hair is up in a high ponytail. It changes the way she looks, and she is almost like a different person. She's wearing a royal blue bikini. I think she feels uncomfortable, so I turn up the music and close my eyes.

"I like your music," she says.

I turn it down, but not too much so we can still listen to it.

"You do?" I'm surprised.

Most of my music is fast-paced, obnoxious, violent, and mean.

"Yes. It's different," she says.

"What do you like about it?"

I am curious to hear Mia's perspective.

"It's real. The person conveys a graphic story in an interesting and captivating way."

"You're deep, sis."

I splash her, and she splashes me back but lightly.

"Thank you?" she says it like it's a question.

Her left arm remains under the water, but she gestures with her right hand like a real girl. It makes me happy.

"Really, I mean it. I like how deep you are. I never thought much about art or why someone says what they are saying in their songs, but you make me look at life in a whole new way."

"I noticed you reading my poetry book. Stepping On Broken Stemmed Violets. Did you like it?" she asks.

"To be honest, I didn't understand a lot of it, but yes, I did like it."

"What stood out to you?"

"There was one where a guy said something about bringing back a girl from the dead," I say.

"She was dead. I was violent. He was lead, I was the pilot. We crash together."

She remembers it word for word.

"Yeah, that one."

Mia has a really good memory for that kind of stuff.

"I like that one, too."

The rain continues to fall, and we enjoy each other's company in silence. Girls know when to speak. They are mysterious without meaning to be. Sometimes girls chat for like an hour but don't say anything. Not Mia. She is the kind of person I wish would talk more because there's nothing dull about her. She thinks she is boring, but she's not.

"Your hair looks nice up," I say.

I hope my compliment isn't creepy, but I'm being genuine. Two strands of hair frame her doll's face and the rest hangs down her back in a disheveled but stylish ponytail. It looks like it's out of a magazine.

"Thank you," she says, but doesn't look at me.

She is focused on the sky that's slate, like Joseph's prison. Two birds fly above us and head for the sea.

"Why don't you wear it up more often?" I ask.

"It feels strange. I don't like to do my hair or makeup like most girls."

Mia is pretty, just the way she is. Her eyelashes don't need mascara. She has this raspberry pink mouth that looks like she's always wearing lipstick. Mia never has a blemish, and her skin is always perfect.

"You don't need it."

"If I did wear makeup, everyone would just say it looks slutty," she says.

"Hey, no they wouldn't. Don't say that."

"Sorry. It's just that I feel people's eyes on me all the time. The attention makes me anxious. I try to blend in and go unnoticed."

"I'm sorry. That sounds terrible. And I hate to say it, but you're never going to go unnoticed because you're too pretty," I say and I reach out and playfully yank on her ponytail. "I'm going to have to beat up so many guys as you get older."

"All the boys at my school are scared of you," she laughs.

I like the way it sounds.

"They should be," I joke, but I'm not joking.

There are nights I dream about broken teeth, shattered bones, and puddles of blood beneath cracked skulls.

"Biora is going out with that older boy," says Mia.

"Shinji? That dick that drove the car?" I ask.

"Yes."

"Is he bothering you?"

"No. Well, not really."

"What do you mean?" I ask.

I don't want to grill her, but now I'm nervous.

"He picks Biora up in his silver Honda. They both look at me funny."

"How so?"

"Shinji gives me this little wave," Mia wiggles her fingers to demonstrate, "and Biora blows kisses at me."

"Has she done anything to you?" I ask.

Mia sits up on the side of the hot tub but keeps her legs in. She swings them and stalls.

"Her and Kim took my bra. They said they were going to sell it for a lot of money," she says.

"When did this happen?"

"Like two weeks ago."

I turn the music off and stare at her. It's burning up in me. The fever that makes me feel like my dad. I sit next to her on the edge of the hot tub and let the cool air bring me back.

"Why didn't you tell me?"

"I don't know. It wasn't that big of a deal."

"It is to me."

"It is?"

"Yeah. I don't like the idea of those mean little queens bullying you or some guy sniffing your bra. I'm not okay with that," I say.

I don't want to make her feel weird, so I turn the music back on to avoid saying dumb shit like I do when I get pissed.

"I love you," she says and puts her arms around me.

I can feel the different textured scars on her arm as it rests against my neck. Her ponytail swishes and I smell violets. I don't like that the boys have been this close to her. Close enough to know her fucking perfume.

"I love you, too, Mia."

I hug her, and we watch the rain. I'm having a great time until I hear my dad sneak up next to me like a snake.

"Hey kids," he lingers on the word "kids."

"Hi dad," I say.

"Hi," whispers Mia.

She and I aren't touching anymore, but who knows how long he was watching?

"What are you two up to?" he asks.

My dad pats my shoulder too hard. He moves to Mia and plays with her ponytail. She looks down and I watch where my dad's eyes are. They are on her neck. He is a snake.

"Just listening to music and hanging out," I say.

"I wouldn't call this music," says my dad.

He keeps playing with her hair and I want to grab his wrist, but I can't. I'll never win. Then he picks up her necklace, grazing her collarbone. Too close for me.

"This is nice. Who got you this?" he asks with imitation fatherly care.

"Ryon got it for me," she whispers.

"He did? It's really pretty, babe."

He lets it go and eyes me up and down. A poisonous viper is readying itself to strike.

"I saw it and it reminded me of her," I say.

He takes another look at my stepsister. I can't tell if he is testing me, but I see him look at her chest and smooth stomach.

"It's beautiful," he says and walks away, leaving a venomous bite.

***

Setsuna invited me out after school. I told her I had time for an iced coffee but that I needed to get home. She seemed sad. I'm waiting for her on the steps. I still can't take anyone on my motorcycle for seven months. It's agonizing thinking about how long I have to wait. Setsuna exits the building and we head towards The Asagao, where everyone from this school hangs out.

"How was your day, Setsuna?" I ask.

"Good. What about you?"

"It was good," I say.

Setsuna is normally bubbly and pointing out everything she thinks is cute, but not today. I wonder what's on her mind. We get to the coffee shop and order our drinks. It's sunny, so we sit outside. I prefer it because it's crowded with people I don't want to be near inside.

"Thanks for inviting me out," I say and loosen my tie.

I hate this stupid thing. My blazer is stiff around the elbows.

"Ryon, can I talk to you about something?"

"What is it?" I try to swallow the lump in my throat.

"That time we hung out at the beach. Did you have fun?"

"Yeah. I thought we had a lot of fun," I say.

I regret drinking this coffee because I want to throw up. Girls always have something to say and it makes the muscles constrict under my skin.

"Why didn't you ever call me again?" she asks.

"I don't know. I figured if you wanted to hang out, you'd just ask me."

"But I wanted you to call me," she says.

"Why?"

"Really Ryon? Isn't it obvious?"

"I don't know what you're talking about," I say.

"I like you. I thought maybe you liked me back, but you never called me. You're always so nice to me at school. I wasn't sure how you felt about me," she says.

Now I really feel sick. I was not expecting this kind of conversation.

"I think you're cool, Setsuna. You're my friend. I'm sorry, but I don't like you like that," I say as gently as possible.

Setsuna nods at me and her wavy ponytail shakes. Her blue-green eyes fill up with tears, and I feel like such an asshole.

"Indigo Midnight," she blurts out the words.

I don't comprehend what she's saying.

"What?"

"Indigo Midnight. It's the name of the perfume your stepsister wears."

"It's not like that—"

I start but Setsuna stands up.

"You don't have to explain. I smell it all over your neck," she says and storms off.

The table behind us is staring at me. It's two girls and two boys from my grade. The table next to them consists of two boys two grades ahead of me. They whisper and I swear I see them mouth my name.

I go back to the school and get my motorcycle. Not wanting to go home right away, I ride around for an hour. I feel bad making Setsuna so upset. The thing that gets me is that I didn't know I was hurting her. She always smiled and acted happy. All this time, she's been wanting to confront me. I'm an insensitive dick.

Mia is probably waiting for me, so I head to the house. Koharu is cooking and I go into the kitchen to greet her. I expect Mia to be sitting at the counter, but she's not. My stepmom smiles at me and continues to chop bok choy. I try not to sound weird.

"Hey Koharu," I say.

"Hey Ryon, how was your day?" she asks.

Her manicured hands slice cucumbers and red bell peppers.

"It was good. Where's Mia?" I ask, hoping not to sound too desperate or worse, creepy.

"She called and said her and Ayumi were going to go to the movies."

"I'm glad she has a friend," I say.

"Me too. He seems like a nice boy."

"He is."

"I wish she had a girl to hang out with though," she sighs.

"Mia tells me the girls are super mean to her," I say and start helping my stepmom.

I set the table and wash her dishes.

"They are. It wasn't always like this. She had two really good friends growing up, Erika and Hosana. Once the girls reached eleven, everything changed. The boy Erika liked told her he liked Mia. Hosana had a crush on Erika's older brother. He also liked Mia."

"She's beautiful and mysterious. Like you," I say.

My stepmom stops chopping and giggles like she's my age.

"Thank you, Ryon."

We're almost done making dinner when Mia gets home. She's wearing an olive green dress, with a long beige coat, and black flats. My stepsister looks pretty and happy.

"Hi," she says and sits down next to me.

"How was the movie?" I ask.

"It was good. We went to see one of the film noirs," she says.

"Cool. I didn't know Ayumi liked stuff like that."

"Yeah. We like all the same old classics. A lot of dramas and dark pieces."

"I'm glad you two had fun," I say.

"Thanks," she says.

We sit down and wait for my dad to come in. He's screaming into his phone. I'm relieved because I was worried it would be one of those nights where he forces us to act like the perfect family and massage his ego. I hate those nights. Lately he's been pressing for Mia to call him "dad." She never does. I can't explain how it's wrong, but it is. Joseph never does anything without some kind of messed up intent.

"Do you want to go shopping tomorrow, Mia?" asks my stepmom.

She smiles and ignores my dad, shouting next to her. She's so good at it.

"What for?"

"Dresses, shoes, whatever! A girl's day. Just me and you," says Koharu, and Mia lights up.

"Yeah! That sounds fun, mom."

"It's a date," says my stepmom.

I shouldn't be, but I'm wary of her. Is she trying to take Mia away from me? No, she said she wouldn't do that because Mia loves me. What if she didn't, though?

It's the middle of the night. I can't sleep. If I do, I know I'll have nightmares about Mia not being in her room and I can't bear the thought of being alone in this house with Joseph again. I face the wall I share with her and attempt to crack it with my mind. Opening the wall and unhinging the barricade that keeps in Mia's thoughts plagues me for over an hour. It's 3:23 a.m., and I can't take it anymore. I get out of bed and sneak into her room.

I'm a bad stepbrother. My hands are shaky and my palms are sweaty. I'm breathing in shallow breaths. I worry that I'm going to wake her. Mia's hair covers her pillow and falls off the edge of the bed. I take out the teal sweater containing her diary. It's not possible for me to stop myself. I need to know that she still loves me, and that she will not leave. I flip through the pages until I find one towards the end. It's dated a week back. Mia wrote another poem about me.

I feel safe
In his embrace
Our lives are intertwined
In lace
He's my saving grace

I retreat into my room and lean against my door and cry. My

stepmom wants to spend time with my stepsister and I'm acting like a psycho. I share so much with Joseph. Maybe I am just like him and don't know it. I have his hair, his face, his build. There's a chance I inherited his crazy. I feel it like a million paper cuts on my brain. Then my blood turns fiery hot and I can't control myself. That's when I rage out and hit people. I felt the sting and swelling in my brain that day I jumped on Fuyuhisa. It hit me again when I assaulted Ben at the park. I want to protect Mia from everything, but I'm wondering if it's just an excuse to act like my dad.

CHAPTER SIXTEEN
STORMS NEAR THE COAST

Anxiety leaves me with little focus. I can't stop pacing around my room until I hear Koharu unlock the front door. Their shopping bags rustle. Mia takes tiny footsteps up to her room. I hear her go in and set her treasures down. Not wanting to seem too eager or weird, I wait to knock on her door. I lay on my floor and try to get my pulse under control. It throbs between my eyes. Twenty minutes seems long enough and I wait for Mia to answer me.

"Hi Ryon," she says.

"Hey! What did you buy?" I ask.

She lets me in and starts showing me her things. Mia holds up several different dresses, all with long sleeves. They are shades of mauve, turquoise, and lavender. She got a pair of black oxfords, knee high mahogany boots, and strappy white flats. All are super small and cute. Mia really is a doll. Her room reminds me of a dollhouse. All the matching teal, sapphire, white, and navy blue hues are vintage looking. Her art studio is organized and neat.

My stepsister is sitting on her fluffy bed stacked with stuffed animals and pillows. Her movements are graceful. The sun is coming through her window and making her hair super shiny. As she pulls out her accessories to show me, I can't help but smile because isn't quite a real girl but not completely a doll anymore either. I pick up the mauve dress. It has a white bow and buttons down the back.

"I really like this one," I say.

This makes Mia happy.

"Thank you. I had a lot of fun with my mom today."

"Good. I'm glad you guys got to spend time together."

I pick up one of her black barrettes with a daisy on it and clip her long bangs out of her face.

"What did you do today?" she asks as she finger combs her hair.

I don't want to tell her the truth. I've been sulking around the house, waiting for her. Worry made it impossible to do anything. Sora and Teo texted me to play basketball, but I lied and said I was spending time with Mia.

"Listened to music, read, just hung out," I say.

"That sounds nice," she says and lays down on her bed.

"Yeah," I exit her room and go back into mine.

It's only 3:30 p.m. I contemplate texting the guys back and taking up their offer now that I can see straight. A new text is in my inbox. It's from Ayumi.

Ryon, you need to see this. I found it last night. There's a link to a website. I click on it. I'm disgusted by what I see. It's a guy's Instagram. He has a powder blue bra with a white rose on it in his hands. I just know it's Mia's. The caption of the picture says "The Sweet Smell Of Violets."

I drop my phone. It makes a loud knocking sound as it hits the wooden floor. My phone buzzes again. It's another text from Ayumi.

There's another guy, he's older than me, probably twenty-five, holding a pair of light pink panties with blue flowers on them. He's sticking his tongue out like he's going to lick the crotch. I don't want to admit it to myself, but these are Mia's as well. I read what the guy writes in his description: Best buy ever. Worn by a sexy ass fourteen-year-old schoolgirl. I paid extra for pictures of the girl these belong to. She had no idea she was being photographed. Makes it hotter. Best service ever, will definitely be using again.

Ayumi texts me again stating Biora and Kim have been stealing her things. Ripping them off her in the bathroom and when she's by herself. Why doesn't she tell me this stuff? I'm getting pissed. Dudes in their twenties are sniffing her bra and looking at pictures of her. I hate those mean queens. If I could, I would bash in their plastic faces with a crowbar. I would crush their skulls into the dirt.

I tell Ayumi thank you. He apologizes for not being able to do more, but he has done enough. I'm happy he walks Mia home. She has someone to go to the movies with. Ayumi might not be the kind of guy to break up a fight, but he is a good person. He cares about other people and tries to do the right thing.

Biora and Kim are going to get it. I don't know what I'm going to do, but I'm going to do something. They will pay for what they've done to her. I wish Mia and I could just run away together. Get her away from this place that doesn't understand her, doesn't appreciate her gentle and beautiful nature. I lay in bed until dinner is ready. Mia is in a good mood and I act like I am, too. We ignore my dad screaming into the phone. I wish I could ignore knowing what I know.

I wake up fifteen times during the night. My neck and hairline are sweaty. I get up and wash my face. I dream about Mia not being in her room. The image of me laying in her bed with all her other items missing haunts me. I dream about boys touching and sniffing her hair. The part where a snake is wrapping around her thigh, leaving bruises, makes me want to vomit. I can't explain why, but it does.

***

School is so boring. Every day is the same as the last. I stare out the window most of the time. Somehow, I pass all my tests. I get good grades on my essays. Everyone thinks I'm smart, but I don't feel smart. I am a fraud. My homework is complete and done on time. The guys always give me shit for being able to barely try and yet excel. I take it as a compliment. Today seems like it's going to be just like every other day until I see three guys a grade ahead of me laughing at their phones and looking at me.

"What?" I ask as I slam my locker shut.

"Nothing," says the tallest boy.

He has green eyes like my dad. I hate him already.

"Tell me what's so funny," I snap.

The other two boys back up, but the snake eyed one just shows me his phone with a smug expression. It's a picture of Mia. Arms with freckles are holding her down, and Biora is kissing her with her tongue in her mouth. Mia's eyes are closed and tears are running down her face. Biora is winking and giving the camera a salacious look. The caption reads "Me and my Girlfriend."

"I didn't know Mia liked girls," hisses the boy with green eyes.

I tackle him and smash his phone.

"She doesn't," I growl.

The other two boys run off down the hall.

"What? Are you mad you had to find out your girlfriend was cheating on you like this?" he asks.

His front two teeth are chipped. I want to crack them into a million pieces.

"She's not my girlfriend. She's my stepsister," I say as I choke him out with his tie.

"People can be two things at once," he rasps.

I let him go before I get in trouble. Standing up, I see no teacher has noticed, but passing students put their heads down and scurry past me. I am dissociating. My classes blur together. Sora and Teo talk to me, but I can't hear. As soon as the bell signifying the end of the day rings, I'm on my motorcycle and ripping out of the parking lot. Mia is in her room reading on her bed when I get home. I don't even bother to knock.

"Hey Ryon, what's going on?" she asks.

"That's what I want to know," I say.

Mia looks at me hurt but I'm also hurt, so I continue.

"I saw two boys post online that they had your bra and panties. They have pictures of you, too. Then a boy a grade ahead of me showed me a picture of Biora kissing you."

I sit next to my stepsister. My eyes narrow. I know I'm scaring her, but I can't turn it off. My rage is making me psycho.

"I'm sorry," she says and sits up to face me.

I don't want her to be sorry. If anything, I am going to make Biora and Kim sorry.

"What's been going on? Tell me the truth."

"Biora and Kim gang up on me in the bathroom. Or if I'm by

myself somewhere in the school. Kim holds me down while Biora unclasps my bra or rips off my underwear and forces me to make out with her. She says she's doing it so she can tell Shinji what it's like to kiss me. Apparently, it would be nice if I wasn't so weird. That's what she said, anyway."

My stepsister holds her arm and hangs her head. I feel bad for yelling at her, so I pull her towards me and hug her.

"Mia, why didn't you tell me?" I ask.

"I was really embarrassed. I'm sorry," she says.

"I'm not mad at you. I just hate seeing guys being gross to you. Now Biora is forcing her tongue into your mouth and I can't beat her up," I say, and this makes Mia giggle.

"What?" I ask.

"Nothing. I like that you're protective of me."

"Even if you didn't like it, I'd still protect you from everything all the time. I'm your brother," I say.

"Everyone thinks you're my boyfriend though," she says and rolls her eyes.

We both laugh.

"Good. Maybe then they'll stop bothering you because they know I'm gonna come smash their windows and kick their asses!"

"Why won't they leave me alone?" she asks.

"I told you. It's because you're too pretty," I say.

Her hair has grown out and is almost as long as it used to be. I pick up a handful and play with it. Even though it's messy, it's really soft.

"Kim told me I was ugly and that the only reason guys think I'm attractive is because they think I'm having sex with you," she says.

"Ugh! Those girls are messed up in the head. Don't listen to them. You're so beautiful. You'd have to be blind not to see that," I say.

"Are you saying that because you're my brother or because you really think that?"

"Both."

***

It's the beginning of winter. Things are tense as ever. My dad hasn't beat me up, but he pauses to look at Mia in front of me. I never took my father for a pervert. An asshole for sure, an abuser, but not a pedophile. He's doing it to put me on edge. It's working. I asked Mia if my dad has been bothering her and she said "no" but she lies to me.

I can't ride my motorcycle because it's too slick out. The house is stuffy. I stand on the back porch for a bit and admire the crisp, clear night. The sky is indigo. I wince as I think about the name of my stepsister's perfume, Indigo Midnight. Apparently, everyone can smell it on me. I don't care. They can think whatever they want. I love Mia and if they want to corrode it with their filthy lies, they can try, but it won't work on me.

It's awful, but I've been drinking. It's only 6:54 p.m. and I'm swaying. My dad and Koharu are fucking really loud and it's grossing me out. I grab another one of his imported beers from the fridge in the garage. He has so many he won't notice. I chug it and throw it into the recycling. Stumbling upstairs, I lay on my couch and listen to songs about love, hate, and revenge. I'm so wasted I fall asleep with the music blaring.

"Ryon! Ryon!"

Mia is shaking me awake. I look at the clock. It's 11:37 p.m. I've been asleep for a while. The music is deafening. I rip out my earbuds. Mia is on her knees, crying.

"What's wrong?" I am panicking, but try not to show it.

"You have to come downstairs," she cries.

I get up, and even though I am still drunk, I keep it together. Mia shouldn't see me like this. I sound like my dad as I lumber down the stairs slowly and with care. Mia turns on the hallway lights and I see broken mirrors all over the floor. Pieces of glass are strewn about the house. Shards stick out from the walls and in the rugs. I turn the corner and walk into the kitchen. There are broken dishes and blood on the floor and counters. Not a lot of blood, but a little puddle resembling spilled wine sits on the kitchen table. Going back down the hall, I look in my dad's study. His desk is turned over. The chair is across the room.

The bathroom is fine. Nothing out of the ordinary here. I brace myself as I open Koharu and my dad's bedroom door. The lamp is still on. It casts an orange glow on the white sheets of the bed. The black blanket lays in a heap on the ground. I walk in and assess the damage.

All of Koharu's clothes are missing from the closet. So are her shoes. Her purse and keys aren't sitting on her nightstand.

I go out to the garage. My dad's car is gone. So is Koharu's. There are tire marks on our driveway. It looks like she got out of here in a hurry. I go back in the house. I'm not drunk anymore, but I'm not sober either. It looks like Koharu kept her promise. She said she wouldn't take Mia away from me, but she never said anything about getting up in the night and leaving.

Mia is freaking out. I'm not in the right mind to handle this. To try and get her to calm down, I make us tea. I put on a movie and let her sob into my hoodie. She doesn't want to be alone, and I let her sleep with me. I keep playing with her hair that coats my pillowcase in violets. Moving and rearranging her wavy hair like she's a doll, and this is just a game, makes me happy. We have school in the morning and I make sure my alarm is set.

I can't sleep, but I'm not upset about it. Mia and I are alone in the house without my father's judgement and I can enjoy my time with her. It's a fucked up wish, but I hope my dad doesn't come back. I like the idea of it just being me and Mia. If only her mother didn't abandon her. I don't blame her. Joseph can drive a woman to madness. His dark magic is powerful. He has made two mothers desert their children. I know my mom loved me. Mia's mom loved her even more.

It's 5:30 a.m. I get out of bed and go out into the hall and call my dad. The need to know if he's coming back makes me excited but nervous. I would love for him to just leave me. Koharu shouldn't have left Mia, but I'm glad she didn't take her with. I wonder if she trusts me enough to leave Mia with me or if she just couldn't be in this house anymore. I'd like to think Koharu wants Mia and me to stay together.

No answer. I call him six times. He doesn't pick up. I call Koharu a couple of times. She doesn't answer either. I go back to my room and look down at my stepsister sleeping in my bed. She's sleeping on my side and holding her necklace. I put my arm around her and try to get some rest. My heartbeat is erratic and keeps me up. I can't tell what I'm feeling. The alcohol has worn off, but I feel weird.

Mia shifts in her sleep and faces me. I rest my head in her hair and drift in and out of sleep. Dreams about the beach soothe me. I'm walking along the shoreline. It's sunny but I'm alone. There's no one else at the beach. Dark clouds roll in, but I keep walking. The waves break white and sea foam green as they hit the sand. I find a patch of purple flowers and start picking them as it starts to rain.

CHAPTER SEVENTEEN

THE MAN WITH RED HAIR

First a week passes. Then another. My dad still won't take my calls. Koharu isn't answering Mia's calls either. It's been nineteen days since the last time we saw our parents. I'm not too upset about it, but Mia can't stop crying. I don't want to show how glad I am that it's just me and her. I'm sure she knows I want her to have her mom, but as selfish as it is, I'm glad Koharu left her with me.

I have told no one except Sora and Teo. The neighbors hardly ever talk to us, so they won't notice. If they do, I'll just say they went on a little getaway. Rich people love shit like that. I told Mia we have to go to school. If we get caught skipping, they'll send truancy officers. Having no legal guardian means they'll send child protective services and separate us. I'll never let that happen.

Surprisingly, I haven't been doing too bad of a job taking care of us. I cleaned up all the glass in our house. It took almost three days to get it all out. I swept, vacuumed, and swept again. Mia and I both know how to cook and take turns cooking each other breakfast and dinner. She does all the laundry. I have almost 250,000 yen. I'm going to have to get a job, but I don't mind. If it can just be me and her, I'll do anything.

Mia and I have had a good routine. I get home from school and we do our homework together. Then we make dinner and hang out like nothing is wrong. Some nights she reads on her bed while I go through her paintings. Or we hang out in the hot tub and listen to music. I'm having a lot of fun, but I know Mia is really sad. She knows I hate my dad and doesn't bring him up.

She's asleep, but gripping onto my tee shirt. I think she's having a dream someone is leaving her. Mia furrows her eyebrows before tossing and turning. I rub her shoulder and whisper to her trying to get her to relax. It takes a while, but she does. She has a pretty baby face. I don't mean to stare at her but we're really close all the time now. Her doll features intrigue me. It's strange to be so close to a living doll. I get out of bed and throw on my red parka.

I'm happy to be free of my dad but the responsibility is heavy. Walking down the street calms me a bit. The cool air touches my face. It's refreshing. I haven't raged out since our parents abandoned us. Biora and those guys are going to pay for what they do to Mia but I can't worry about them right now. I need to make sure we're okay. It could be my imagination but I think someone is following me. I turn around to see a tall dark figure approaching.

"Hey," he says.

As he nears, I see he is a little older than me but still young. He has tousled red hair and a big diamond in his left ear. His button up is silky and black. He has on tight leather pants and short black boots with a heel.

"Hey," I say.

He's smoking a cigarette and grinning at me. I look around and see no lights on in the houses. The sidewalk is empty. Only a cat slinking across the road stirs in the blackness beyond the streetlights.

"I like you, kid."

He exhales, and a big plume of smoke fills the air between us. I cough.

"Who are you?" I ask.

"My name is Noburu," he says.

Now that he is closer I see that he is also white. Red sideburns accent his face. No other facial hair. There is a bump on the bridge of his nose like me. His eyes are the color of honey and mischievous. They reflect gold in the dark.

"Why do you like me? You don't even know me."

I am about to walk off. This guy seems like a weirdo.

"I've been watching you," he says.

"Fuck off, dude."

I cross the road to evade this creep. He follows.

"Hey! Wait! I got a job for you."

"What?" I ask.

Who is this guy?

"I'm The Soul Keeper. I could use your help, kid."

I laugh, because I'm deliriously tired and confused. Noburu lights up another cigarette and shows me his teeth but doesn't smile.

"I'm serious," he says.

"Prove it," I say.

Noburu ushers me towards town. There seems to be no one out but then I hear it. The sound of a girl crying.

"Please, let me go!" she shrieks.

As we turn the corner Noburu stops me. We watch a girl my age being hassled by two older men.

"If you don't want to be bothered why are you out so late?" asks one of the men.

"I was at work. I just wanna go home. Please, let me go!" she repeats.

The other man is holding her arms and kissing her neck.

"Work? Is that what you whores are calling it these days?" he growls as he forces his mouth on hers.

Noburu approaches the men very confidently.

"Hey assholes," says Noburu.

The men stop and stare at him.

"Piss off! This one's ours," says the man holding the girl.

She has watery eyes and long wavy hair. Her arms are thin and she is wearing a dress. She reminds me of Mia.

"I don't think so," says Noburu.

The man not restraining the girl lunges at him. Noburu hits him in the chest with a piece of paper. The man is surrounded by a neon glow. He holds his neck like he is choking. The man is gasping and being lifted off the ground by a hand that isn't there. Noburu charges at the man holding the girl and does the same. He drops her. She backs up slowly and runs away. I see her frightened face as she darts past me.

The two men attempting to hurt that girl are floating in Noburu's neon aura. It looks like they are being sucked dry. Their eye sockets are sunken and their lips are chapped. The men kick their legs but don't move from their suspended places.

"Go back to hell," says Noburu, and the men evaporate into neon green mist.

"What the fuck?" I say.

"I told you, kid. I'm the real deal," he says as he lights up another cigarette.

His fingers are covered in silver rings with red jewels and diamonds.

"What's the job?" I ask.

We start walking back towards my neighborhood.

"You'll be my assistant. I need someone to help me send demented souls back to hell."

"Huh?"

"You see, there are a lot of souls wandering the earth. The bad ones are overpopulating the planet. It's my job to send them back to where they belong," he says as he takes a long drag.

"What do I do?" I ask.

Noburu reaches into his pocket and pulls out a stack of papers with writing on them.

"These are demonic sutras. You'll use these to send the souls back. But there are a few rules," he says as he pushes the papers into my hand.

"What are they?"

"The first rule is don't tell anyone. I mean it. The second rule is don't get caught. If someone sees you, I'll have to kill them. That's bad for business. The third rule is no kids. Souls rarely get tainted by the darkness until about age twelve, so no one younger than that, okay? The last rule is you have to give me one good reason why the soul needs to be sent back to hell. Got it?"

"How much do I get paid?" I ask.

Noburu stops walking and laughs.

"Of course. How could I forget," he says and pulls out a black credit card with red numbers on it. He hands it to me, "Every time you bring me a soul I'll put 55,00 yen on that card."

"I thought a soul would be worth a lot more," I say.

Noburu almost falls over in a hysterical fit.

"Not the bad ones," he says.

"Why do you want me to be your assistant?"

"Your soul is pure. Despite having a shitty dad, no mom, a sad stepsister, and anger problems you manage to be a pretty decent guy. I think you will be a good judge of character," he says as his cigarette hits the asphalt.

Noburu stomps on it with the heel of his boot and sparks fly. We're right outside my house.

"What if I need to get a hold of you?" I ask.

Noburu fishes a small black phone out of his pocket. It's a flip phone, old school, with red buttons.

"My number is the only one in there. Thanks, Ryon. I'll see you soon," he says.

Noburu fades into the ghostly realm and I unlock the front door. Placing the sutras, credit card, and phone in my top drawer I smile. Now I'll be able to help Mia.

***

I thought it was just a dream. A psycho fantasy. But for the past week I have checked my top drawer and there they are: the phone, the credit card, and the sutras. I keep using my cash because I'm skeptical about this job. Am I really The Soul Keeper's assistant or am I a lunatic? This seems like something out of a movie.

Even though I don't fully believe that this is real, I've been gathering information. I got Biora and Kim's addresses. It made me feel like a creep, but I asked some of the shady kids to help me out. Everyone thinks I'm odd, anyway. What's another rumor? It's chilly but no snow and the ground isn't slick. I'm playing at the park with Sora and Teo while Mia reads on the bench by the fountain.

"How are things?" asks Sora.

"They're actually pretty good without my dad around. I feel bad for Mia though. She misses her mom," I say.

"Has your dad talked to you at all?" asks Teo as he shoots.

141

He misses but tries again.

"No. He won't take any of my calls. Koharu won't answer me either. She won't take Mia's calls," I say.

"What do you think happened?" asks Sora as he bounces the ball that Teo just passed to him.

"I think Koharu had been planning on running off on him for a while. She took Mia out for a girl's day right before. I confronted Koharu about what my dad said. She told me she wouldn't take Mia away from me, that she wouldn't separate us. I guess she kept her promise," I say.

"What about your dad?" asks Teo.

He passes the ball to me. I shoot and score.

"Koharu's closet was empty. My dad must have caught her packing up her things. He is the kind of person to hunt someone down. That's why my mom didn't take me with her," I admit.

"Do you think she's okay? You said there was blood in the kitchen," says Sora in a whisper.

We are the only ones on the court but it's better to be cautious.

"She was okay enough to get in her car. I think some of the blood was his," I say.

"What will you do if he comes back?" asks Teo.

We stop playing and stand closer to each other.

"I'm not sure. I like it just being me and Mia," I say.

"If he is willing to hurt Koharu, what does that mean for Mia?" asks Sora.

"I'd kill him before he could get close to her," I hiss.

It disgusts me to hear his voice come out of my mouth but it does more and more frequently now.

"I hope he stays away. You two could be happy together," says Teo.

He takes a drink of his water, reminding me to do the same. I haven't been hungry or thirsty. Mia has been making sure I eat but I don't really want to. Food doesn't appeal to me. I feel hungry for something else. It hurts to say, but it's true: I'm bloodthirsy.

"I'm going to go check on Mia," I say.

She's writing in the diary I got her. I wonder if this one is happier. The yellow one is filled up with depressed entries, sad poems, and some that bring me to my knees because they're about me.

"Hey," I wave to her and she closes her journal.

"Hey," she says.

"Everything okay? Are you getting cold?"

I ask as I adjust her pink scarf. She has on her white jacket and black shoes. A sad doll with big eyes.

"I'm okay. I like the cold," she says.

I hug her because I know she's sad and there's nothing I can do to bring her mom back. My dad likes to take things that aren't his. At least Mia is mine. I couldn't stand the thought of being in that house alone with Joseph. The nights I thought Koharu was going to take Mia away I thought about leaving in the night, too.

"I'm going to play a little longer and then we'll go home," I say and stand up.

She holds her diary to her chest and nods.

"Okay," she whispers.

I go back to the guys and we mess around on the court for a while. Mia and I walk home and I bounce the ball on the sidewalk periodically. It reminds me of the first time I attempted to be close to Mia. I said I would be her friend, and she jumped on me. The memory makes me smile. I wish I had tried harder to be a good brother sooner.

I cook, and Mia takes a shower when we get home. Looking through our stack of bills I am reminded of my responsibility as The Soul Keeper's assistant. I've had a lot of thoughts about killing someone but never thought I would act on it. I let the rage wash over me and swirl me in its red aura. Thinking about Fuyuhisa's hand in her shirt, Akito saying gross things to her, and Ben's hand in her skirt and other places causes me to cut my finger because I'm not paying attention. It's not bad but there's blood on the zucchini I was chopping. It's an impulse and I stick my finger in my mouth. The blood is metallic, like pennies, and bitter.

We eat together even though I can barely stomach anything. If I don't eat, she won't eat. Mia and I watch a black and white movie that she likes in my room. She leans on me as she falls asleep. It seems like she's always tired now. I worry that maybe it's part of being a doll and she's losing the vibrancy she had. I cradle her in my arms and think of her painting of the baby bird. She has been sleeping with me but I tuck her into her bed.

I set my alarm and prepare myself for Monday. It's hard to pretend to care about school when all I want is to be with Mia. Now that I know she's alone in this house until I'm here I speed all the way home. Mia is the kind of girl I double check the locks for. I make sure the windows are locked, too.

Falling asleep comes easier than usual tonight but I wake up to the smell of violets and a skinny arm around my shoulder. Mia doesn't like being left alone. It's probably bad, but I let her do whatever she wants. If she wants to be with me I let her stay. I think about that picture of Biora making out with her and that horrible caption, Me and my Girlfriend. If I couldn't do it before I can now.

For Mia I will kill. I'll murder everybody that's ever made her cut herself. No matter who it is. I open my eyes at my fucked up thoughts. Mia is breathing tiny breaths into my neck. I put my arm around her and my hand in her hair. She's wearing the sweater I got her. The rumors about me are true. I am the white devil, a blond demon. I sleep with my stepsister every night. The way I love her is wrong, but it's not what everybody thinks.

***

"Mia, I need to ask you something."

"What is it?"

She's wearing her royal blue bikini. We're sitting in the hot tub listening to my heavy rock music.

"What all happened in that car?" I ask.

I don't look at her because I know she's still shy.

"I told you," she says.

"Did anybody else do anything like what Ben did?"

"Ryon, I don't want to talk about this."

"Please, I really need to know," I say, trying not to snap at my stepsister.

Her hair is up and she can't hide her face from me. A dark shadow enters her eyes. Mia's been keeping something from me.

"Why?" she asks.

"Because I'm your brother. What happens to you is important to me," I say.

Mia sighs and turns away from me. She stands up and crosses her arms.

"Akito forced me to make out with him. Fuyuhisa made me touch him. It was so gross," she's crying but trying to keep it in.

I jump up and stand beside her.

"Mia, why didn't you tell me?"

It pains me to hear something so ugly happen to my beautiful stepsister.

"They said you would think I liked it anyway," she mumbles into her shoulder.

"You know I would never think that," I say and start playing with her ponytail.

I tickle her face with it and get her to laugh.

"I know. It's just so embarrassing."

"It's not embarrassing for you. It's embarrassing for them. You didn't do anything wrong," I say.

"I wish I was invisible."

"Hey, don't say that!"

"It's true though. All I want is to exist without a man staring at me or trying to touch me. Boys walk by and smell my hair. They snicker at me because they say your neck is covered in my perfume," she says and touches her heart.

My stepsister reminds me of a flower that will wilt at any moment.

"Like I told you, sis. You're just too pretty," I say and reach out to touch her doll's face.

The hot tub is making her cheeks rosy, and she looks more real this time.

"The other pretty girls don't get bullied like I do," she whispers.

"The other girls aren't as pretty as you."

"You always say that."

"It's true. I'm going to keep saying it until you believe me. No girl is as pretty as you. No one can paint like you can. You are beautiful, Mia."

This makes her smile like a real girl.

"Thank you, Ryon."

"Are all the boys at your school still scared of me?" I ask.

"Yeah, they are."

"Good. That means I just have to beat up all the high school boys," I joke and splash her.

She splashes me back and we go back and forth until both of us have soaking wet hair and can't stop laughing. I'm laughing now but I wonder how I'll feel later when I reap the souls of the guys who molested my stepsister.

I wait for her to fall asleep. She's clinging onto my hoodie. I'm trying to break from her grasp as gently as I can. She's wearing her lavender pajamas with stripes on them. The sleeves are loose and her left one falls to her elbow, exposing her scars. I take in the image and allow it to fuel my hatred. In order to murder someone I'm going to have to get pissed off.

It's cold tonight. I pull my checkered comforter over her. It reminds me of playing house and tucking in a toy. Her hair falls over the edge of the bed, cascades over my pillow, and spills over the white sheets. I brush it to one side. The moon is full, and it illuminates her tiny face. I make sure the window is locked. Even though I locked them earlier, I check all the windows in the house. I make sure the back door is locked as well. Walking out to the garage and getting on my bike causes my thoughts to blur. As I leave the driveway, I wonder what Koharu was thinking at the exact moment she left the tulip lined road.

I head for Fuyuhisa's house first. For some reason him forcing Mia to do things to him angers me more than what Ben did. Both of them will pay, but I decide to take out the one that makes me the most angry. Fuyuhisa violated her in front of me. I know other boys have touched Mia, but that was the first time I saw someone do something inappropriate to her. I park my bike two blocks away from his house. Everyone knows I have a motorcycle. I put up my hood. My joggers are black and so are my shoes.

It's 2:13 a.m. and the streets are empty. The houses are dark. I walk up to the address Ayumi gave me. He said he wouldn't question why I asked for it. I figure I can trust him. The Soul Keeper said don't tell anyone, and I didn't. Now I have to make sure not to get caught. I walk around the two-story house and inspect inside. There's the living room, dining room, and kitchen. The bedrooms must be upstairs.

I climb the oak tree next to the house and peek in through the windows like a common criminal. I find Fuyuhisa's parents' room first. They have purple curtains. A small lamp is on and I see they are asleep. Fuyuhisa's dad is sleeping sitting up with his glasses on. It appears he was in the middle of reading something. His mom is sleeping facing the window. It makes me nervous, so I move swiftly to the next branch and inch closer to the room that I know belongs to Fuyuhisa.

He also has purple curtains. His room is covered in rock band posters and girls in bikinis. He has no light on but the glow from his computer screen gives me enough to see him. He's sleeping on his stomach. Books are on the floor next to him. I hope for the window to be unlocked and it is. This is it. The moment I've envisioned since the day I saw him put his hand up her skirt.

It's too easy. He doesn't even see it coming. I sneak up and place the demonic sutra on his back and the neon glow appears. It takes only a second. The wind blows through the window and Noburu appears. He runs his fingers through his hair and grins.

"You finally got one," says Noburu.

"I thought you were just a dream," I admit.

"That's what a lot of people think. Until they have to deal with me," he says with a mischievous expression.

His nose is pointy, and his eyes are narrow. He reminds me of a fox. "So tell me, why should this soul be sent back to hell?" he asks.

"He kidnapped her. This boy forced my stepsister to touch him," I say and as I do, I want to brush my teeth.

It feels disgusting in my mouth.

"Nice catch," says Noburu.

He approaches Fuyuhisa and places two fingers with big rings on his back.

"Go back to hell," he says.

Fuyuhisa rises from the bed and levitates. He swings his feet and reaches for his neck like the other men. His eyes bulge and it looks like his tongue is drying out as he screams silently. He turns to neon green mist and disappears.

"Did that really just happen?" I say.

"It did, kid. Thanks. Money's on the card. I'll see you soon," says Noburu.

He's gone by the time I turn around. I exit Fuyuhisa's room and close his window. Sneaking down the tree I peek into his parents' room again. I wonder if they knew what a piece of shit he was. They'll probably still miss him. I get on my bike and arrive home by 3 am. Mia is sound asleep. I take off my hoodie and get into bed with her. Mia reaches for me and I pull her to my chest.

"Where did you go?" she asks.

"To get some air," I say.

I pull the blanket over my shoulder. It seems like such a big deal to take someone's life but I feel fine. I don't feel bad at all.

CHAPTER EIGHTEEN
RED WINTER

I'm watching the news in my room. Normally I never watch this stuff but I have to because it's about Fuyuhisa. The police found no evidence of forced entry. They assume he ran away. His parents are begging for him to come back. I don't think they know the kind of darkness that was in their son's heart. His mom has soft features and big brown eyes. His dad is trying to be strong, but his voice is shaking and his hair is graying. Mia walks in my room unannounced. I turn off the TV.

"Hey Mia, what's up?" I ask.

She's got big tears in her eyes and I feel my stomach drop. "What's wrong?" I ask.

Mia stands in front of me but doesn't say anything. She's wearing the teal dress I got her.

"My dad is gone and my mom is, too."

Mia covers her face with her tiny hands and sobs.

I don't know what to say, so I just open my arms to her. She sits with me and cries into my shoulder. I didn't even think about that. First, her dad dies and now her mom abandons her. All she has is me. I hope I can be enough.

"I'm sorry. I'm right here. I'll always be here for you," I say.

This does the opposite of what I want and makes her cry more.

"It's okay, Mia," I say and run my hand through her hair.

"I love you," she says.

Great, now I'm going to cry.

"I love you, too."

I hide my face in her hair and let her sob until she falls asleep. She barely weighs anything. I stand up and put her in my bed since I know she won't sleep in hers. It's early evening and I get on my motorcycle. I head into town and search for scumbags to steal souls from. The heat from Fuyuhisa needs to cool down before I go after Akito and Ben.

I drive a couple towns over. As I ride through the streets, I witness petty thefts and couples fighting. This is a bad part of the city. Good, that's what I need. There are a lot of love motels and hookah bars. I smell boozy vomit on the sidewalk. It's sickening and reminds me of my dad. I park my bike in the darkness of an alley. Since I'm so tall, no one fucks with me. Guys with gold teeth and big boots walk by me with evil eyes, but don't say anything.

"Please, leave him alone!"

"Oh, c'mon. How much do you want for him?"

"He's my son! He's not for sale!"

"Look at you, old man. Living on the streets. I can take better care of him."

I round the corner to see a little boy, probably six or seven, being grabbed by the hood of his jacket. The man is obviously wealthy, with a nice suit, nice shoes, and an expensive watch. His face is tan and young looking, probably late twenties. A homeless man is gripping onto the hand of the little boy. His face is leathery and covered in grime. His clothes are dirty but the boy's are relatively clean.

"No, you're not taking my son," says the homeless man.

The wealthy young guy throws money at him and yanks on the boy's hood.

"Give him to me!"

The man rips the little boy out of the homeless man's grip and shoves him into his fancy red car. He takes off and the homeless man starts bawling his head off. I go back and get my motorcycle and take off down the road where I saw the man with the red car go. His vehicle is flashy and easy to find. I follow him and he swerves and takes turns at the last minute to get me off his tail. It doesn't matter though, I keep chasing him.

Homeless people and stray dogs back up against building walls as me and this guy race through the streets. He is driving recklessly, and so am I. I remind myself to be safe for Mia. She said I can't die until she dies. Who would take care of her when I'm gone? I stop driving like a maniac and focus. The guy puts on the brakes and jumps out of his car.

"What the fuck do you want, kid?" he asks as he gestures with the wrist wearing the expensive watch.

"Give me the boy," I say.

"No way."

He puffs his chest. Tufts of curly hair pop out from the top of his tacky button up. His shoes are shiny and he reeks of hairspray. Fuck this guy.

"Give me the boy," I repeat.

The man lunges at me, and I hit him in the chest with the demonic sutra. The neon aura appears. Through the veil of existence walks Noburu, who is smoking and looking casual as always.

"Hey Ryon. What we got here?" asks Noburu.

"This man stole another man's child for unsavory purposes," I say.

"Lovely," he says as he approaches the man. "Go back to hell."

The man is reaching for his neck. The watch glistens neon green and gold. His eyes are bulging out of his skull. They become empty sockets and as the man attempts to scream, his tongue evaporates. I hear people waking up and see a light come on in someone's apartment.

"I better get going," I say.

"Money's on the card. See you around," says Noburu.

He crosses through to the other side. It feels like the wind has picked up, but it's just The Soul Keeper's wake. I walk up to the car and find the little boy hiding in the backseat, covering his eyes with his hands.

"Hey, are you okay?" I ask.

The little boy nods his head "yes." I smile at him to let him know I'm not trying to hurt him.

"I'm going to take you back to your dad," I say.

The little boy jumps out of the car. I pick him up and put him on my motorcycle. My helmet won't fit him, so I drive extra cautiously back to where I saw the homeless man.

"Tobi!" exclaims the homeless man as I approach with his child.

"Papa!" says the little boy and runs to his dad.

"Thank you, young man," he says.

"You're welcome."

I pull out the last of my cash. It's only 10,000 yen, but it's better than nothing. I hand it to the homeless man, who stares up at me with shiny eyes.

"Take care of each other. Bye," I say and wave to the little boy who is smiling.

"Wait! What is your name?" he asks.

"Ryon," I say over my shoulder.

"You are a good person, Ryon."

"Thank you," I say.

I put on my helmet and head home. It takes over an hour. Mia is still sleeping. I'm not tired, so I lay on the couch and watch one of the foreign films Mia likes. I don't really get the plot, but it makes me feel closer to her.

***

To pay our monthly expenses, I find two more pieces of garbage to collect for The Soul Keeper. I was hanging out with Sora and Teo at the park last week. They went to talk to Koga and Kirin. I walked off because I thought I heard something. It was a young girl and a boy about my age. He was kissing her, and she was kissing him back, but he kept trying to get her to go down on him in the bushes. She started crying, but the guy didn't knock it off. I approached, and the girl ran off back towards the middle of the park. He didn't see it coming.

The other one was a woman. The first female soul I've collected. She was yelling at her husband as he was putting groceries in the car. Their baby was crying. Instead of comforting her child, she smacked them. This made them cry louder, and the woman kept yelling at her husband to "do something about this." She stormed off to smoke a cigarette. I heard her talking shit about her husband and baby to her friend on the phone. The woman didn't even look at me as I walked up to her.

I have extra money on the card, so I asked Mia if she wanted to go out with me. At first she declined, but I begged her to come hang out with me. She goes back upstairs to change. When she comes back down, I'm happy to see her wearing one of her new dresses and she has her hair up. Mia picked her mauve dress and mahogany boots with the white coat. She looks super cute, like a little doll.

"You look nice," I say.

She looks embarrassed.

"Is it too much?" she asks.

"What? No! I'm going to put on something nicer," I say and go through my closet.

I never wore the black button up Koharu got me. It's formal, but also casual. I put it on and look at myself. My reflection reminds me of Noburu. I head back downstairs and we walk into town. There's a high end sushi place on the corner next to the bookstore and I choose there.

"Why do you want to go there?" she asks.

We are the youngest people here. The host looks at me funny, but I smile at her and she seats us. The waiter is also skeptical of me, but I would be, too.

"I want to do something different," I shrug.

I order us sparkling yuzu drinks that are served in fancy glasses with wedges of fruit. Mia and I scan the room together. A lot of wealthy couples in black dresses and black suits. There are groups of businessmen wearing different colored ties and drinking sake. A group of older women give me the side eye. A table with four young women, probably in their mid-twenties, keep looking at me and giggling. I order for Mia since she's too shy and we observe the pink and yellow paper lanterns. There are white and orange string lights. The walls are red and black. It's very chic but festive.

"This is nice," says Mia.

"It is. I like that nobody from school is here," I say.

"Same. It's like I'm just a normal girl. Right now I'm not anybody. I like that," she says.

"You're somebody to me. You're my stepsister," I say and playfully tug on her ponytail.

She pulls back and fake glares at me. It makes me laugh.

"You know what I mean," she says and sips her bubbly drink.

"I know. I just like teasing you."

The waiter approaches us as I put my arm around her.

"The table over there bought you two this," says the waiter—he is gesturing to the table of young women.

He places one of the fancy desserts in front of us.

"Thank you. May I ask why?" I say.

Mia is blushing, but I think it's funny.

"They said it was nice to see such a sweet young couple," he says.

I want to laugh because Mia is dying next to me, but I smile and tell the waiter "thank you" again.

"Even people that we don't go to school with think you're my boyfriend," she says and tries to cover her blushing face.

"They just think you're cute and want to buy you stuff," I say.

I have no problem digging into the green tea ice cream with a bunch of toppings.

"Why would someone like you like someone like me?" she says, and it makes me choke on the bite I just took.

"Hey, what does that even mean?" I say and roll my eyes.

She always thinks I'm cooler than her, but I think the opposite. Mia has way more to offer the world than me.

"You're popular. You're smart. You're handsome. I'm just the weird girl," she says into her sparkling yuzu drink.

I reach for her and pull her closer to my side.

"Don't say that. Nothing about you is weird or embarrassing, okay?" I say.

Out of the corner of my eye, I see one girl from the table that sent the dessert looking at me and covering her smile with her hand.

"Do you really mean that?" she asks.

"Of course. It's everyone else that is weird and embarrassing," I laugh.

I excuse myself to the bathroom. I'm examining myself in the mirror. My shaggy hair is even more disheveled, but Mia says it looks good. The button up fits me nicely. I don't normally wear stuff like this, but I don't hate it. There's a guy four sinks down, checking out his teeth. I ignore him until I notice something strange. He takes out a condom from his wallet. In the small pocket of his suit jacket, he pulls out a needle and pokes a hole in it. He takes out another condom and does the same. I feel my face get hot. I have a demonic sutra in my wallet and I take it out. As I walk by the guy, I stick it to his back. They never see it coming.

"Snazzy place," says Noburu as he saunters out of one of the stalls. He's smoking, but he flicks the cigarette in the sink without a care.

"Can we make this quick? I'm having dinner with my stepsister," I say.

"Sure thing. Why should this soul be sent back to hell?" he asks as he lights up another cigarette.

He didn't even finish the last one. Noburu is wasteful in habit and dresses extravagantly but also kind of trashy. He's wearing a black bomber jacket with no shirt and black leather pants. Instead of the chunky boots today, he's wearing checkered slip-ons.

"He was poking holes in the condoms he was about to use."

"Ugh! Guys who infringe on the rights of women are the worst," he says, and puts his jeweled fingers to the back of the man. "Go back to hell."

I watch the man struggle for breath in the mirror as the neon aura consumes him. He flails and struggles. It doesn't matter. He's gone in a matter of seconds.

"Thanks Noburu," I say.

The Soul Keeper drops his cigarette on the ground and walks back towards the stall.

"No, kid. Thank you. See ya soon," he says and disappears across the spectral plain, which happens to be in the stall of a sushi restaurant bathroom.

I run water through my hair and calm myself down. This wasn't planned. I wasn't prepared to kill someone while out at dinner with Mia. Not wanting to keep her waiting, I walk back out and act cool.

"Ready to go?" I ask her.

She nods and I see the young ladies looking at her like she's something in a department store. They have glossy eyes and rosy cheeks. I pay the waiter and I see his eyes go wide when the card goes through. He didn't really think I'd have the cash for this place. In his effort to be kind, he is extra polite as he sees us out.

"I had fun," says Mia.

"We can do fun stuff all the time now," I say.

"I'd like that."

***

Ayumi is calling me. This can't be good. I pick up on the fourth ring. My hand is shaking. Ayumi is a good guy, but he always has bad news.

"What's up?" I ask.

"Ryon, I need to show you something. Please don't freak out," he says, but I already am.

"What is it?"

"I found Biora's alternative Instagram account. I'm going to send you the link. Shit, I'm so sorry." He hangs up.

I get a text from him with a link to the account. It's not her real name, it's *bby_chinadoll6969*. Clicking on it with a tremble in my hand, I wait for it to load. I almost drop my phone, but collapse onto my bed instead. Her profile picture is a tame one of her and Mia, with their ties loosened and the first two buttons undone. Mia looks scared, but Biora is winking and has her arms around her.

I search through the posts and become increasingly alarmed. They are mostly pictures of Biora wearing slutty clothes and lots of makeup. But then there are the ones with Mia. I find the one with the caption Me and my Girlfriend. Swiping through photos, I find shit that makes my blood boil. It's incinerating me from the inside. Rubbing the back of my neck, I feel sweat. It's building at my hairline.

The photo with the most likes horrifies me. Biora is sitting in a chair with Mia straddling her. My stepsister's shirt is undone and her pink bra is exposed. Biora has her hand in it and is kissing her neck while looking at the camera. The caption reads My Boyfriend is Jealous and so is Hers. Unable to stop myself, I keep swiping.
Biora has her hands all over her. She's giving Mia a piggyback ride while grabbing her ass. This photo has hundreds of likes. There's

another of them laying in the grass outside the school. Biora has her hand down Mia's skirt and another pulling her hair. Towards the "beginning" of their relationship, there is one photo that isn't as graphic as the rest. They're both on their knees, embracing each other and kissing.

I can't read the comments from the guys or I'll go crazy. All I see are hundreds of dudes drooling over Mia, seeing her stomach, watching Biora use her as a prop. The dream I had of a snake leaving indents on her thighs comes to mind. I think of her painting of the yellow snake with green eyes. Does she have nightmares like I do? I'm sure Mia's are worse.

How can someone so innocent be treated like an accessory for some sick sex fantasy? Mia said Biora liked me once. I wonder if this is some fucked up way of getting back at me. My heart stops on a photo of Biora and Mia, cheek to cheek, with Biora's hands tousling her hair. This one is captioned She Smells Like the Color Blue. It's wrong, but I'm jealous. I don't want anyone to know her perfume or touch hair, especially not Biora and all these horny dudes.

These photos go back two months. I walk into her room without knocking again. It's becoming a bad habit. I think I'm getting too comfortable with my stepsister, but I'm upset. Mia stops painting to look at me. She's working on a portrait of her mom. It stops me in my tracks.

"What's wrong, Ryon?" she asks. I unclench my fist.

"Mia, I need to talk to you."

"What is it?"

She gets up and walks up to me. Mia has to crane her neck to make eye contact with me. She is so small. I kneel down and take her hands.

"What's been going on with you and Biora?" I ask it as gently as I can. Mia stares at her feet but I make her face me. "Please, tell me."

"She has us pretend to be girlfriends, even though she hates me."

"What?"

I am so confused by girls.

"Biora says all the guys think I'm hot, and she wants to make them jealous. That's why she makes me kiss her," she says.

"I saw her account, bby_chinadoll6969. It looks like she does a lot more than just kiss you," I say.

Mia recoils from me and crosses her arms.

"Why are you always spying on me?"

"I'm not! Why are you mad at me? Do you like being Biora's girlfriend?" I ask.

I've never gotten upset with Mia, but I'm getting really pissed off.

"No! I hate it," she sobs.

I try to put my arms around her, but she backs away from me. It hurts me worse than any punch to the chest from my dad.

"Then why are you mad at me?" I ask again.

"You can't save me from them! Biora and all the girls in my grade have terrorized me for the last three years. Nobody can stop them," she cries.

I know it will make her mad, but I pick her up and sit with her on her bed.

"I'll do anything for you. You know that, right?" I say.

Mia's bottom eyelashes are soaked in tears. The double lashes look like they are coated in mascara, but they aren't. I wipe them away. She opens her mouth like she wants to say something but can't. I hope Mia doesn't turn back into a doll. One that doesn't talk.

CHAPTER NINETEEN

AN ARROW AIMED AT THE QUEEN

It's been three weeks since Fuyuhisa went "missing." I lay in bed with Mia and contemplate what I'm about to do. It's 2:27 a.m. on a Saturday. It's indecent of me but I asked Teo for help. I wanted him to find out from Fumika the next time Kim was going to stay the night at Biora's. They are together constantly but I need to time this right. Two birds with one stone was fine by me.

Mia is tossing and turning. Her tiny hands claw at the maroon sheets. I rub her shoulder and pull her closer to me. This seems to calm her down. I wish Mia felt better. It makes me feel guilty about how happy I've been. I can't enjoy it knowing she's miserable. There's no way for me to bring back her dad. My father drove her mother away. I can't fix that, but I can get rid of those mean little queens.

Once I'm sure Mia has fallen back asleep, I get out of bed. I'm starting to feel like I'm doing something dirty. Not only do all my zip-ups smell like violets, but I'm about to start up my motorcycle and crash a middle school girls' slumber party so I can steal their souls. I told everyone, including Mia, that my dad left me a lot of money and that's how I've been paying the bills.

I check the address for Biora's house again. It's only about eleven minutes away on my bike. I drive through the dark streets and find a spot between two black cars to park. It blends in. I sneak up to the two-story house. There's no tree next to this one. I hope her room is on the first floor. There's the kitchen, lounge, and dining nook. I find a big window with frilly magenta curtains. This has to be her room.

Looking in like a robber, I see Biora and Kim. They are laying in Biora's big bed that is covered in lacy blankets, pillows with ruffles, and lots of glittery stuffed animals. It looks like Kim is snuggling Biora. She must be the one who takes the pictures. I wonder if she is secretly in love with Biora. The window is locked. Damn. I go around the house until I find a small rectangular window that's cracked. It leads into the bathroom. I open it the rest of the way and manage to pull myself through the limited space. Stepping on the toilet and onto the floor, I take a deep breath.

I'm in.

I open the door and make my way down the hall towards Biora's room. Her dad is snoring upstairs. It's so loud I can hear him clearly down here. I step quietly in my white sneakers until I reach the door with pink butterfly stickers all over it. Her room reeks of sweet pea perfume, plastic, and hairspray. I almost have to hold my breath. I'm glad Mia's perfume is subtle and soothing, like the beach on a rainy day. Biora and Kim's girly miasma gives me a headache.

Cracking the door, I peek in. The girls are still sleeping. Their hair is shiny and they have glossy lips. The kind of girls that sleep with makeup on. I walk up and place the demonic sutras on their tar black hearts. The neon green aura envelops them and Noburu is standing beside me.

"Two this time," he purrs as he exhales a plume of cigarette smoke.

He's wearing the bomber jacket and no shirt again. Noburu has on jeans that are barely there. They are shredded to bits and hanging way too low, exposing the tops of his red pubes. I avert my eyes.

"These girls have been bullying my stepsister. They force her to make out with them and take dirty pictures of her," I say.

"There's a special place for mean bitches like these," says Noburu as he puts his cigarette out on one of Biora's stuffed animals.

He burns a hole right in the middle of its head. "Go back to hell."

The girls rise from the bed and reach for their long, skinny necks. They choke and scream voiceless screams. Their round cheeks sink and so do their eyes. Biora and Kim fade into nothingness and the green mist escapes through a crack in the window sill.

"Thank you, Noburu. These girls were horrible people," I say.

"I know. I can see into their soul when I touch them. Theirs was black as night and acidic, like bleach. They got what they deserved," he says before walking to the other side through Biora's closet.

Not wanting to be in here another second, I open the window and run.

Riding my motorcycle home, I feel accomplished. They can't hurt her anymore. Mia will be safe. I will make sure she is happy. Her birthday is coming up. We haven't seen our parents in thirty-four days. I want to get her something special. It'll come to me. I get home just as it starts to snow. Mia wakes up when I open my door.

"Where did you go?" she asks sleepily.

I open the curtain and lay down with her.

"To look at the snow," I say, and we enjoy the white ribbons swirling down until we fall asleep.

***

All the girls have stopped talking to me except Chisaki. Naomi doesn't flirt with me anymore. Neither does Nina. She still waves and smiles at me, but she doesn't talk to me much or try to hang out with me. People from school heard what Setsuna said to me that day at The Asagao. I'm sure everyone has made me out to be that guy.

Chisaki comes up to me between classes and shows me her photos. We chat for a bit during our lunch period about classes, people, and art. I'm not insightful like Mia, but I try. Chisaki seems to appreciate my input.

She's a cool girl. Chisaki isn't popular or unpopular. She is pretty, but not in a traditional sense. Her hair is super short, but it suits her. "The girl with no friend group" or "the girl who is a friend to many." She's never said anything weird about Mia and I. That's what I appreciate the most about her. I think she is a genuine friend, even though we don't really hang out.

Setsuna walks past me like I'm a stranger. I feel bad for hurting her. Not that I had any idea that I was. I probably hurt Naomi and Nina, too. It might not make sense to anyone, but I'm focused on making sure Mia is happy. After our parents abandoned us, I feel like I have to try twice as hard, but that's okay.

"What did you do to him?" asks a boy in my grade.

His name is Hojo. One of Fuyuhisa's friends.

"I didn't do anything," I snap.

I grab my books and head for class, but he grabs my elbow.

"I know you did something, psycho."

"Fuyuhisa ran away like the little bitch he was," I laugh.

Hojo tries to hit me, but I slam him into the ground.

"Don't fucking touch me," I hiss.

I shudder because I hear it again, my father's voice. My peers stare at me as I walk to class. I act like nothing happened. A girl who saw me hurt Hojo makes eye contact with me but quickly looks down even though I smile at her. Everyone is starting to figure out I'm not Mister Nice Guy.

I make it home without getting a ticket. My zoning out and dissociating is getting worse, but I focus enough to drive. I'm not sure what's happening to me. Is it the stress? Or my new job? Besides being mad about Mia's abuse, I've been super happy. We get to hang out all the time. I have gotten used to her sleeping with me and now I don't know if I can sleep without her. She shows me old movies and I have her listen to my rap music. It's been a lot of fun. Except the nights she can't stop crying because she misses her mom. I know she misses her dad, too.

"Ryon, have you seen this?" she asks as soon as I walk in the door.

Mia has the TV downstairs on. I don't think I've ever watched anything down here. She has it on a news channel. It's about Biora and Kim. Two fourteen-year-old girls missing after a weekend slumber party. No foul play. No forced entry. Family is distraught. The girls went missing while they were asleep in their bedroom upstairs.

"Wow," I say.

"Fuyuhisa went missing, too."

"Yeah," I trail off.

I'm not sure what to say.

"How was your day?" she changes the subject.

"It was good. How about yours?" I ask.

"I feel bad saying it, but it was a great day. Since Biora and Kim weren't in school, the other girls left me alone. They don't really act on their own. They need someone to tell them what to do," she says.

"Like the news said, no foul play, no forced entry. They probably upped and left with their older boyfriends."

I roll my eyes and Mia laughs.

"I'm going to take a shower and do my homework," she says and runs down the hall.

I go upstairs and do the same. Even though I bought all new soap and shampoo, I can't stop smelling the gingery scent that reminds me of Joseph. I got a mixed assortment of bath items: cherry blossom shampoo and conditioner, pear body wash, and tea tree face scrub. I buy anything as long as it's not coconut or ginger.

I get out of the shower and take out my books from my bag. I only have a little bit of homework and finish it within an hour. Checking my top drawer, I see that I only have one more demonic sutra. I pick up the flip phone and hit the call button. Noburu steps out of my bathroom with his messy hair and low hanging jeans. Today he has on a blood red leather jacket and the chunky boots with the heel.

"What's up, kid?" he asks.

Noburu is kind enough not to smoke in my house.

"I need more of those sutras."

"Of course." He takes out a small stack from the coat pocket and hands them to me. I reach for them, but he holds on to them for a second with a harsh grip. "Be careful, Ryon."

"What do you mean?"

"I know no one has seen you, but I don't want anyone to get suspicious. If you have to take the souls of people who terrorize your stepsister, just be sure to space them out, okay?" he says.

I thought I had waited long enough, but I guess not.

"Sorry. I'll do better from now on," I say.

This is a good paying job. And rewarding. I don't want to get fired.

"Whoa, kid! No biggie. You're not in trouble. I'm a laid back boss. Just be cautious," he says as he steps back into the starry abyss.

I take a couple of sutras and put them in my wallet, never know when I might need them, then I hide the rest in my drawer with the flip phone.

I go into the kitchen and start dinner. Mia is good at cooking but doesn't really like to do it. I actually think it's fun, so I do it more often now that I know how she feels about it. I wish she'd tell me how she felt more. We talk a lot, but she avoids being too personal with me. All I want is for us to be close, but she shuts me out. I don't blame her, though. Everyone has let her down. I vow to always be there. No matter what.

CHAPTER TWENTY

INTO THE DARK

I asked Mia what she wanted to do for her birthday and she said she just wanted to watch movies and hang out in the house. It's cold and dark during the early hours of the day. I don't mind staying in. I'm excited to give Mia her present. I spent over an hour picking it out. It's a vintage white gold ring with a blue topaz gemstone. I hope she doesn't think it's weird. The lady at the store told me if it reminded me of her, then I should get it. She was probably just trying to make a sale, but I believed her at that moment.

We're watching movies in the living room. When my dad was here, none of us spent any time here. Mia and I have the coffee table covered in bowls of popcorn, candy, ramen, and lychee soda. I got her a cupcake with a daisy on it. I'm having fun watching this black and white American comedy about rich people. The moment seems perfect, so I pull out her gift.

"Happy birthday, Mia."

I hand it to her and the way she holds it reminds me of the painting of someone cradling a baby bird. She removes the light blue ribbon and unwraps the silver paper. When she opens the box, she gasps. I don't know if it's a good or bad noise.

"I'm sorry. Do you not like it?" I ask.

"It's beautiful, Ryon. Thank you," she says.

My stepsister doesn't talk as quietly but it's soft when she speaks. She puts the ring on her left index finger.

"You don't think it's weird?" I ask.

"No. I never think anything you do is weird," she says.

This puts me at ease, and we watch another movie. This one is also an American classic. I realize I left my phone upstairs and feel the need to check it. I tell Mia I'll be right back. As I open my door, I can hear it buzzing on my nightstand. It's Koharu. I pick it up just in time.

"Ryon," she says in a low voice.

"Koharu! Are you okay? Where are you?" I ask.

"Tell Mia happy birthday for me," she's cries.

I don't like this. There's the sound of traffic and rushing water in the background.

"Wait, Koharu! What's going on? Where's my dad?"

"Your dad won't stop following me. I'm really far away. I don't think he'll be coming back, Ryon."

"Koharu, you're not making any sense. Where are you?"

I'm freaking out.

"Take care of Mia. I'm glad you two have each other," she says.

Then I hear a loud splash. Metal creaking and water pouring in.

"Koharu! Koharu!"

I call for her but I know she's dead.

She must have driven off of a bridge or something. No. Not on her birthday. I put my phone in my pocket and try to get it together. I knew my dad was a shitty guy but I can't believe he drove my stepmom to kill herself. What has been going on for the past two months? I hope she is right about him not coming back. Mia and I can manage on our own.

I walk back downstairs and smile at my stepsister because she is smiling, and it's her birthday. The ring on her finger is pretty and unique, like her. I sit down next to her and act like I didn't just hear her mom kill herself. We watch the rest of the movie. She gets up to make more unnecessary snacks. I throw popcorn at her and she takes her cupcake and smashes it into my face. This is the happiest I've ever seen Mia.

She makes gyozas and cucumber salad. She puts on another movie. It's an American horror movie, but it's not very scary. The plot is something like a lady's husband sacrificing her to the devil, but she doesn't know it until the end. I find myself engrossed in this one. I'm glad Noburu never mentioned any deals involving Mia. Not only would I turn him down, but I'd have to kill him, too.

Even though he is kind of a weird dude, I like my boss. He gives me a lot of freedom. So far, he hasn't let me down with the money. It's always on the card as soon as I bring him the soul. I don't have to wait for a check to clear or anything. It's awesome. I'm not sure if Noburu is a devil, a demon, or maybe a human like me, but with special abilities. It's hard to say how old he really is. He looks like he's twenty, but I have a feeling he's been at this for quite some time.

Mia falls asleep as she often does, but it's late for her. Almost 2 a.m. I carry her upstairs and put her in my bed. She's wearing a black dress with a white collar and gold buttons. I tuck in the little doll and do something bad. In her room, I paw through her items in search of her blue diary. I find it under her mattress. I turn a couple of pages and land on a poem.

A blond angel
Is the light
In the dark
Where it is most painful

It hurts me so badly to be like this, but I can't help it. I put her journal back and go downstairs. In my dad's study, I find a bottle of scotch that's half full. I don't want to get wasted, but I take three pulls off the bottle so I can numb myself. Lately I've been feeling things so deeply I can't take it. I brush my teeth and get into bed. Mia puts her arm around my waist and I have creepy dreams all night.

First there is a snake with Chartreuse eyes. It bites me, so I stomp on it. I think everything is fine now that I've killed it, but then I see Mia. She's laying in the tall grass surrounded by violets and dandelions. I try to wake her up, but she won't move. There is an ocean in the distance, but it evaporates. The beach becomes a desert. I can't wake up my stepsister. Everything is my fault. I can't do anything to help her.

I wake up and reach for Mia. She's sleeping, facing away from me. I move her hair and attempt to get a better look at her mind. Long, black locks of hair are her shroud. I imagine parting her skull so I can see what she's thinking. Mia reaches for her necklace and touches her heart in her sleep. I feel like such an asshole. Sometimes I wonder if I am just as bad as everyone else.

***

Today is my seventeenth birthday. I can start taking Mia to school and picking her up on my motorcycle soon. She says the boys don't bother her anymore, but I feel the need to make my presence known, just to remind them. Sora and Teo knock on the door and I let them in. They brought me a red cake with a motorcycle on it.

"Happy birthday, Ryon!"

They both say at the same time.

"Wow, thanks, guys."

I let them in, and we walk to the kitchen.

Mia made me dinner. Chicken katsu, broccoli stir-fry with noodles, rice, short ribs, and salmon sashimi. I thought it was really nice of her, considering she doesn't enjoy cooking. She didn't complain about it, though. She said she wanted to.

"Hi Mia," says Teo.

Mia is wearing a yellow dress with flowy sleeves and a white belt. She looks up at Teo and smiles. I can hear him gulp.

"Hey Teo," she says.

"How are you, Mia?" asks Sora.

He sits down. I join him and put the cake on the table.

"I'm good," she says.

It's been just us for the past four months. I think Mia is happier than she has ever been, but is still quietly sad. She misses her mom. I never told her about Koharu calling me. It haunts me, but I can't bring myself to do it. Maybe it's wrong, but I think it's better if Mia thinks Koharu abandoned her. Knowing she's dead might kill her, and I can't let that happen. I think I need Mia more than she needs me.

I pay all our bills on time. So far, no one has noticed our parents haven't been around. That's how close we are with the neighbors. I've picked up a lot of garbage off the streets. There was a man pimping out his underage daughter to a sex club. I took his soul and the soul of the guy working the club. He knew she was underage. I saved a homeless man who was getting beaten up by a gang of teenage thugs. That time I got four in one night. Another time, I found a girl passed out in an alley. A guy was about to rape her. He had her panties down and everything. I touched him with the sutra just in time.

I've been waiting to get Ben and Akito. The heat has died down, but I don't want to get in trouble. Noburu told me I had to space them out. It's been two months. That seems long enough. Right now I'm trying to enjoy my birthday with my friends and stepsister, but I have so much on my mind. No wonder adults are always drinking and smoking.

"Thank you for making such a beautiful feast," says Teo.

"No problem," she says.

Mia doesn't whisper anymore.

"Thanks again, sis," I say.

The guys hand me a present. "Oh, thanks, guys. You didn't have to get me anything."

"We wanted to," says Sora.

I open it up. It's a black leather jacket, expensive.

"Wow, thank you. This is really cool," I say.

"We figure every guy with a motorcycle needs a leather jacket," laughs Teo.

Mia nods her head to agree. I put it on. It's not my usual style, but it's nice. I like the feel. This must be why Noburu wears leather jackets all the time.

The four of us eat dinner and hang out in the living room. The guys brought their swim wear and race out to the back porch to sit in the hot tub. To my surprise, Mia joins us. She's not as shy anymore, but still reserved. It makes me happy to see her be a part of my group. Sora and Teo are good guys.

"How's your birthday, Ryon?" asks Sora.

"I'm having a great day," I say.

"I like your house," says Teo.

The guys have stood outside but have never been in. My dad made it a very unwelcoming place. Without him, it is nice. The house is big, the hot tub is fancy, our home is comfortable.

"Thanks," I say.

Mia readjusts her ponytail and I watch both the guys turn red. Girls have this weird power over guys. It makes us blush when they look at us or talk to us. We can't talk if they play with their hair or touch their necklace. I am The Soul Keeper's assistant, but I don't know how magic works.

It gets late, and the guys go home. Mia and I are hanging out in my room. We're playing cards. I let her win, and she smiles. She gets up and runs into her room. In her hands is a piece of paper when she comes back.

"I made you something," she says.

I take it from her. The paper is thick. She filled the page with violets and mystical blue flowers. In the middle is a poem in her handwriting.

> *A heart of gold*
> *Like his hair*
> *I don't care*
> *If they stop and stare*
> *Wherever he is*
> *I am there*

"Thank you, Mia. I love it," I say.

My stepsister hugs me, and I want to cry. I guess I start crying because Mia pulls back and touches my face.

"Don't be sad about it, silly," she teases.

It makes me laugh.

"I'm not sad. It just happens when I feel something really deeply," I say.

She lets me cry and doesn't make me feel weird about it. Mia knows what it's like to hold a feeling so heavy it breaks bones. I look at the snowflake, wishing I could touch her heart and know everything in it.

CHAPTER TWENTY-ONE
STEPSISTER DEAREST

At Ume Park is a derelict bathroom. I'm waiting there. Through the cracked and moldy window, I watch Akito and Ben head this way. I got information from the shady kids that this is where they drink the booze. They bribe people to buy it for them. I see the two of them laughing with smug expressions. My throat is dry. I'm honing in on the pulse in my ears.

"They bought us good beer this time," says Akito.
He cracks one open and hands it to Ben. Reaching into his bag, he grabs another beer.

"Right. So sick of that piss water," says Ben.

They light up cigarettes. I step out from my hiding place in the shadows.

"Ryon!"

Ben's eyes are wide with surprise. Akito drops his cigarette. I charge at them and hit them in the chest with the demonic sutras. Noburu talks into my ear behind me.

"Hey kid. Another set of assholes. Tell me, why do these souls deserve to be sent back to hell?" he asks.

I feel a raw, unadulterated hatred in my veins. It doesn't feel like enough to just take their souls. I wish I beat them to a pulp first.

"These two molested my stepsister," I say.

It tastes sour in my mouth. The image of her crying in the car as I chased them comes to mind.

"Your stepsister has shitty luck. Good thing she's got you around," says Noburu. He flicks his cigarette and steps up to the scumbags. "Go back to hell."

The neon aura lifts them off their feet. They choke, but it's not quenching my thirst for blood. I haven't been myself lately. Mia hasn't said anything, but I think she notices a change in me. It's difficult going to school, taking care of my stepsister, and stealing souls.

I want to grab their ties and choke them myself. Their eyes melt in their sockets. I enjoy their gasping for breaths that won't come. Ben looks at me and I show him my teeth but don't smile. Akito was the most afraid of me. He looks like he's shitting his pants. They turn to neon mist and escape through the broken glass of the window.

"Thank you, Noburu."

"No problem, kid. Your money's ready. See you soon," he says as he walks out the door like a normal person.

I wait a while before exiting, just to be cautious. The sun sets and I head home. The sky is pink and orange. Mia is probably looking at it right now. Even though we spend so much time together, I miss her.

I park my bike in the garage and grab a beer. Not really thinking I chug it. I grab another beer and do the same. Feeling the need to zone out, I grab one more and sit in the living room. I hear Mia taking a shower. Not wanting her to see me like this, I drink my beer and throw it in the trash. I head upstairs and lay down.

She and I have been happy, but my job is fucking with me. It used to make me feel like a badass. Sometimes I actually feel guilty even though they are shitty people. Why should I be the one to judge? I'm a seventeen-year-old-might-be-psycho. There are nights I stare up at the moon and I wonder if Noburu is real or if I am really just the crazy white boy. I planned on just laying here until the alcohol wears off but I fall asleep.

My hand feels like it's somewhere it shouldn't be. I open my eyes. Mia is wearing a light pink sweater and leggings. I find my hand on her bare stomach. Not wanting to wake her or make her uncomfortable, I remove my hand slowly. I'm still buzzed. I wonder if I am being too intimate with my stepsister. We've been together nonstop for the past four and a half months. I told myself she'd eventually go back to sleeping in her room but she hasn't.

What I did earlier cracks parts of my already fragmented mind. Ben did something so fucked up I could never forgive him. I thought he was my friend. How could he do that to Mia? Akito pissed me off, but it's Ben's face I keep seeing. The green aura stealing the air from his lungs, eyes bulging, and mouth open. I go back to sleep but wake up a bunch. Mia and I are face to face and she's hugging onto me. It's comforting. Ben and I didn't connect. I don't regret anything.

I focus on my hand. It's flat on the sheets. Mia's hair is covering my arm like a blanket. She smells like the color blue. I dream about violets, snakes, and ocean waves. Then it hits me suddenly. The smell of vanilla. I'm groggy from the alcohol and slow to react. She's touching my hair. Mia's lips are on mine. I open my eyes.

"No," I say and gently push her away.

"Why not? Everyone thinks we do it anyway," she says.

"Because I'm your brother."

"You're not really my brother, Ryon."

I know she didn't say this to hurt me, but it does. It hits me like my dad's concrete fists. She looks at me apologetically. Mia would never say anything mean to me on purpose. I pull her back to my chest and cry in her hair. The saltwater makes my pillowcase smell like the beach.

"Yes, I am."

***

I got Mia her own helmet. It's turquoise with chrome accents. She's excited for me to take her to school and pick her up. I'll forever be grateful to Ayumi for watching her when I couldn't. He has a kind soul.

Ever since Mia kissed me, things have been kind of weird, but not. She hasn't tried to be romantic with me, but we still sleep together. I've been worried that maybe I gave her the wrong impression with my hand on her stomach. We are happy, but she's withdrawn. I wish she wasn't so skittish. As soon as I get to know her, I scare her away.

"Are you ready?" I ask.

She nods "yes" and puts on her helmet. It only takes a few minutes to get to the middle school, but I don't want her walking by herself. As she gets off my bike, I scan the steps. I see Nero and his crew of perfect haired douche bags glare at me. Mia smiles as she bounds up the stairs. Nero stares at her ass as she walks into the school. I know he is doing it to piss me off.

I get to school on time and head to class. I've been trying to be on my best behavior. If anyone notices something strange or I get into any fights, they might get nosy. Having Mia taken away from me is my worst nightmare. I would rather die than be without her.

The way I love her is wrong, but not like that. I feel bad for rejecting Mia's advance, but she's my very beautiful, very vulnerable stepsister. She shouldn't be sleeping in my bed, let alone kissing me. I could tell her "no" and lock my door, but the image of her sitting outside my room waiting for me is unbearable. We've had only each other for a long time. I can't do that to her.

I take notes, pass my test, and fake laugh with my classmates. It's scary how easy it is to pretend to be normal. I collect souls at night. My stepsister wants more from me. I haven't told Mia that her mother is dead. My dad still won't take my calls. Not that I care. I just want to know he isn't coming back. I go into the boy's bathroom on the second floor and find graffiti about me in red paint across the mirrors.

Ryon fucks his stepsister

It's unoriginal but vulgar. I walk out and use the bathroom on the first floor. Setsuna bumps into me. I say "hi" but she doesn't acknowledge me at all. As I'm walking down the hall, I catch Naomi looking at me. I wave at her, but she slams her locker shut and rushes past me without a word. Nina says "hey" in her pretty voice, but brushes by me like I'm not a person. All the girls must know about the writing on the mirrors.

As soon as school is over, I go pick Mia up. I'm waiting for her outside and watching the parade of tiny girls with black hair in uniforms scurry past. None of them are her. They aren't as unique. All their faces blend together, but Mia's stands out. Boys watch her walk up to me and whisper to each other. She puts on her helmet and I take us home.

"How was your day?" I ask.

"It was okay," she says.

"Did something happen?"

"Not really," she sighs.

We're sitting in the kitchen drinking blueberry tea. I'm sad she won't share with me. She was secretive before, but ever since I pushed her away, she pushes me away harder. Her vanilla kiss has been on my mind, but I'm not sure what to make of it. Koharu told me to take care of her. Putting my hand on her bare skin and her lips on mine felt like I was committing a crime.

I don't think Mia really likes me that way. We've been through so much together. Our trauma has bonded us. To allow her to throw herself at me feels like I'm taking advantage of her. My stepsister is very beautiful, very sweet, and very vulnerable. I love her, but not like that.

"Tell me. I want to know what's going on."

I try not to be too eager, but she lies to me a lot. It's irritating me but I can't be mad at Mia.

"Someone's been writing stuff about me in the girl's bathroom."

"What kind of stuff?"

I peel a tangerine to try and steady my hands.

"Last week someone wrote 'Mia doesn't put out because she gets enough at home,' then today it said, Mia aborted Ryon's baby."

I hear static, and my pulse slows. Something snaps in my head. The loose screws fall and make sharp metallic sounds. It feels like tiny snakes are slithering around across my skull.

"Fuck them," I say.

"It's stupid. I shouldn't have even brought it up," she says and gets up.

"Wait! Mia."

I get up to follow her. She goes into her room and locks me out.

"Leave me alone, Ryon."

I could go to my room. To make myself feel better, I could face the wall I share with her, but I slump down on the blue and white rug in front of her door and wait for her.

***

* * *

I go to sleep alone for the first time in almost five months. My dreams are morbid and creepy. There are cobras with green eyes. All the boys have green eyes, too. I can't find Mia. Everyone is keeping me from her. I try to ride my motorcycle through the crowd, but they block me. Fuyuhisa gets on top of me and takes off my helmet. His eyes are my father's eyes. He licks my face and whispers in my ear, "she tastes like raspberries." I sit up and find Mia sleeping next to me. She hasn't spoken to me much for the past two days.

Even though she's mad at me, I miss her and I put my arm around her. She's wearing the teal sweater she hides her yellow diary in. I wonder where it is now. Shaking the thought from my mind, I try to go back to sleep. Now that she is here, I relax. I'm about to doze off when I hear loud yelping next door. I get out of bed and go downstairs.

Heading for the back door, I listen again. A dog barks. I hear a hefty thwack and then another yelp. It's warm outside. I smell fresh cut grass and tulips. I hear the man next door yelling at his beagle. The poor thing keeps crying and whining. Our neighbor is drunk and kicking the shit out of his pet. Stepping into the shadows, I sneak up behind him and place the sutra on his back.

"Hey kid. What do you have for me now?" asks Noburu.

He's got on the leather pants and a black button up. His cigarette illuminates his fox face as he takes a drag.

"This man was abusing his dog," I say and gesture to the beagle with sad eyes.

"I hate people who abuse animals," says Noburu. He puts his cigarette out in one of the man's flower pots. "Go back to hell."

"I need more of those sutras," I say.

Noburu chuckles and reaches into his pocket.

"You've been doing a good job. I'm going to give you a raise."

"What?" I ask.

"I like you, kid. What can I say? How about 85,000 yen a soul? I'll even throw in a, what should I call it—a bonus."

Noburu lights up another cigarette. He exhales and looks up at the stars.

"A bonus?"

I look up at the sky and wonder what the fuck I'm doing.

"Yeah. If you bring me a soul that's darker than night, uglier than sin, and poisonous like anthrax, I'll stock that card with unlimited funds. You wouldn't have to work ever again," he says and puts out his cigarette with the heel of his boot.

He immediately lights up another.

"What kind of person possesses such a soul?" I ask.

"You've brought me some genuine pieces of shit. Their hearts are tarry and soiled, but they aren't what I'm looking for. I need someone so twisted even the gods recoil as I summon them back," he says.

Noburu holds the cigarette in his mouth and fiddles with his rings. He looks at me with piercing amber eyes. They shimmer gold in the shadows.

"Thanks for everything, boss," I say.

Noburu hits his knee and almost falls over. I'm worried the neighbors are going to hear his cackling. The Soul Keeper is amused and can't contain himself.

"Just call me Noburu. 'Boss' makes me sound old," he says.

"How old are you, anyway?"

"I'm almost a thousand years old."

"No way."

I roll my eyes at him.

"It's true. The Soul Keeper before me lived to be six thousand. I'm still in my prime," he flexes and licks his lips at me.

"What are you exactly?"

I've never talked to Noburu for more than two minutes until now.

"I'm a demon," his smile is wide, and he exhales smoke through his teeth.

"Are there other demons like you?" I ask.

"Everything in the human world is connected to our world. I am The Soul Keeper. I cross over from the ghostly realm and restore the balance over here. Your seasons are controlled by demons. The weather is influenced by spirits. We are part of your sun and moon. The gods watch us from above. They can't cross over like demons. We are sent to do their bidding," he explains.

The beagle is at Noburu's feet, begging for a belly rub.

"Do demons regularly ask humans for their help?"

I give him a smirk to show I'm half serious.

"Not a lot, but it's not against the rules."

The dog is jumping on Noburu's legs, signaling he wants to be picked up. The Soul Keeper obliges and bounces the beagle like it's a baby.

"What is against the rules?"

"We can't make anybody do anything. We can only suggest. There's no way for us to make anybody love anyone or anything like that. I can give you money and fame, but I can't guarantee everything will work out in the end. The creators of Fate can see the future, but I can't. I simply try to make the world a better place."

He puts the dog down, and it runs into the house.

"Thank you for choosing me, Noburu."

"No problem, kid. I'm glad I went with my gut. I knew you were the right guy for the job. Take care. I'll see you soon," he says and walks into a tear in the fabric of space.

I go back in the house and double check that the windows are locked. Mia isn't in my bed. I open her door and find her sleeping in hers. It's overstepping so many boundaries, but I don't want to be alone. If she tells me to go away, I will, but I go into her doll house and get into her bed.

Her sheets are powder blue. The blanket is sapphire and white. Mia's sweater is teal. I put my arm around her, hoping she doesn't yell at me. She lets me hold her and I fall asleep wondering who has hurt my stepsister the worst. Who has a soul of sticky black tar? One that's nothing but anthrax and blackness. I dream about cracking open porcelain skulls and finding poems inside.

CHAPTER TWENTY-TWO

SNOWFLAKES MELT IN THE SUMMER

I know that Mia and I are codependent. I don't try to stop it. If anything, I've been encouraging it. I intended on being there for Mia no matter what, and now I really am. We eat together even when neither of us is hungry. She makes sure we do our homework. I can't sleep by myself anymore. We do everything together. Cook together, clean together, shop together. It feels like playing house. Maybe I'm turning into a doll, too. I keep dissociating. My grades are good but I'm not retaining anything.

Mia is watching a black and white movie. She's painting her nails sky blue. I'm brushing her hair. It's back to her hips. I'm holding handfuls of it and brushing from the bottom so I don't rip any of it out. I like it and would hate to damage it. Remembering the gum in it that one day causes a dark shadow to enter me, but knowing they can never hurt her again, and that helps me to act casual.

"How has school been?" I ask.

She's painting the index finger of her right hand.

"It's okay. I wish you were there though," she says.

"Yeah, me too."

"Nero asked me out again."

I stop brushing her hair.

She keeps painting her ring finger. I pick up more dark wavy hair and keep brushing the pretty mess. There is so much of it. It's the blackest black, almost unreal. People pay to dye their hair this color. It has a blue sheen to it. Mia never styles it or uses any product, but she has magazine hair.

The back of her dress is lacey, and I can see her white bra. She has freckles on her spine. Her shoulders make tiny movements as she paints her nails. I am reminded of wind-up toys and imagine Mia having clockwork pieces turn to make her come to life.

"How did he handle being told 'no' again?"

"I was thinking about saying 'yes.'"

I stop brushing, but don't let go of her hair. It's not that I want to yank it, but I need control. I need to hold onto something.

"What? Why?" I ask.

"Why not? You don't love me," she says.

I get up and kneel down so I can talk to my stepsister. She is so little. Her lips pout and she shrugs at me.

"That's not true. I love you so much."

"It doesn't seem like you do."

"How? I try to show you how much I care all the time," I say, and touch her petite shoulders.

"Am I not pretty enough?" she asks.

My stepsister is the most beautiful person. She is also the most sad. The most mysterious.

"What are you talking about?"

"Is that why you wouldn't kiss me back?"

"You shouldn't be kissing me."

"My dad is dead. My mom is gone. I don't know what happened to her. All I have is you and you don't even love me," she starts to sob.

Her dress is blue, her nails are blue, everything about her is indigo and midnight. I can't talk because my rib cage is collapsing. She needs me, though, so I do.

"I really do love you so much, Mia."

"I miss my mom," she has large tears pooling down her face.

I pull her to my chest and let her cry on me. It's wrong keeping a secret like this from her but I can't tell her. Koharu trusted me to take care of Mia. I wonder what she was thinking. Can she see me right now? I should have asked Noburu.

"I know you do. I'm sorry," I say.

She holds up her hands so her nail polish doesn't get ruined but continues to lean on me and cry.

"Please don't leave me, Ryon."

"Hey, why would you think I'm going to leave you?"

"My mom said she loved me. We had so much fun shopping and getting iced coffees. She took me to all my favorite places. But she left me," she chokes on her sobs.

"She didn't leave you. My dad is a bad person. He drove her away," I say.

"I don't want to be alone," she keeps crying and my heart hurts.

"You're not alone. I'm right here."

"You're not really my brother. You're probably going to leave me, too."

I'm getting frustrated. I know she's upset, but she's digging in deeper and deeper. Lately, it feels like she says things just to hurt me. I grab her face, but not hard. It scares her as I look at her with our noses practically touching.

"I am your brother. You can disagree, but I am. And I really do love you, Mia. I love you so much."

She cowers from me. I let her go. My arms are slack. Everything is getting hazy. I'm trying really hard not to go somewhere else. Mia puts her arms around my neck and it brings me back to the present moment.

"I love you," she whispers.

Her palms are on my shoulder blades. I'm tense. Every muscle has gotten tighter since I started soul collecting. Mia is crying into my neck, breathing next to my ear. I smell her vanilla chapstick. It's fucked up, but I can still taste it.

***

There are bad guys everywhere. I haven't sent as many female souls back to hell, but there have been a few. Moms who hurt their children, girls who bully someone so hard they cut themselves, and women who prey on other women. Mia knows I'm leaving in the night. She hasn't asked me where I go or what I do, but she clings to me more than ever lately. I know she's sad, but I wish she'd trust me. She thinks I'm not going to come back.

I've been trying to get her to sleep in her room, but she won't. There was one night I locked her out. I didn't get any sleep because I could hear her crying through the wall we share. At one point I put on my headphones to drown it out, but I knew I wasn't going to be able to live with myself if I let her cry by herself all night.

With Noburu's raise, I can pay all our expenses plus extra. I am always on the prowl for the most wicked soul I can find. Once I have it, I'm going to ask Mia where she wants to live. We could go anywhere. All I know is we're not staying here.

I'm sleeping in the doll house hoping I can get Mia to feel comfortable in her room again. The sapphire string lights illuminate the room with a soft blue glow. She has a lamp in the shape of a star. Her arm is around my waist and I have to move her. I slip out of bed and throw on my leather jacket and grab my shoes. It's 2:32 a.m. and I go to a town I haven't been to before.

The streets are empty. I hide my bike in the shadows. There are a few neon lights on in businesses, but not many. The apartments are shabby and derelict. I see a bar is open and three thug looking dudes throwing a thin guy with stylish hair out the door. His square glasses fall off.

"Get out of here, you queer!" screams the fat one.

"Fucking freak," laughs another. He has hairy arms and a mustache.

"People like you disgust me," spits the other.

This man has a shaved head. The thin guy is scrambling to get up, but the fat one kicks him. He goes to pick up his glasses, but the hairy armed man steps on them.

"Look at this little freak! He's crying. What kind of man cries?" laughs the dude with a shaved head.

The thin guy with glasses runs, but the fat man grabs him.

"He's got a nice mouth. I bet he would like it!" yells the hairy armed man.

"Me first!" says the fat man.

I walk up slowly and methodically behind them as they drag the thin guy into the alley.

"This is going to be fun," laughs the hairy armed man.

I fan out the sutras in my hand. One for each of them.

"Please! Please, let me go!" cries the thin guy.

The fat man is dragging him by his tight black shirt. His jeans are cuffed and his shoes are retro.

"What a pussy," laughs the guy with a shaved head.

They push the thin man onto the ground. I throw the sutras onto the backs of the men. They are frozen in the bright green aura. Noburu appears and touches the thin guy with two bedazzled fingers. He falls over unconscious but Noburu is polite and catches him. The guy never even saw me or The Soul Keeper.

"Three's a lucky number," says Noburu as he exhales smoke. He stands up to inspect my catch. "Tell me, why do these three souls deserve to be sent back to hell?" he asks.

"They assaulted that man. They used homophobic slurs. Then they dragged him back here to do horrendous things," I tell him.

Noburu takes another drag and nods his head thoughtfully.

"Homophobes are usually gay but in the closet," he says and flicks his cigarette. The cherry burns red in the darkness. He approaches the men and touches them individually. "Go back to hell."

The men squirm. I can almost hear their collective screams, but they can't breathe. The green aura dries them out the way the sun would kill a starfish. They evaporate and rise up into the night sky.

"I don't know where to find the most vile soul. But I will," I announce.

Noburu lights up another cigarette. I don't think he can go one minute without smoking. Maybe it's a demon thing.

"I believe in you, kid," he says with his mischievous fox face.

"Thank you for the raise. It's helped me out a lot," I say.

"You deserve it. I've never had an assistant, but I'd say you're the best."

Noburu leans on the grimy alley wall and looks up at the moon. I wonder if a demon is communicating with him through it.

"Why did you choose me?" I ask.

"I saw something in you," he says with a sly grin.

The smoke leaves his parted mouth in slow, steady ribbons.

"What did you see?"

"Your heart. I saw how much you loved your stepsister. It told me what you were willing to do. Most people say they would kill for someone, but they are insincere or tainted by the darkness. You are neither," he says.

Noburu makes intense eye contact with me. His gold eyes are intimidating but kind.

"You can see that?" I am perplexed by demons and their ways.

"Yeah, it's a Soul Keeper thing." Noburu shrugs and this makes me laugh a real laugh.

"That's cool. I wish I could see into Mia's heart," I admit.

"I've seen it," says Noburu as he fishes out another cigarette.

"What's in there?" I ask.

"Sorry, kid, I can't tell you that."

"Why not?"

Now I'm irritated. Why even mention it?

"It's against the rules. Privacy regarding matters of the heart is kind of a big deal," he says with casual flare.

Noburu is formal, but not. I roll my eyes at him as he lights up his cigarette.

"Can you tell me anything about it?" I ask.

"No. Mia has to be the one to tell you what's in her heart," he says.

I feel defeated. She's never going to do that.

"Have a good night, Noburu. I better get going," I say.

Noburu walks backwards into his world.

"Your money's on the card. I know you can find this soul, kid."

Noburu flicks his cigarette on the disgusting ground. It lays burning. The thin man starts to wake up and I run back to my bike. I made a lot of money tonight. Maybe Mia will want to do something fun with me. The ride home is calming. After taking souls, I get this rush and I can't relax. It's almost like being buzzed, but not quite.

I get home before 4 am. School starts in a couple of hours. I head upstairs to get some sleep. Mia is still in her bed. I turn off the star lamp. It dims the room and allows me to fall asleep faster. Her long hair swirls around the pillows. The blue light makes me feel like I'm in the ocean. Mia has mermaid hair. I put my arm around her tiny waist. Not expecting it, I'm startled when Mia grabs my hand.

***

"You doing okay, Ryon?" asks Sora.

"I'm okay. I haven't been sleeping very well," I say.

It's not a lie, but not really the truth.

"Is something wrong?" asks Teo.

He takes off his glasses to wipe them off. The sun is out, we're at the park, but I'm days away.

"Mia's been distant from me," I admit.

"What happened?" asks Sora.

We're sitting in the shade of an oak tree. People are enjoying the beautiful day. Mia is hanging out with Ayumi. I'm glad she has someone other than me, but I've been depressed. She and I were so close and now I feel rejected. We still sleep together but she doesn't talk very much. Her moods change without warning. I'll think she's fine, but then she's crying silently but won't tell me what's wrong. She doesn't need to tell me, though. I already know.

"She kissed me, but I pushed her away."

I wince as I say it out loud.

Sora and Teo are my friends, but I'm not sure what they're going to think. The guys look at each other and then at the ground. They seem to be concentrating.

"It makes sense. She likes you. For a long time, she didn't have anyone. She was bullied, and you stopped that," says Sora.

He runs his hands through his dark hair and smiles. I look up and watch sunlight come through the leaves. The grass is cool under my hand. I lean back into the trunk and sigh.

"Why did you push her away?" asks Teo.

He takes a drink of his raspberry tea and I grimace, thinking about my nightmare. The one with all the boys with green eyes. I've been having bad dreams more often.

"It didn't feel right. She shouldn't be kissing me. We've been alone in that house for almost six months. It would be taking advantage of her. I know she doesn't really feel that way about me," I say.

"How do you know?" asks Sora.

"I don't think I'm Mia's type. Besides, I'm her brother."

"Stepbrother," says Teo.

"Do you feel that way about her?" asks Sora.

I see a young couple holding hands walking through the park. They are both Japanese. The boy has shiny black hair and so does the girl. Their eyes are dark and they walk like pale ghosts. No one pays any attention to them as they pass by.

"I don't know. I didn't think so. But ever since she kissed me, I've been wondering. I spend most of my time worrying about taking care of us. I haven't allowed myself to think about stuff like that," I confess.

If Mia and I met under different circumstances, maybe things would be different.

"Maybe you should," suggests Teo. He smiles to himself. "I think you two would be cute together," he says.

I punch him in the arm, but not hard.

"C'mon guys, knock it off."

"I think Teo is right. You both have been through a lot. I know you think it's wrong because she's vulnerable, but I think she already felt this way," says Sora.

The friend who is the wisest. I know he's not teasing or making a joke. Sora is serious.

"You really think so?" I ask.

"Mia is a very deep person. I don't think she kissed you on impulse," says Teo.

The one who is close with his sister. The friend who knows what it's like to have a girl change your perspective.

"You've said 'no' to every hot girl that's liked you. Maybe deep down you have felt the same," says Sora.

"For the past two years, all I've cared about is making her happy," I say.

"What if kissing her back is what would make her happy?" asks Teo.

The wind picks up and blows through our hair. Sora and Teo got haircuts, but I've kept mine shaggy.

"I never thought about that," I say.

Even if that's what it took to make Mia happy, I don't know if it's moral. I don't want my dad to be right about me.

CHAPTER TWENTY-THREE
GRAB A SNAKE BY ITS TAIL

Mia is with me all the time. My stepsister hardly leaves my side but has many secrets. I tried asking her what would make her happy. She said she is happy but misses her mom. The guilt weighs heavily on my shoulders. I've been trying to be understanding, but I'm getting really fucking pissed. She is acting like everything is fine, but deep down, I know she wants to cry. I can see it when I look into her doll eyes.

I'm laying with her in her bed. She won't sleep in here unless I'm with her. Mia is wearing the white sweater I got her two years ago. It has a hole in the left sleeve, but she says it's her favorite. I don't know why, but I keep tugging at it and making it bigger. Her hair tickles my face. I'm moving and rearranging it when I see her phone light up. She always has it on vibrate. It's 12:48 a.m. Who is texting her this late?

It's so quick I don't realize her phone is in my hand until I'm relieved that it's unlocked. I open her text messages. It's Nero. My blood fills with ice. It burns, it's so cold.

Nero: Are you up?

I scroll through. She's been talking to him for over two weeks. I land on a conversation from five days ago.

* * *

Nero: I miss you. When can I see you?
    Mia: Saturday :)
    Nero: What about Ryon? :/
    Mia: I'll tell him I'm at Ayumi's house again.
    Nero: Do you think he knows?
    Mia: No

I keep scrolling.

Nero: Hey babe. You looked really hot today ;)
    Mia: Thank you
    Nero: Wear that bikini again later. My parents won't be home.
    Mia: Okay <3

And another one.

Mia: How do I know you really like me?
    Nero: I've asked you out eleven times. I've liked you since sixth grade.
    Mia: You don't even know me.
    Nero: You won't let me. Please give me a chance.
    Mia: Is this your idea of a joke?
    Nero: I'm not joking. I really want you to be my girlfriend.

What's happening? I look at my stepsister, who is so beautiful but a fucking liar. I recall all the times she told me she was with Ayumi. She supposedly went to the movies with him, hung out at his house, and went to the bookstore a few times. Now that I'm thinking about it, I've only seen Ayumi stop by once. I want to call him, but I already know the truth. My eyes widen in horror as I go through her photos.

There are a lot of nature shots: flowers, butterflies, and sunsets. There are pictures of us. She looks happy. Then I find the ones of her and Nero. My worst nightmare starts coming true. Photos of her wearing the blue bikini in his pool. She's sitting on his lap and smiling. They're kissing and I can smell his stupid hair just looking at it.

I find more. It kills me, but I keep snooping. Mia breathes quietly next to me. It's almost like she's not alive. More photos of her and

Nero. He has his arm around her. She is kissing his cheek. They are laying in his bed and light is streaming through venetian blinds. It is artistic, but I hate it. She is smiling in all of them.

He knew I was clueless. That's why he stared at her ass in front of me. I hear static and imagine breaking his teeth. To see pieces of enamel shattering like white plates brings me joy. He lied about her, spread rumors about her, and bullied her. Nero has too much money and too much confidence. Mia, how can you let this guy touch you?

***

I don't confront Mia. I let her do what she wants. She lies about where she goes, spends the day with him, and then lays in bed with me. Her clothes smell like hairspray and chlorine. I never thought a guy like Nero would be Mia's type. I asked Sora what he thought. He said she didn't like Nero, that she wants me, but because I rejected her, she is using him to fill that void. I hope he isn't right. Maybe they are happy. They smile from ear to ear in their pictures.

I didn't think Nero was a bad guy until he lied about her. She might have forgiven him, but I don't. I think he is a snake, just like the rest of them. Everything is falling apart, including me. In a desperate attempt to numb myself, I tore through my dad's bedroom. I found another bottle of scotch in his dresser. It's a really expensive brand. It smells like vanilla. I can't place my sadness, but then I remember her kiss. Unable to be bothered any longer, I pour myself a rocks glass full of it and sulk in my room.

Mia is painting in her dollhouse. The alcohol is warm in my stomach. It makes me feel better and I decide to have another and sit in the hot tub. I put on my rock music really loud. Loud enough that it would annoy my dad. I lean back and sip on the whiskey. The sound of the bubbling water mixes with the music.

The sun is setting. I enjoy watching the sky turn pink. Before it turns indigo, I close my eyes and space out. I smell violets and chlorine. I'm in my own world and I don't notice Mia join me until I open my eyes. She's wearing a teal bikini with yellow flowers on it. Her hair is braided off to the side. My stepsister is smiling at me, but I'm glaring at her.

"What's wrong?" she asks.

"Nothing," I say and turn my music up.

"Are you okay?"

"I'm fine."

I close my eyes and ignore her. She does it to me, I can do it to her. I down the rest of my drink and dissociate. The oak notes from the scotch mixes with her vanilla chapstick. Her lips are on mine. She's touching my face. My very beautiful, very vulnerable, very confused stepsister is kissing me again.

"What are you doing?" I snap.

"I'm sorry," she says and puts up her arms defensively like I'm going to hit her.

Mia is afraid of me, but I can't stop.

"What has gotten into you lately?"

I'm agitated.

The neighbors can probably hear me yelling at her, but I don't care. I'm not being a good stepbrother or person. There is something ugly in me. I got it from my dad.

"I thought you loved me," she cries.

Not this again.

"I do love you," I sigh.

Why doesn't she believe me? I do everything for her.

"Why won't you kiss me back then?"

"I'm your brother," I say.

"You're not my actual brother," she says.

It's worse than the time my dad threw me down the stairs. I feel it crack every rib. It's hard to breathe. I hate being alive at this moment.

"It's wrong for you to cheat on your boyfriend," I hiss.

Joseph's voice is in my throat. Mia looks surprised. She knows I know.

"I don't want him to be my boyfriend," she says.

Mia looks into my eyes with such intensity I can't meet her gaze.

"Then why are you dating him?" I ask.

"I don't want to be alone."

"You're not, though."

I'm getting impatient with her, but she touches her heart and I soften my tone.

"I worry that one of these nights you're not going to come back.

Who will I have then?"

Mia is holding onto the snowflake necklace like it's the most precious thing in the world to her.

"I'm not going anywhere."

I hug my stepsister, but it's not the same. The normally loving embrace feels perverse, with all her bare skin touching mine.

***

Dissociated days, restless nights, and endless nightmares. Dreams about Mia's empty dollhouse. Everything is gone. All her art, her clothes, and books. I have nightmares where I can't find her. Obsessive thoughts plague my waking hours. Terrifying fears play like black and white movies in my dreams.

Everyone at school is afraid of me. Hojo and his gang think I have something to do with Fuyuhisa, Akito, and Ben. They are right. I haven't been a suspect in a criminal investigation but I have anxiety that someone has seen me. This job is harrowing, but I like it. It gives me the power to restore justice in my own way.

Biora and Kim are still considered missing. No one really misses them. They were mean as hell. Now they're where they belong. Mia is sleeping in my arms. We are in my room. I gave up on trying to get her to sleep in hers. She broke up with Nero. I didn't want her to be with him, but I'm not sure it's safe for her to be so close to me. My very beautiful, very vulnerable stepsister has been acting strange.

She hasn't tried to kiss me again, but the way she holds me is different. I wake up to her hands in my hair all the time now. Mia has gone back to being quiet. I pretend nothing is different. It's the middle of the night and I can't sleep. I keep thinking about finding the most vile soul. One that can guarantee a lifetime of happiness for Mia and I. Unlimited funds for the soul of the biggest piece of garbage I can find? I'll take it.

Mia stirs in her sleep and grabs her necklace. It's very sweet, but it makes me sad. Her breathing changes and I think she's awake. I pretend to be asleep. It's been hard for me lately. I want us to be close, but we are further apart than ever.

"Ryon, are you awake?" she asks.

I want to ignore her, but I can't.

"Yeah," I say.

She turns to me and puts her hand on my shoulder.

"What's wrong?" she asks.

"Nothing."

"I know something has been bothering you."

"I've had a lot on my mind," I say and keep my eyes closed.

"Why won't you tell me?"

"Why won't you tell me anything?"

I don't mean to, but I sound more and more like my dad. Always hissing. Snarling at everyone like a dog that has rabies. Maybe I need to be locked up. Mia reaches up and plays with my hair that's getting too long.

"I like your hair," she whispers.

"Thanks," I grumble.

Mia stops touching my hair and reaches for the snowflake. I decide to ask her what I've been afraid to know.

"Mia, what's the worst thing that someone's ever done to you?"

"Why do you want to know?"

"I want to know everything about you," I say, and she sits up.

"I can't tell you that."

"Why not? Please," I beg. It's so pathetic, but I do. "Please tell me."

Mia has tears forming in her doll lashes. The moonlight makes her skin shine like porcelain. She covers her face and turns away from me.

"I can't," she cries.

"Yes, you can."

I sit up so I can comfort my stepsister.

She sobs quietly, but it makes her body convulse.

"What happens to you is important to me," I say.

My room is dark. Only a sliver of moonlight is coming through the part in the curtains.

"When our parents first got married, your father didn't pay any attention to me. We hardly spoke. Then one night he came into my room," she's not crying anymore but she's gripping my arms so tight with her tiny fists.

"No," I whisper. It can't be. I'm not drunk, but I am dazed. This isn't real. It can't be real. "Why didn't you tell me?" I ask.

My face burns as salty tears pour out. How could something so ugly happen to my beautiful stepsister?

"I couldn't tell anyone."

"When did it happen?" I ask.

My vision is blurry. I hold my stepsister like a baby bird. Her hair doesn't smell like chlorine anymore. The violet perfume is everywhere. All my hoodies and tee shirts. It's on my pillowcases and sheets. I thought my blood was the only blood all over the house, but I was wrong.

"On your fifteenth birthday," she says.

I cry uncontrollable silent tears, remembering the day. Sora had a party for me at his house. Teo, Koga, and Kirin came over. We played basketball all day and stayed up late playing video games. While I was goofing off and being stupid, my stepsister was being assaulted by my dad. I feel sick to my stomach.

Noburu must have known Joseph was the darkest soul. Blacker than the bottom of the sea. Toxic tar for a rotten heart. I knew he was capable of unforgivable acts, but I didn't expect this. Maybe I didn't want to see it because then I would have to take responsibility. It's loud in my brain and I want to tear him apart.

I think of all the times my dad touched her. Running his meaty hand through her hair and she shuddered. His condescending tone towards her at brunch. She could somehow sit at the same table with him. He took everything from her. Her childhood, her innocence, her sense of security. It makes me want to vomit thinking of all the meals we sat together, and I was clueless. I am always the last to know.

"Where was your mom?" I ask.

"She didn't feel well, so she took her sleeping pills. She didn't wake up until noon the next day," says Mia.

She lays down and hides from me.

"I'm so sorry, Mia."

"It's not your fault. You didn't do anything wrong."

"I should have known. My dad is a bad person. I'm sorry I didn't protect you from him."

I am unconsolable.

It's my fault Mia is depressed. She was already a sad girl, but I was callous and thoughtless. By the time I took an interest in Mia, it was too late. I should have known my dad did something. All his accusations make sense now. He saw himself in me.

"You're nothing like him, Ryon. You have a good heart," she says and touches her own.

I put my hand over hers. Maybe it's too invasive, but I want to know everything about it.

"I love you," I say.

"I love you," she says it back and even though I need her to say it, I'm upset that she does.

How can she let me touch her when I look just like him?

CHAPTER TWENTY-FOUR
CLEVER PREDATORS

I drop Mia off at Ayumi's. It's not that I'm trying to control her, but I can't leave her alone in the house. Her behavior has been scaring me. I hate to say it, but I don't trust my stepsister. She might do something bad to herself. I check her wrists while she's sleeping. If she leaves her phone unlocked, I go through it. I haven't read her diary because I don't think my heart can take it.

Am I trying to protect her the way a real brother would, or am I being possessive and jealous like a boyfriend? The lines have blurred so much over the last three months. I go into her room without knocking. She puts her hands in my hair and under my shirt when I'm sleeping. I pretend not to notice, but I do. We spend too much time together. I've been making a point to distance myself. I don't want to, but I know I have to.

The summer heat is enjoyable as I ride my motorcycle through small towns until I reach the countryside. It's a nice change of pace to be welcomed by groups of trees instead of buildings stacked on top of each other. The grass is dark green and tall here. A man wearing a sunhat is working out in the field. He stops what he's doing to watch me drive by.

As I pass cedars, black pines, and oaks, I am met with shadowy limbs. There are patches of sunlight on the road. It smells floral and aquatic out here. The wood notes of the forest are refreshing. I find a secluded place to park my bike and lay in the grass. I am up on a hill. The farmland and road I took to get here are visible except for the stretch that is hidden by the dark woods.

Clouds pass overhead and I lay in their shadow. I cover my face with the crook of my arm. The sleeve of my white tee shirt is damp from my crying in a matter of minutes. I can't stop thinking about what happened to Mia. How I was too late. The Christmas he gave her the ridiculous charm bracelet and his hand on her tiny shoulder as she sat at his desk hit me over and over again.

I told Sora, but not Teo. We were hanging out at his house. I could barely get the words out. The look on his face was sympathetic, but horrified. He put his head down and cried, too. Sora said it's not my fault, but I feel like it is. I should have seen it coming. Joseph is the kind of person to take whatever he wants. Poor Mia, so sweet and innocent, ruined by my father. I hold her in my arms and wonder how I don't repulse her. My dad stared her down in my bed and she didn't say a word. She didn't tell me anything. I take out the red and black phone to call Noburu.

"Hey kid," he answers right away.

"I need to talk to you about something. It's important," I say.

"What's up?" says Noburu.

He's standing right behind me. I wipe my eyes and stand up. Noburu looks me up and down with his curious fox face.

"I know a soul that would make the gods recoil as you summon him back."

"You do?"

Noburu's eyes light up and he stops raising his cigarette to his mouth in surprise.

"Yes."

"Who is it?"

"My father," I say and clench my fists, thinking about what a piece of shit he is.

He drove my mom away, he beat me, and he is the reason my stepmom killed herself. But nothing compares to what he did to Mia.

"What did he do?" asks Noburu.

His amber eyes narrow, and he examines my face. He looks at my heart.

"Joseph is a bad person. He made my mom have me. She was very young. He hit me all the time. My dad drove my stepmom to kill herself," I say. My palms are bloody from my nails digging in. "He raped my stepsister. She was only thirteen." I choke on what I have to say.

Noburu's eyes widen for a second, then he smiles. Or maybe he's grinding his teeth.

"A soul as black as night. Be careful, Ryon."

"What do you mean?" I ask.

"The darkness is being tempted in your own heart. You're not the same as your dad but he gave you that heart. Be sure not to let it be consumed by hatred," says Noburu.

He inhales slowly and blows out a plume of smoke that is carried by the wind. His messy red hair dances in the breeze. The silky black shirt he's wearing has waves in it. The Soul Keeper is elegant but disheveled.

"I hear his voice in my throat. I've been snapping at everyone. There is something ugly inside me. I feel his rage in my heart," I admit.

"Remember Mia."

"What?"

"When the darkness threatens to take over, remember Mia. She is the one who will bring you back. Her heart is connected to yours," he says.

"I don't understand."

"Sorry, kid. I can't say anymore than that. Here, take this."

Noburu hands me a demonic sutra that is written in red.

"What's this?" I ask.

"An unholy soul like your father's will require a stronger demonic sutra."

"He won't answer my calls. Is there any way you can transport me to where he is?" I ask.

"That would be against the rules. Any and all souls must be collected without the use of my magic," says Noburu.

He gestures with his hands and gets ash all over the grass.

"Okay. Thanks Noburu," I sigh.

"You can do this, kid. I believe in you," he says as he crosses over.

I pull out my real phone and call my dad. No answer. I'm not even sure if this is his number anymore. I call again and let it go to voicemail.

Dad, it's Ryon. Please call me back. I really need you.

I wait until the sun is about to set to go home. Before I get on my bike, I call again. I leave another voicemail: Please, dad. It's important. I'm out of money. I don't know what to do.

***

"Ryon?" Someone is talking to me, but I can't hear them. "Ryon?" It sounds like my name is being said underwater.

"Huh?" I say.

My teacher is standing at my desk.

"Thank you for joining us," he says.

"Sorry. What was the question?" I ask.

"What was the name of the military dictators in feudal Japan?"

"Shogun," I say.

My teacher doesn't stop looking at me until it's uncomfortable. They walk back to the front of the room and continue to write on the board. Out of the corner of my eye, I see my classmates watching me. Girls whisper and cast wicked stares in my direction. The boys snicker and glare.

I am still considered popular, but for all the wrong reasons. Everyone thinks my stepsister is my live-in girlfriend. The girls want to ride my motorcycle. All the guys want to smash it. I'm a "bad boy." The Blond Demon. Everyone either thinks I'm cool or is scared of me.

My demeanor is friendly on the surface, but underneath is a simmering pool of chaotic rage. I hide the psycho in me by smiling at people. It relaxes them. I joke with my friends and hang out in the park. We wait in line to get coffee and talk about nothing at all. It's all so casual. It's scary how easy it is to fit in.

I'm walking out of school to the parking lot. Hojo and his gang approach me. They all have cropped black hair with bangs and brown eyes. Their mouths are snarling. They have crooked teeth and chapped lips.

"What do you want?" I growl.

My helmet is in my hand and I think about bashing in his skull with it.

"What did you do to them?" he asks.

The guys behind him back him up.

"Nothing. Fuyuhisa was a little bitch," I say.

"You're up to something. I see the psycho in your eyes, white boy."

"I didn't do anything. He ran away."

"What about Ben and Akito?" Hojo gets in my face but I put my helmet on and mount my bike.

"They were pussies, too."

I take off before they can harass me anymore. Picking up Mia gives me a sick surge of power. She takes tiny steps up to me and smiles. Nero watches her with a longing gaze. Mia's touch has been making me feel awkward, but I enjoy seeing Nero's face fall as she wraps her arms around my waist. We get home and I wait for her to get in the shower to drink. I pop open another bottle of scotch I found under the kitchen sink. I've been drinking a lot.

I do my homework as fast as I can so I can drink more. My focus is somewhere else. I keep thinking about what happened to Mia. As I go into my room, I look at her door. I open it and peek into the dollhouse. Blue lights, blue blankets, blue sweaters. I walk in and kneel down at her paintings. They're beautiful. I hold the one of the baby bird and try to see it from Mia's point of view. I walk over to her bed and sit. So many nights I slept here. I lay down and stare up at her ceiling. The sapphire lights make me feel like I'm being consumed by ocean waves.

Her violet perfume sits on her nightstand. It's a round bottle with blue liquid. The top is sparkly and silver. A small chain with a purple flower hangs from the cap. In metallic writing is the name Indigo Midnight on the front. I pick it up and smell it. It's nice, but it's missing something. I like it better on Mia.

The wall we share is slate. It's like a prison. I thought I had it bad, but Mia had it worse. She is stronger than me in so many ways. My dad's fists are nothing compared to his evil intentions towards his stepdaughter. I thought he was just a shitty dad that hit his kid. Apparently, he was a molester, a pedophile, and a rapist. I stare back up at the ceiling and want to throw up, knowing that Mia's eyes were on it as my dad was on top of her.

I run to the bathroom in my room and vomit. It's slithering snakes in my brain. Their squirming and writhing causes me to empty my stomach completely. I hear that static again. The more I think about my fifteenth birthday, the sicker I become. I can't stop, though. Every minute of that day, I run through and try to find the gaps. The places where I should have seen the signs. All the red flags that I missed. My hair is damp with sweat. I shower, hoping to feel better, but I never feel clean anymore.

Mia washes my clothes. They all have a hint of violets and rain to them. I put on a red tee shirt, but it smells blue. My black zip-up also smells like midnight. I brush my teeth and comb my hair. It's shaggy and messy, like Noboru's. I could be his younger brother. Mia is cooking downstairs. I use this opportunity to call my dad again. It rings endlessly. I leave a voicemail.

Dad, it's Ryon. Please, please call me back. I need your help. Please don't abandon me like mom.

It hurts to say the last part, but I know I have to convince him I'm on his side that I see him as my savior. My dad needs that admiration. The only way to give it to him is to insult the woman who broke his heart.

***

The waning crescent moon curves like a wicked grin. I'm staring at it through the parted curtains. Mia is sleeping behind me with her hand on my heart. I wonder if she thinks I'm going to die. Her small palm is cool on my skin. I've tried to set boundaries with her, but she accuses me of not loving her. She's probably doing it to guilt me. It's working because I let her do whatever she wants. Her touch is more intimate than it should be. I keep my hands off of her as much as possible, but she is all over me.

We sleep in my room. I can't be in hers for very long anymore. Knowing what happened there churns my stomach and brings up emotions I have no words for. I don't want to even look at the slate wall we share, so I'm faced away, watching the night sky smirk at me. We have bills to pay. I need to go out and get a soul. My dad hasn't returned my calls.

I slip out of bed. Mia's hand falls onto my maroon sheets. She's wearing a black shirt with long sleeves. Her other hand is on her heart. The ring I got her shimmers in the moonlight. I kneel and brush the hair out of her pretty baby face. Her double lashes are blackest black, like her hair. I can tell she's dreaming by the way they move.

"I love you," I whisper.

I grab my leather jacket and black sneakers. The motorcycle is a familiar friend. So is the night. I ride towards a shitty part of the city. There's a nightclub that's known for being divey. A place with a lot of sleazeballs. I'm not old enough to get in, but they let me through the door without hesitation. My height and face have always made me appear older than I really am.

The music is extremely loud. It vibrates through the floor and walls. Everything is blue like Mia's doll house. The floor lights up blue and white. The DJ is wearing a purple suit and hat. Strobe lights mix with the erratic movement of everyone dancing. I can't hear anyone talking, but I see their mouths moving. Electronic pop music is overbearing, pumping through the speakers. I walk through the club and survey the people inside.

Girls come up to me and tug on my sleeves. They all have tiny sparkly dresses and high heels on. I brush them off me gently and they frown as I walk by. Dudes in white coats give me cold stares. A guy that doesn't look old enough to be here smiles and waves at me like we're friends. There's a group of men in business suits sitting at the rack watching a half-naked girl dance. She winks at me when we make eye contact.

Topaz string lights remind me of Mia's room. The floor flashes white, teal, and indigo. I see couples making out behind pillars and up against walls. A guy in a fedora is following a girl that looks really mad at him. I keep going further into the blue wonderland until I hear what I am looking for. A woman's scream. It's coming from the bathrooms. I can barely hear it over the music but I was waiting for it. I open the black and gold door to find a man bending a girl over the sinks. He's trying to force himself inside her.

"Let me go, asshole!" she yells and tries to kick him.

"C'mon! You feel so good," he says as he runs his hands over her hips and grabs her ass.

He's in his late twenties, wearing a nice suit and tie, sporting a vulgar smile.

"Stop!" she shrieks.

He grabs her ponytail and bashes her head into the mirror.

"I'm going to have fun with you."

He licks his lips and pushes up her dress.

I should use my demonic sutra, but I don't. I use my fists. The man doesn't see me coming. His expression changes rapidly as I throw him on the ground. I kick him in the ribs. The pretty girl looks at me with big brown eyes. Her cheeks are covered in freckles and her ears have big dangly earrings in them. She has blood running down the side of her face.

"Thank you," she says and runs out the door.

I pick the guy up by the collar, the way my dad would pick me up, and I bring him to my face.

"What do you think you're doing?" I ask.

The man kicks but can't get out of my grasp.

"Hey, now. I was just messing around," he says in a soft voice.

"She didn't seem to like it," I hiss.

"We were just having fun."

He rolls his eyes and I shove him into the wall. I punch next to him and he flinches. It feels good to have this kind of power.

"You were having fun. She wasn't."

"I'm sorry! Was that your girlfriend or something?" he asks.

I throw him into the mirror and break it more.

"She's somebody's girlfriend. She's somebody's daughter, sister, friend."

"What are you getting at?"

"No matter what you do, you'll never be anything but trash," I whisper in his ear.

The sound of my fist hitting his cheekbone is a satisfying crack. I hit him again. He spits out a tooth, and it hits the dingy nightclub floor.

"She was just some slut. Don't get so worked up about it," he says as blood drips down his jaw.

I grab his collar and throw him on the ground next to his disgusting tooth. Sitting on his chest, I get nose to nose with him.

"She wasn't a slut. You tell yourself that to make yourself feel better about violating women the way you do. Rot in hell," I say and hit him with the demonic sutra.

Noburu appears from the stall of the nightclub bathroom.

"Whoa, kid. What happened here?" asks The Soul Keeper.

He has on the ripped jeans that hang too low and the black bomber jacket with no shirt on. I can hardly look at him when he wears this outfit. He's practically naked.

"This man tried to rape a woman. Then he said she was a slut when I confronted him," I say and stand up.

"What a fucking loser," he says. Noburu tosses his cigarette into the sink. He puts his jeweled fingers to the man. "Go back to hell."

The man rises and I watch him suffocate with joy. The way he kicks his legs and flails pleases me. Neon green aura consumes him. His eyes bubble and turn to liquid that dries out immediately. He tries to pry off hands that don't exist from his neck. The man evaporates and green mist is pulled into the fan.

"You okay, Ryon?" asks Noburu as he lights up another smoke.

"I'm fine."

"Next time, try not to damage the goods before delivery," says Noburu.

He is casual, but I think he is upset with me.

"I'm sorry. I've been under a lot of stress," I admit.

"It's okay. He was going to get it, anyway."

Noburu pauses and smokes slowly as he continues. "I don't want the darkness to take a hold of you though. Once it does, it's hard to stop. Most people are unable to fight the darkness. It spreads like a disease. Rots you from the inside out," he says.

His gold eyes are kind but serious as they stare into mine. I get what he's saying.

"I understand. It won't happen again."

"No worries, kid. Money's on the card. Take care of yourself. Mia needs you," he says as he returns to his world.

I get back on my bike. My knuckles are bruised and bloody. When I get home, I wash my hand and bandage it. I change my clothes and get back into bed. Mia's hair is fanned out all around her like a mermaid. She has her hands on the snowflake guarding her heart.

CHAPTER TWENTY-FIVE

A WHITE DEVIL DRESSED IN BLACK

I've been in an atrocious mood. The ugliness inside me tempts me to give into the dark. I keep drinking to drown out the fucked up thoughts. I'm in my father's study tearing it up. The desk is knocked over and I've broken all his rocks glasses. There isn't much in this spacious room, but I trash everything. I find his business cards he had Mia make for him and burn them.

After picking up his chair and smashing it into the hardwood floor, I snoop through all the drawers. He took his laptop with him. His important documents and paperwork. I wish I could strangle him. I want to feel his pulse in my palms as I choke him out. All he ever cared about was money. I fucking hate him.

My fist is in the wall. The knuckles on my right hand are bruised, and it stings. In my other hand is the half empty bottle of scotch. I sway around the room and inspect the damage I have caused. I don't want Mia to see this or clean it. She's at Ayumi's. I've been asking him to keep her company. I lock the door to the study and stumble into the kitchen. Mia made me dinner before she left. There's a note by it: I love you. I haven't been hungry in days. My appetite and sleep have been nonexistent.

I bring it with me up to my room. She's worried about me and I should try harder not to be such an asshole. I take another pull off the bottle and set it down on my coffee table with the food. My head feels heavy and I rest it in my hands. I miss Mia. I miss the way things were. Everything is overwhelming and confusing.

I love her so much I do horrible things. Is Noburu real or is he a figment of my imagination? I checked three times to make sure all our bills are caught up and they are. The credit card works. It always clears at the grocery store and all the restaurants. I must really be getting paid to take people's souls. My dad still won't call me back. I'm agitated, so I call him and leave a message. I don't care if he knows I'm drunk. Maybe it will help him sympathize with me.

Hey dad, it's Ryon. I really need to talk to you. You haven't returned any of my calls. It's been almost nine months since I've seen you...

That's when I get a brilliant idea. This should get his attention.

Mia is pregnant. I don't know what to do. I'm sorry, I really messed up. Please call me back.

I smile with my teeth. My dad will love to rub this in my face. I'll beg him to help me out. That will give him the leverage over me he wants. It's the need for power over people that drives him even harder than the desire for money.

It's been a while since I've been in Mia's room. I'm drunk and feel nosy. I open her door and observe the tiny sapphire lights like they are stars. It's 8:48 pm and I have to use the wall to steady myself. I'm so drunk it's hard to stand. I shouldn't be in here, especially like this. Her book of poems is on her bed, Stepping on Broken Stemmed Violets.

I sit down and lean against her turquoise and pink bed. It's a reflex, and I put my hand under the mattress. I hold her blue diary in my hand. Her private thoughts. My vision is hazy. I don't know what's wrong with me, but I thumb through the pages. I stop on an entry from a week ago.

No one bullies me anymore, but I'm lonely. I miss Ryon. He's different.

I turn the pages until I find what I'm looking for.

* * *

If he loved me
The way I love him
Would it wake me up
Or be a dream

There is so much I don't understand about my stepsister. I'm not an artsy person. In the years I've grown to love her, I find myself more sensitive, but not in a bad way. It actually feels good to have a greater sense of depth. I never would have cared about art or seen things the way I do without her. Feeling like a criminal, I put her diary back in a hurry.

I hide the bottle of scotch under my bathroom sink. It's almost 10 p.m. Mia will be home soon. To make her show up faster, I fall asleep. I fade in and out. My dreams aren't as scary. I'm walking on the beach. The waves are breaking on large boulders. I keep finding stems and leaves but no flowers. It looks like they washed up on shore. I walk closer to the ocean. Leaning on a rock, I watch a mermaid with long black hair bite the top off of the flower and throw the stem into the sea.

Mia is always in my arms when I wake up. I hold her close to my chest. My heart beats hard but slow. She's wearing a thin gray shirt with long sleeves. I check her wrist. No fresh cuts. Mia wrote that she missed me, even though I'm always here. She turns around to embrace me. It's not a dream, but I don't feel real.

***

Mia is brushing her hair. She's sitting on the floor. It's so long it almost reaches the ground. I'm laying on the couch in the living room looking at her turn her head this way and that as she untangles her messy hair. I have the urge to yank on it and open up her skull. I cringe at my intrusive thoughts and close my eyes.

"What are you thinking about?" she asks.

"Nothing," I say.

"Why won't you talk to me? I really miss you."

"I'm sorry. I've just been tired," I say.

Mia turns around and puts her hands on my shoulders. Then she starts playing with my hair. It annoys me and I sit up.

"What's wrong?" she asks.

Her face is innocent despite all the fucked up things she's been through. It's hard to look at her. Mia sits next to me and puts her arms around my neck.

"Do you have to do that?" I snarl.

It was a slipup, but the damage is done. Mia shrinks back and holds up her arms defensively again.

"Sorry," she whispers and runs up to her room.

I don't mean to, but I keep snapping at her. She's clinging to me every moment, and I have too much shit on my mind. I go upstairs and knock on her door.

"Please, come out. I'm sorry. I didn't mean it," I say. She doesn't say anything. I contemplate breaking the door, but hear that static and feel that sense of shame again. "I love you," I say and go into my room.

I lay in my bed and put my hand to the wall. My phone is buzzing in my pocket. It's my dad. I get up and go into the bathroom so Mia can't hear me.

"Dad," I say.

"I thought I told you to use protection, son."

I can tell he's smiling. His viper smirk with fangs is audible.

"I know. I'm so stupid. Please, dad. I need you to help me out."

"I'll send you some money, but don't call me anymore."

"Wait, no! Dad -" I make it up on the spot. I need him to come to me. "Mia's been sick and missing a lot of school. The truancy officers already came by. Child services are getting involved. Please, dad. Don't let them take Mia away from me." I am impressed with my acting skills.

My dad is silent, but I can hear the clockwork pieces turn in his brain.

"You're only seventeen. I don't think you're old enough to handle all this responsibility," he says in his deep and horrifying voice.

"Help me out this one time and I'll never bother you again, I swear. Please, dad. I love her. Don't abandon me like mom did," I say it even though it pains me to.

At this point, I can't tell if my desperation is genuine or not. I think it is. There is a heavy pause between us. It's raining outside and the drops of water hit my window softly. The tension is palpable in the air, even though we are far apart.

"Okay. I'll be there in a few days," he says. Now he's going to bite me. "I knew you were going to give in to that little whore," he laughs and hangs up on me.

I want to throw my phone across the room, but I don't. Green and yellow venom in my ears. I can't wait to kill him.

I go downstairs and start cooking dinner. My hands need something to do. I keep thinking about stabbing him in the chest with the chef's knife. Tomatoes remind me of cutting into the flesh of an arm. Stirring egg yolks with chopsticks gives me visions of scrambling the eyes out of his socket. Everything about me is wicked, evil, and violent. I put on some music and try to remember what I used to be like. Right now I'm volatile.

I get Mia to come out of her room. She keeps her head down. I'm in a better mood knowing my dad is going to pay for what he did. Mia sits with me, but doesn't say a word. Great, now I want her to pay attention to me and she's not going to. It's always like this now. I try to get over it but I'm hurt.

"I miss you, too," I say to break the silence.

"Why are you always mad at me? I just want you to be happy. You yell at me all the time now," she cries and clutches her necklace.

I'm such a dick. I get up and put my arms around her. She reaches for me with the hand her ring is on. Mia never takes it off.

"I'm not mad at you. It's hard to explain. I've been really stressed out. I need to stop snapping at you. I'm sorry."

"Please don't leave me."

"I will not leave you."

"Do you think my mom's okay?" Mia sobs.

It takes me a minute, but I realize it's Koharu's birthday. My blood stops in my veins. It's frozen, icy, and still.

"I hope so," I whisper.

It's the truth.

"I dream about her coming home," she says.

"That's a nice dream."

"What do you dream about, Ryon?"

"Lately my dreams have been different," I admit.

"How so?"

"I used to dream about taking a test or winning a game. Now I dream about all sorts of things," I say as I sip on my aloe green tea.

"Like what?"

"I dream about a beach with purple flowers. There are doll skulls with poems in them like fortune cookies. I don't know. They're weird," I laugh.

"They sound profound," says Mia.

She wipes away her tears. I should have done it for her, but I've been causing them. Mia is wearing a powder blue sweater that's super fuzzy. Her nails are sparkly indigo, her ring is blue, her face is blue. I smile at her and she smiles back, but it doesn't reach her eyes.

***

To make up for my aggressive behavior, I've been trying to be extra nice to Mia. I bought her a bunch of books I thought she'd like. She looked surprised at how many I got her. We went to the park where Chisaki took our picture. Mia admired the gold and red leaves while I admired her. I don't know how I feel about her, but I want her to trust me again.

I bought a bunch of stuff for her with my surplus cash. There was a scumbag trying to rob a small convenience store the other day. I learned that Noburu can distort images in cameras, so he never appears in them and no one sees what he does. He said it was "a demon thing." I went to the store that all the girls in my grade like and got Mia a black dress with long sleeves that I thought would look good on her. I got her a dark blue scarf with silver accents. It reminded me of winter, which always makes me think of her. I found another vintage ring. This one has a really thin silver band and an aquamarine gemstone.

It's probably weird, but I sent her flowers at school. I got her roses with cosmos and lilies. She thinks I don't love her, so I try to show her that I care. It's selfish, but I also wanted Nero to see them. I still hate that guy. It makes me happy to see his disgruntled face when I pick her up. His pretty boy teeth don't show if he's frowning.

Mia is laying on me. We're watching a horror movie about a family that is haunted, and the dad tries to murder his wife and kid. It's not actually scary, but we're having fun. Things aren't back to normal, but we're close again. She doesn't act like she's afraid of me anymore.

"All the girls were jealous of my flowers," she announces.

"Are they still being nice to you?" I ask.

Mia is eating popcorn. Her eyes remain focused on the movie.

"No one is mean to me anymore. I sit with a girl named Rei during our lunch break. She likes poetry and classic movies, too."

"Good. I'm glad you have a girl to hang out with," I tease, as I playfully tug at her hair.

She shoves my hand away but smiles.

"Me too. Girls are different. I haven't had a girl to talk to for years," she says.

"It's because you're too pretty. You make everyone nervous."

"How?" she rolls her eyes at me as she watches the movie.

The dad is looking for his wife with an axe while the wife is hiding from him in a large building.

"All the girls think you're going to take their boyfriends," I joke and she giggles.

"Whatever," she says, but I can tell she's happy.

"I got you something," I say.

She sits up and I go into my room and get her the gifts I bought her. I hand her the fancy boxes the ladies at the store put everything in. It seems wasteful, but it's a thing girls like, I guess. Mia opens the one with the scarf in it first.

"This is sweet of you, Ryon. You don't have to keep buying me stuff," she says.

Her tiny hands grip the fabric and look too small to belong to a real person.

"I wanted to," I say.

She opens the box with the dress and holds it up. The sleeves are sheer and lacey. More doll clothes. Mia looks more grown up now. I like her style. She's always been unique.

"Thank you."

"There's one more."

Mia puts the dress in her lap and picks up the last present. She pauses like she's not sure if she should open it. Her toy hands open the black and gold box. My stepsister holds the ring between her fingers.

"I love it, Ryon. I really do. But what's going on? Why are you being so nice to me?" she asks.

"I've been kind of a jerk the last couple months," I make a face at her and she laughs.

"Only a little bit," she teases. Mia takes her gift and puts it on her right hand. It fits her ring finger. "It's beautiful. Thank you," she says.

"Are you still mad at me?"

"No. I can never stay mad at you."

"Really?" I ask.

I rest my elbows on my knees and think about all the bad shit I've done. If Mia can forgive me, then I guess I don't really care.

"Yes. I love you too much to stay mad," she plays with her new ring and smiles to herself.

"Wanna watch another movie?" I ask.

"Yeah," she says.

I go to the bathroom and run water through my hair. Looking at myself in the mirror, I see my dad's reflection. I'm glad I don't have Chartreuse green eyes. I wonder where my indigo eyes came from. Noburu said Mia's heart was tied to mine, and she is blue. I wonder if that has something to do with it. The Soul Keeper is an interesting character. I wish he could tell me more about Mia's heart.

Back in the living room, Mia picks another horror movie. My stepsister is eating popcorn like everything is fine. It's almost like our parents didn't abandon us and we've always just lived like this. Soon my dad will be here. Having the pleasure of taking his life excites and terrifies me. I'm sitting next to the arm of the couch and she goes back to laying on me. Her hair falls over my wrist. I like this movie. This one is about a psycho that doesn't know he's the crazy one until the end.

CHAPTER TWENTY-SIX
WHEN A FLAME ENTERS WATER

Mia and I meet Sora and Teo at the park. She takes a seat on the bench with her books and I walk up to the guys. Teo is bouncing the ball. He passes it to Sora to take off his glasses and wipe them off.

"Hey guys," I say.

"Hey Ryon. I'm glad you wanted to play ball. It's been a while," says Sora.

He knows why I've been distant. Teo knows things are awkward between me and Mia, but doesn't know what my dad did. I can't tell him. Not that Teo isn't trustworthy. More like the secret is so hideous, I couldn't burden someone as nice as Teo with it. Sora is the most mature person I know. That's why I had to confide in him.

"I miss hanging out with you. I hope you and Mia are doing okay," says Teo.

"They're a lot better," I say, and Sora passes the ball to me.

I shoot and score as I always do. The guys give me fake glares and we all laugh. It feels nice to be normal. We mess around on the court for a while. I take off my gray zip-up. There's sweat dripping from my hair, but I'm not concerned. It's the first time I'm not thinking about fucked up shit in what seems like forever.

The guys and I play like nothing has changed. Everything about me is different. I wonder what transformation Sora and Teo have been through. The thing about changing is no one can see it. I didn't see it, or at least I didn't want to see it. There is no turning back now.

Mia has made me a better person. I never took the time to notice certain things until she came into my life. A photo, a painting, or a certain song, emotions I can't explain, they all touch me so deeply in a way I never felt before. Most of my life I've just been goofing off. Only skimming the surface. Mia has taught me what it means to hold something so precious you never want to let go.

Every time I won a game, I could zone out the dread of going home. All the good grades, the praise, and the attention made me feel like I fit in. I didn't care enough to know what it would be like to be the outsider. Everyone liked me, so I liked myself. It's sad, but it's true. That's who I was.

"That was awesome! The Blond Demon plays a mean game!" says Sora as he jumps and shoots.

It goes in the basket and we cheer for him.

"You're really something," says Teo.

All of us are out of breath and sweaty. I feel like my old self. The person who just wanted to hang out with his friends and be happy.

"Thanks guys," I say as I run my fingers through my frizzy hair. "I'm going to go check on Mia."

I approach her and she closes her journal.

"Hey," she says.

"What are you writing?"

I ask and sit down next to her.

"Nothing," she blushes.

"C'mon, please."

I smile at her, and she laughs.

"Okay, but don't make fun."

"I would never do that."

"Autumn leaves, halo of gold, wishes untold, my soul I sold."

Mia recites her poem to me. I feel my jaw drop. Her voice is adult and pretty. She doesn't whisper or mumble. Mia sounds sure of herself.

"That's beautiful, Mia."

"You think so?" she asks as she holds her diary to her chest.

"You're going to be famous someday," I say and pick up a handful of her hair.

I tickle her face with it. She pushes me away, but not in a mean way.

"I would like to be published. I've always wondered if my poems would affect people the way I have been affected by other people's art," she says.

My lungs give out on me. She doesn't know about all my snooping. All the times I read her private thoughts and they hit me so hard I cried in my room all night. Her poems are amazing. They have kept me going when I thought it would be better just to die.

"I think you're deep and unique. No one else has your heart or your mind," I say and stand up to hang out with the guys a bit longer.

Sora and Teo are smirking at me.

"What?" I ask.

"Did you ask Mia to be your girlfriend?" asks Teo.

He is holding back a giggle. So is Sora.

"What? No!" I say.

The guys are acting weird.

"Why are you looking at me like that?" I ask.

"Fumika told me all the girls think you asked her to be your girlfriend. They think you proposed to her with that ring," says Teo.

He passes me the ball and I feel the wind get knocked out of me as I catch it.

"I got it because it reminded me of her," I say.

"So you didn't ask her to be your girlfriend?" asks Sora.

I shoot the ball even though I'm far away and I make it. The ball echoes on the ground as it bounces. It sits on the concrete, waiting for someone to pick it up.

"No. Nothing like that," I say.

"What about the flowers?" asks Teo. "All the guys are apparently really jealous because The Blond Demon not only picks her up on his badass motorcycle, he is a gentleman as well!" he jokes.

"Okay guys, I get it. It's weird all the stuff I do for her," I say and walk across the court to get the ball.

"It's not weird," says Sora.

"Then why are you guys acting so goofy?" I ask.

"Because it's funny. You spend all your time making her happy and you won't even let yourself think about how you really feel about her," says Sora.

Teo nods to agree.

"Wouldn't it be wrong of me?" I ask.

I bounce the ball a few times and pass it to Sora. He shoots and misses. Teo picks it up and bounces it but doesn't shoot it. He passes it to me.

"Why would it be wrong?" asks Teo.

"I don't know. She's my stepsister. It's just been us for nine months. I feel like I'm doing something bad having those kinds of feelings," I admit. I shoot the ball without looking and make it. "If I met her another way, maybe things would be different," I say.

"If you met her another way, you may not have paid any attention to her," says Sora.

"You're right. I don't know. Girls drive me crazy," I joke.

The guys agree, and we play until the sun is about to set. Mia and I part ways with the guys and walk home. She seems to be in a good mood. I catch her staring up at the pink sky.

"Do you like sunsets?" she asks.

"Yes," I say and look up at the swirling orange clouds. "They remind me of California. I would always watch the sunset on the beach with my mom."

"Do you ever talk to her?"

"No. I don't know where she is. Maybe someday I'll hire a private investigator to find her," I am half joking.

This makes Mia turn up the corners of her mouth.

"I miss my mom," she says.

"I know. I'm sorry."

I reach for her hand.

"I'm glad I have you, though. I don't need anybody else," she says.

Koharu trusted me. She left Mia with me because she wanted us to have each other. I hope I can be enough.

***

It's been two days since I talked to my dad. He will be here soon. I'm

217

on edge but try to hide it. We need money, so I have to go out tonight. I don't want to be away for too long. Mia's arms are wrapped around me. So is her hair. She has her hand on my heart. I move her as gently as possible and slip out of bed.

I don't want to ride my motorcycle tonight. The neighborhood is full of assholes. I put on my black hoodie, black jeans, and black sneakers. I stay in the shadows and avoid the streetlights. My breaths are visible in the cool autumn air. It smells like wet grass and roses. All the houses have big windows and nice cars in the driveway. They are all boring colors like periwinkle, white, and gray. The cars are black, white, and silver. Everything is dull but flashy. Shallow people have poor taste.

Mia worries I will not come back. I hope leaving my bike in the garage calms her down if she wakes up. My moods haven't been as erratic. I hope she knows I'm trying my best. She thinks my dad is paying all our bills, but really, I'm the one who's going to make him pay.

I sneak into the backyard of a house with white curtains and kid's toys in the front yard. The place gave me a feeling. I go with my gut and patrol around the back of the house and peek in. I see the kitchen, living room, and a bedroom. There is a smaller bedroom off to the side. As I press up against the glass to see, I hear it. A child crying.

Creeping around the corner, I peer in through the small part in the curtain. I am disgusted. It's our neighbor's brother. He's taking lewd photos of his niece. She's only four. Her name is Sayomi. She has short black pigtails and big blue eyes. I can hear her uncle trying to coax her into certain poses, but she's distraught. Her red swimsuit is sinister in this situation.

I go back towards the kitchen. The window is cracked. I open it and let myself in. My shoes get dirt on the counter. I step down slowly and walk towards Sayomi's room. I can hear her sobbing. The orange lamp makes the house look like it's something out of a horror movie.

"It's okay, sweet girl. Just a few more pictures for your favorite uncle," he purrs.

"I don't wanna," she cries.

He is taking off her top. She is fighting him with her tiny fists.

"Just do what I say, you little brat!" he spits.

He has a thin mustache and stubble all over his cheeks. His eyes are bulging from his rage. I am right next to him, but he doesn't see me. Noburu appears and puts Sayomi to sleep. He tucks her in and plays with her pigtail the way a brother would.

"What do we have here?" he asks, but I'm sure The Soul Keeper already knows.

"A pedophile. Taking pornographic photos of his niece," I say.

"Sick bastard," says Noburu. He isn't smoking. With jeweled fingers, he touches the man. "Go back to hell."

We watch with satisfied grins as the man asphyxiates in the neon aura. I know I enjoy seeing shitty people die. It's graphic, but it gives me a surge of energy.

"I wonder what else my neighbors are up to," I say.

"Didn't have to stray too far from home to get this one," he says.

The green mist is pulled through a crack in the window. We use the back door. Noburu and I walk towards my house. He lights up a cigarette.

"You said Mia's heart is tied to mine. I was wondering...is it wrong if I love her as more than just my stepsister?" I ask him.

Noburu takes a long, thoughtful drag. I get the feeling he might make a joke, but he doesn't. His heels hit the pavement and make menacing noises in the quiet night.

"You and Mia have always been together. In your past lives, you have been best friends, lovers, and acquaintances. In this life, you happen to be step-siblings."

"So these feelings that I have, they aren't bad?" I ask.

Noburu puts his hand on my shoulder like he's my friend. I suppose he kind of is.

"You have always loved her. It doesn't matter how," he says confidently.

We're almost at my house.

"Everyone makes me feel like I don't love her right."

"Everyone else isn't like you guys. Not everyone is fated together. You two are different," says Noburu.

He stands in front of the house and waits for me to go in.

"Why are we meant to be together?" I ask.

"I'm not sure. All I know is your hearts have been intertwined for centuries. Later, kid. Get some rest," says The Soul Keeper.

He puts out his cigarette with his heel and walks across the spectral plain.

Mia is still sleeping. I kneel down and study her doll's face. Her dark pink mouth is covered in vanilla chapstick. The truth is, I'm not sure how I love Mia. All I know is I would do anything for her. If my dad has to die so she can be safe, then I will do it. I get into bed and bring her close to my chest. She holds my hand as I dream about snakes leaving indents and bruises on her. I rip them in half and purple flowers fall out of their stomachs.

***

I dream about ocean waves bringing me bottles with poems in them. They are in languages I can't understand. I'm by myself, but I'm not afraid. I dream about yellow snakes with green eyes. They slither across a beach that turns into a desert.

I dream about finding seashells, purple flowers, and blue jewels. I step on them and scoop them out of the sand. I find a deer skull and crack it open. It turns into dust and leaves behind a ring. I dream about mermaids with long hair. They eat violets and throw the stems into the sea. They reach out to me and say I love you.

I dream about dolls with love notes inside. They are written in blood. I drop one of the porcelain skulls and it shatters. I dream about holding a baby bird in the palm of my hand. It's soft and sweet. I need to protect it and I hold it close to heart.

I dream about drowning. The sea is blue and black. There are teal lanterns leading to the bottom. I catch a glimpse of a mermaid. She has sharp teeth and long hair. I try to swim, but another mermaid is dragging me down. She has blue-green eyes like Setsuna.

I dream about silver charms. It's raining and they keep falling from the sky. They make a ringing noise as they hit the cement. I pick them up one by one. They are sparkly and lavish. Big koi fish with diamond eyes, rabbits made of gold, and hearts with red jewels in them.

I dream about bridges. The river below is forceful. Cars keep driving into the water. I dream about bruises on my chest. They decorate my torso purple, green, and yellow. I dream about playing basketball in front of trophy people that keep falling over.

I dream about cigarettes. The glow of a red cherry in a dark alley. I dream about pretty girls with wavy hair. They're ripping the sleeves off my shirt. I dream that I'm riding my motorcycle through empty city streets. There are no lights and even the stars don't shine. I dream about it getting darker and darker.

"Ryon?" I wake up to Mia.

She's touching my hair and whispering my name.

"Yeah?"

"You were having a nightmare," she says.

"Thanks," I say and stare out the window.

The moon is full. I wonder if it has anything to do with my dreams. Noburu makes frequent glances at it. Maybe the moon affects humans because of the demons who control it. Am I a lunatic?

"What are you looking at?" she asks.

"The moon is full," I announce into the pillow.

"I had a weird dream. A snake was following me. I was crossing a river to get away from it and I got swept up by the current. Right as I was about to go over the waterfall, someone grabbed me," she says.

"Sounds like the moon is messing with both of us," I tease.

My dad will be here any day. I want to keep Mia away from him.

"You have pretty eyes," she says.

Mia's staring up at me. I wonder if she knows she's the color blue.

"So do you," I say and play with her hair. I do whatever I want. If she tells me to stop, I will, but I have given up on analyzing everything we do. "If you could live anywhere in the world, where would it be?" I ask.

"Italy," she says.

"Why Italy?"

"Some of the greatest artists are from there. It's beautiful and romantic," she says.

Mia would fit in there. People would understand her sensitivity. Japan is beautiful and romantic, but it is also cold. Love and distance are often two sides of the same coin. People in Italy seem uninhibited. They are passionate and soulful. I think she would be happy there.

We would be by the ocean, and I would get to be with Mia. I'd ride my motorcycle through the city. I would admire the art and history. It would be a fresh start. A new beginning for us. I'm ready for it.

"What would you do there?" I ask.

Mia closes her eyes and thinks about it.

"I would want to live by the beach in a house that has a lot of windows so I can paint the ocean. I'd hang my art in a local gallery and read my poetry at cafes," she says.

Whatever Mia wants, Mia gets. As soon as I get the funds, I'm going to find her the perfect place. I imagine her sitting by the window with the breeze in her hair as she presses paint into canvas.

"That sounds really nice."

"Where do you want to live?"

"I want to stay with you, silly."

"We could visit California. I want to see where you're from," she says and reaches for my hair again.

It's been so long since I've seen a palm tree next to an American flag. I'd show her my favorite beach. The one my mom would take me to.

"I'd like that."

"I want to go wherever you want to go."

"Well, that's too bad because you're going to have to pick all the places that we go."

I grab the blanket and pull it over my shoulders. Mia's violet perfume lulls me to sleep. I have more strange dreams. I'm in a field. Mia is standing in front of me, watching the sunset. The sky is pink but turns dark too fast. A snake rushes past me. I stomp on it, and black blood splatters across my face.

I dream about blue petals scattered on my pillow. There's a trail of them on the hardwood floor. They lead me to Mia. She's wearing the black dress I got her and playing with her ring. I watch as blood drips down her thighs, but she's still smiling. I wake up to her sitting up, staring out the window.

"What is it?" I ask.

"I saw a man with red hair smoking across the street. He had a big diamond in his ear," she says.

"It was probably just some weirdo," I say.

CHAPTER TWENTY-SEVEN
REMOVING THE HEAD OF A SERPENT

I'm going through old photos. There aren't many with my mom. I've been hiding them for years. My dad would probably burn them. I have one picture of the three of us. We had more, but he threw them away before we moved to Japan. I rescued this one. Somehow he hasn't found it. Or maybe he did. My father is unpredictable.

My dad and I have a lot of newer photos. He smiles with his eyes in the pictures where I'm receiving trophies and winning games. His hand is on my shoulder and we both look happy. It's fake, but it hurts how real it looks.

I have a picture of my mom at our favorite beach. She's wearing aviator sunglasses and laughing. Her blond hair is being picked up by the wind. I took this picture using a Polaroid camera. My mom may have abandoned me, but I know she loved me. I can see it. The way she is looking at me take this picture of her. Maybe one day I'll see her again.

The photo of all three of us stands out. My mom has her hands on my shoulders. She is smiling and so am I. We both look happy. Our faces are similar, but I look more like my dad. He is smiling, but it's not genuine. His eyes are dark and dead like a shark's. They remind me of Fuyuhisa's. He has his arm around my mom. Now that I look at it closer, I think she is cringing as he touches her.

"Ryon?"

Mia is calling me from downstairs. She's home. I've been dropping her off at Ayumi's after school. I can't let my dad anywhere near her.

"I'll be down in a second," I say.

I hide the pictures back in my old textbook. Mia is making tea in the kitchen.

"Hey," she says.

"Hey. How was your day?"

"It was good. Rei and I exchanged some of our poems. Ayumi and I hung out at the park by his house. We watched a movie, too."

Mia sets the tea down and gestures for me to sit with her.

"I'm glad you're making friends," I say.

"Yeah, I guess I am."

Mia is in a good mood and I'm about to ruin it. But I have to.

"Mia, I need to ask you something."

"What is it?"

She stares into her teacup and tucks her hair behind her ear, revealing her pretty face.

"Did my dad," I see her eyes fill with fear as I mention him, "do anything else?" I ask.

"Why do you keep asking me these things?"

My stepsister has a soft voice, but she is being harsh with me. I don't like it. It makes me brace myself because I know she's hiding something.

"I'm sorry. I just can't stand knowing he hurt you, and I had no idea."

"He only came into my room that one time. I think he wanted to teach me a lesson," she says.

"What kind of lesson?"

"That he could do whatever he wanted."

I rest my head in my hand. Mia is right. With my other hand, I reach out for her but don't make eye contact.

"I want you to be honest with me. I know you keep things from me, but I love you. I want to know everything about you. It doesn't matter what you tell me, I will always love you," I say.

Mia squeezes my fingers. Her thumb is grazing my knuckles. They're not bloody and bruised anymore.

"A month after it happened, your dad caught me throwing up. He called me out of school and took me to a clinic an hour away. I remember sitting there in the uncomfortable chair, listening to the ticking of the clock. It was so quiet in there," she says.

I don't know what I'm feeling. My head is in my hand. It's heavy on my wrist.

I'm so pissed I want to break everything in his study again. Mia puts her other hand on mine. I feel both of her rings. They are cool against the heat of my rage. I'm pissed I didn't stop him. I'm pissed she didn't tell me. How could she keep something like this from me? I wonder how many times I made her uncomfortable with my touch because I look just like him.

I am unhinged. I'm so angry I can't see straight. The table is blurry and so is my cup of tea. I hear static. I can't tell who I am more angry at: my dad or myself. He is the cruelest person that I know. I should have been able to tell he did something horrible to her. She is beautiful, and it has always attracted attention and bad intentions. I stifle my rage so I don't scare her.

"I'm so sorry, Mia. I should have protected you from him."

My voice is hoarse and barely audible. My father, the most wicked man I know, the darkest soul. The one that will bring me endless fortune.

"I don't blame you for what happened to me, Ryon."

"I know. I blame myself. I should have been paying attention."

"It made me really happy that day you said you would be my friend," she says.

It brings me back and I look into the face of my stepsister. She looks stronger than she used to.

"I wish I tried harder to be a good stepbrother sooner," I confess.

Mia gets up and sits next to me. She puts her arms around me. They feel fragile, but they are elegant as they wrap around my shoulders.

"I think you try too hard to make me happy," she whispers.

"I thought that if I made you happy, I would be happy, too."

"I am happy."

"How can you say that?"

I don't mean to, but I snap. Mia doesn't recoil from me. She hugs me tighter.

"Because I am. I was lonely for a really long time. Then you came along and showed me what it was like to have someone truly care. I'm sorry I hid this from you. I thought you wouldn't want to be close to me if you knew the truth."

"Are you really happy, though?"

I feel the words get caught in my throat.

"Yes. I know I don't smile all the time, but I'm happy. I miss my mom, but I like it just being us. In a way, I feel like we've always lived like this," she says.

Noburu said we have been together for centuries. Mia can feel it, too. I put my arms around her. Even though I want to cry, I don't. I feel glad knowing my dad is going to die.

***

My intuition says he will be here today. I keep checking my phone. What if he calls her out of school and takes her from me? The heartless bastard would do it just to teach me a lesson. So far, no calls or texts from Mia or Ayumi. I finish my work and space out until the end of class.

As I arrive at the middle school, I see Nero and his gang of pretty boys watching me with envious stares. Good. I'm glad he thinks she chose me over him. In a way, she kind of did. I can easily hide my grin in my helmet. Mia walks past him like he doesn't exist. His friends snicker, but she doesn't pay any attention to them. I take her out for coffee and drop her off at Ayumi's.

The tulip lined neighborhood has a dark energy to it. I park my bike in the garage. Something seems off. I go to the front door. It's unlocked and ajar, but only an inch. I hold my breath and go inside. Nothing is out of place, but I sense him. I know he's in the house.

"Dad?" I call.

The kitchen sink is dripping. The sound of it makes me tense and I turn it off all the way. I go into his study. No one is here. My heart is pounding in my chest. I hope he can't hear it. Can snakes hear your heartbeat or feel it? I open the door to his old bedroom. He isn't here.

"Dad?" I call again.

There is no one on the porch or in the laundry room. He must be in my room. I walk up the stairs. It seems like I'm going in slow motion as I open my door. No one. My heart stops out in the hall. He's in Mia's room. I push open her door and find him reading her diary. He's sitting on her bed and grinning.

"Hey son," he says and stands up.

"Dad! I'm really glad you came. I need your help," I start begging to distract him from what I am going to do.

"You shouldn't have called me, Ryon."

"What?" I ask.

My dad pulls a gun out of his coat. It has a silencer on it. Expensive, lethal, and American. I put my hands up.

"Why are you doing this?" I ask.

"Where's Mia?" he asks his own question as he picks up her perfume.

"She's not home," I say.

He throws the bottle, and it breaks behind me.

"Where is she?" he hisses.

"I'm not telling you," I growl.

"Once I get rid of you, I'm getting rid of her, and that thing inside her. Koharu did me a favor and got rid of herself," he laughs his deep and horrifying laugh.

Koharu was a sweet woman, a wonderful mother, and a stepmom. I haven't really thought about it much, but I miss her. She took care of me, even though I wasn't hers. Somehow she loved me even though I look just like this psycho. He shoots, but I run down the stairs. I duck into the laundry room. It's dark in here.

He takes calculated steps that thud each time his heel touches the hardwood floor. I hear him looking for me. My heart is racing. I hope he can't sense the heart he gave me. In my pocket is the sutra Noburu said I would need to use on him. I'm glad I've been keeping it on me.

"Her poems about you are really sweet. Too bad she's a little tramp," he speaks into the empty hall.

I clench my fist and hold back my anger. He is trying to bait me into coming out.

"I tried to warn you, son. That girl is nothing but trouble."

I hear him rip the door off the closet.

Wood splinters, and he continues towards the kitchen. I come out of hiding and follow him down the hall and step into his room. He's thrashing things around in his office. I should have just left it dirty.

"I know why you couldn't stop yourself, Ryon. You're just like me. You take what you want," he snarls as he exits the office and goes back towards the living room.

I'm livid. Noburu said my dad gave me this heart, but it doesn't belong to him. It's mine, and it's tied to Mia's. Even though I want to rage out on him, I keep my composure.

My dad is a bad person. I have known this for a long time. The depths of his cruelty surprise me. I think about my mom and how she looked afraid of him. Remembering Mia cowering from his touch and him telling her to call him "dad" has me grinding my teeth. I can't afford to fuck this up.

Koharu wanted me to take care of Mia. I can't do that if I die. Mia told me I can't die until she dies. I touch my heart and feel it. The unexplainable connection. Even though I hate my dad, there is a part of me that loves him, too. I stand up with the sutra in my hand. If my dad can kill off his family so easily, then why am I pausing as I ready myself to take his? His steps are heavy and making their way back towards me.

"I got her to call me 'daddy' once. I was hoping to hear it one last time," he hisses.

Wrong move. I don't hesitate as I lunge at him as he steps in front of the door. He tries to shoot me, but I knock the gun out of his hand. I put the sutra on his tar black heart. The green aura appears, and he is frozen in place.

"You did it," says Noburu. He is standing right next to me.

"I did."

I'm in shock. Noburu puts his hand on my shoulder. It steadies me a bit.

"So this is your dad," he says.

He blows his smoke into Joseph's face. We watch as he levitates, suspended in the neon green light of The Soul Keeper.

"Yes. A man with a soul blacker than night."

Joseph and I have the same face but not the same eyes. I don't have my mother's eyes either. Maybe they're blue just for Mia. I put my hand to my heart. It doesn't ache anymore. Noburu walks up to my dad and puts his hand on his chest. Noburu's young and carefree face looks alarmed. He furrows his eyebrows and appears disgusted. Pulling his hand back, he shakes it like something gross got on it.

"That's a black soul, alright. Go back to hell," he says and we watch my father struggle for breath. He kicks his legs. His eyes are wild and so is his screaming mouth. I watch him deflate and feel no remorse. He hurt the person I love the most. If his death means Mia's happiness, then I am forgiven. I don't feel bad at all. No one will miss him. "You and Mia can do whatever you want now," says The Soul Keeper.

He is polite and puts his cigarette out in his hand instead of just tossing it or putting it out with his heel on the hardwood floor.

"She wants to live in Italy," I say.

"Then you better buy your plane tickets. Money's on the card, kid. It was a pleasure doing business with you," he says as he goes to exit out the front door like he's not a demon.

"Wait—" I grab his arm.

Noburu turns around with wide eyes. His fox face is perplexed but still smirking.

"What is it, Ryon?"

"Will I ever see you again?" I ask.

For whatever reason, I'm going to miss Noburu. He was my boss, but I'd like to think he was also my friend.

"I'll be around. Bad souls are everywhere. Even in Italy," he pats me on the back.

"See you around," I say, and The Soul Keeper walks out like nothing happened.

CHAPTER TWENTY-EIGHT
THE COLOR BLUE

There are paintings of ocean waves kissing the sand. Large pieces with romantic florals and exotic animals. There are paintings of angels, demons, and gods. I find myself looking at those ones a lot. I walk by a painting of a fox and a young man. It reminds me of Noburu.

I stop at a painting of a beach with purple flowers. The clouds are gold and the sky is pink and orange. I hired a private investigator to find my mom. It took a month, but he found her. I was surprised she cried when I called her. She said she missed me and never stopped thinking about me. I didn't tell her Joseph was dead. It doesn't matter. I just said he abandoned me. My mom and I talk on the phone every couple of days. Even though I haven't seen her in years, I feel close to her. We are going to visit her in California next month for my birthday.

Mia is talking to someone about her art. She is standing in front of her paintings. Her most popular piece is a painting of me and her. She used the photo Chisaki took of us. People ask to buy it, but Mia always refuses to sell it. It's the only one she won't part with. The man talking to her takes her hands and smiles at her with his eyes closed. They part ways and she goes back to looking at her work.

This gallery isn't the fanciest, but it's nice. There are a lot of local artists and a few international ones. Mia is new, but her paintings have attracted a lot of attention. Everyone is surprised when they meet her. Not only because of how young she is, but because of her name. I walk up beside her. She is looking at the painting of us, but I'm admiring the plaque with her name on it: Mia Smithart.

No one expects her to be Japanese. She has the same last name as me. I hate my father and resent owning anything of his, but I don't mind sharing it with Mia. He might have given us his last name, but it's ours now. We are our own family.

People in Italy stare at her a lot but it's not like back in Japan. They watch her with admiration. I am the one who blends in here. She stands out with her long hair and almond eyes. Everyone comes up to me to tell me how pretty she is. One time a man proposed to her at a cafe. She declined, but he said he had to ask her because she was the most beautiful person he had ever seen. Everyone sitting on the patio felt bad for the man when I came back to sit with her. He shook my hand and told me to take good care of her. I promised him I would.

We live in a small house by the beach. Our neighbor is a woman in her forties named Isabel. She is always smoking and drinking wine. Her skin is tan and leathery, but she is still an attractive woman. Isabel is a fun and lively person. She fawns over Mia. At first it made Mia nervous, but they've become good friends. Isabel enjoys dressing Mia up and doing her hair like a little doll. I gave Mia the credit card and told her to buy whatever she wanted. Mia was unsure, but Isabel clapped her hands with delight.

They came back with at least twenty bags and boxes. Isabel chose a dozen dresses in different colors for Mia. They are too short, in my opinion, but all the girls in Italy wear skimpy clothes. Isabel also insisted on high heels. She says all women in Italy wear heels. It's true. Even the waitresses and traffic conductors wear them.

Isabel dressed Mia up from head to toe one day. She did her hair up beauty queen style. Mia always wears dresses, but not quite like this. Her black dress was very tight and short. Isabel accessorized her with black heels and a hair clip with purple flowers on it. She even put mascara and red lipstick on her. When she showed me her work, Mia was super shy, but she looked amazing. I took her out and everyone told me how lucky I was everywhere we went.

The men here aren't subtle about their infatuation with her, but they aren't creepy either. Their straightforwardness is admirable.

They never say anything inappropriate or rude. They simply tell her that they had to talk to her, they had to hear her voice, that they had to see that she was real because she looks like a doll. She always just says "thank you" and turns to me. Her shyness is sweet. It melts the men's hearts.

Mia still wears violet perfume. I'm happy she didn't change that part. Isabel gave her some Italian perfumes, but she doesn't wear them. They smell nice, but they're not her. Mia got her nails done, so she has white tipped nails like her mom did. She just turned sixteen, but she looks older.

"What did that man want?" I ask her.

It draws her out of her thoughts. Today Mia is wearing a tiny pink dress and yellow heels.

"He asked if he could buy that painting," she says and looks up at the one of us.

People have offered her thousands of dollars, but she never takes them up on it. She doesn't need to.

"What did you tell him?"

"I said I couldn't."

"Yeah?"

I ask and put my arm around her. She embraces me, and we admire the wall that is dedicated to her. Everyone looks at the paintings, but I keep looking at the plaque: Mia Smithart.

"He said he understood. That he could feel the love in this picture. He told me he could sense it in the paint. That's why he wanted it," she says and silent tears fall down her face.

I am quick to kneel down and wipe them away.

"What's wrong?" I ask.

"Nothing. I just got that really deep feeling again," she smiles.

I stand up and tickle her face with her hair. It makes her give me a small laugh.

"Do you enjoy living in Italy?" I ask.

We've only been here three months, but I feel like we've been here before.

"I love it. Everyone is so nice here," she says.

"It feels like home."

"Wherever you are is home to me."

***

Girls are cooler than boys. I love the guys. Ayumi, Sora and Teo are the only people from home I still talk to. But they agree that girls are way more interesting. Ayumi is going to visit us during summer break. Sora and Teo plan on visiting after graduation. I can't wait to see their faces. The faces of all the people that influenced me flash through my mind.

I knew a girl who was happy to be alive for no reason. She loved the beach. I used to know a girl who missed her brother. Her sister was a musician. She wanted to be an actress. I hope she makes it. A girl with a beautiful singing voice was in love with me, but I didn't know it. I still know a girl who takes the best photos. Chisaki and I don't talk much, but we still keep in touch. She sent me a photo she took that won a prize. It's a black girl playing chess against a Japanese boy. She titled it: The Game. I framed it and put it next to the poem with purple flowers Mia made me for my seventeenth birthday. There's a knock on the door.

"Ciao! It's me! Want a glass of wine?"

Isabel is holding out a too full glass of red wine to me. She is the person who treats everyday like a party.

"Thanks Isabel," I say and she grabs me hard by the arm and yanks me into the garden.

We sit down on the grass. The sky is light blue, and the sun is white gold. Isabel lights up a cigarette and puffs on it. I kind of miss The Soul Keeper and his strange ways.

"Where's my beautiful Mia?" she asks.

"She's at the market. She should be home soon."

I sip on the wine Isabel gave me, but there's too much. The glass should be half full, but it's almost spilling out of the top. Isabel laughs as I try not to spill it on my white tee shirt.

"Don't leave her alone too long. Another man will snatch her up," laughs Isabel, in her raspy voice.

"I told you, Mia is my stepsister."

Isabel thought we were a young married couple when we first moved in. She ignores what I say, though.

"Love is love! In Italy, nothing is more important than love!" Isabel is kind of drunk but it's not annoying. She is passionate and bold. A lot of Italian women are this way. It's very different from Japan where all the girls are shy.

"Okay, okay, calm down Isabel."

I am only half joking. My wine glass isn't as full, but I am still worried I'm going to splash it on myself. Our house is surrounded by daisies and white oleanders. The breeze is light and kicks up the floral fragrance. The oleanders remind me of California.

"Why aren't you two together?" asks Isabel as she downs the last of her wine and lights up another cigarette.

"I already told you."

I laugh, but Isabel isn't having it. She sticks her cigarette in my face as she talks. Italian women gesture wildly with their hands and have booming voices.

"C'mon Ryon! It is so obvious. I know a man in love when I see one," she grins at me as she takes a long drag.

The cherry turns bright red, and the ash looks like it's about to fall off.

"I don't know."

I throw up my hands, and my wine sloshes into the grass. Isabel takes it away from me and takes a large gulp before handing it back.

"You think because she is your stepsister that you can't be in love? I don't know how love works in Japan, but here there are no rules. Love is love. It is the most wonderful thing in the world. It would make Mia very happy," she says matter-of-factly.

Isabel and Mia keep secrets from me like most women do. It doesn't make me mad, though. They don't have bad intentions.

"How do you know?"

"Mia has been proposed to twice." Isabel has an impish grin painting her face.

I shake her shoulder playfully.

"Hey! I thought it was just the one time," I tease.

"Three days ago when we were getting coffee, a man stopped her in the street. Told her he was in love with her! He didn't hesitate. Why can't you be more like him?" she teases and acts like she's going to pinch me.

"I guess I'm worried I'll mess things up," I admit.

Feeling Isabel eye my wine, I down it in one gulp. It's dry but good. It has hints of chocolate.

"Pshhh," says Isabel as she paws at me.

We get up and head back to the house. Isabel stops to admire my new motorcycle. I sold the black one my dad got me and bought a red one. Mia says this one suits me better.

"I'm making puttanesca tonight! I'll bring some over!"

Isabel shouts at me over her shoulder. Her wine glass is empty, and she hurries back to her house to refill it. Her orange dress is loose and flowy. She has dark brown hair that she keeps in a loose French twist, with pieces that frame her face. Isabel is always wearing red lipstick and heavy eyeliner, even at 9 am.

"Thank you, Isabel! See you later," I call and go back inside.

Mia should be here any minute. I got us a two-bedroom house, but she still refuses to sleep in there, so she uses it as an art studio. There are canvases and tubes of paint everywhere. She has tons of brushes in every shape and size. Mia uses everything: acrylic, oil, and watercolors.

"Hey kid," says a familiar voice.

It's The Soul Keeper. I turn around and see him sitting on the windowsill like a cat.

"Noburu, what are you doing here?" I ask.

"Just came to check on you. I like your new place. Real cozy," he says as he runs his hands along the yellow curtains.

"Thank you. I can't thank you enough."

"Don't sweat it. I miss having you as my assistant."

Noburu looks out the window and admires the ocean waves. There are seabirds calling to one another. The sun is in Noburu's eyes, but he doesn't squint. He looks straight at it. I wonder if the demon that controls the sun is speaking to him.

"Noburu, can you tell me what's in my heart?" I ask.

The Soul Keeper hops off the windowsill and walks up to me. He puts his jeweled hand on my chest.

"Mia," he says.

Her name leaves his mouth and I hear her opening the door. By the time I look back, The Soul Keeper is gone.

***

We are walking on the beach. She's wearing a white bikini. It's new. She looks older, but still sweet and innocent. Her hair is down and the wind moves it around her in black swirls. She is laughing and smiling at me. We splash water at each other and run down the shore. Mia is real.

She reaches up for a bird that flies over her. It is small and cute. I almost think it's going to let her touch it, but it flies just an inch too high. The blue jewels she wears sparkle in the sunlight. The one on the snowflake is the biggest and brightest. I decide to lie down in the warm sand and enjoy the sun. Mia likes the cold ocean, but I like the heat.

There are clouds shaped like hearts. They float by and expand into elephants and whales. I put my hand in the sand. A million broken flecks. My ribs have been broken multiple times. I have been broken inside. The beach reminds me we can be lost and broken, but life is still beautiful.

Mia reads her poems at a cafe twice a month. They all love her there. It's amazing to see the way people love her here. No one makes fun of her poems or paintings. All the men want to marry her but aren't aggressive about it. The girls think she's a doll and want to be her friend. Mia was never appreciated in Japan, but in Italy she is the popular one.

Everyone likes me, but I'm the quiet one now. While they all speak about the complexities of art and human emotion, I listen, but don't have much to say. I think I understand Mia more. There are times I want to speak but don't know what to say. I am usually the confident, talkative one, but I enjoy letting Mia take the lead.

Last week, Mia read a poem that made everybody applaud. Isabel did her hair again. Mia wears high heels every day now. Her lips were red and so was her dress. She is still blue, but it mixes with red and makes purple. I listened to her speak with no shake in her voice, no whisper, and no softness. Mia reads her poem with conviction.

At midnight
In my dreams

Velvet flowers
Every time I see a palm tree,
I think of ya
every day, I wonder
If angels are born in California

Her accent makes her more adorable. She hugged me after and people covered their hearts as they looked in our direction. Mia waved goodbye to them, but they didn't want her to go. The people of Italy love that she's different. She never needed to change. I just had to take her somewhere she belongs. All of a sudden, there are wet legs straddling me and her cold hands are touching my face. It makes us both laugh. This time, I don't push her away. She kisses me and I kiss her.

Yesterday, I saw Mia standing in front of a fountain. She was wearing a light blue dress. Her purse was yellow, and she rummaged around in it until she found a coin. She held it in her palms like she was praying. Mia kept it close to her heart for a moment before tossing it into the water. I walked up behind her. It startled her, and she seemed embarrassed. I asked what she wished for. Of course, she didn't want to tell me, but I finally got her to. She said she wished for me to kiss her, so I did. I picked her up, which made everyone watching really happy. People in Italy make out everywhere and don't care if you kiss your girlfriend in public.

No matter what I do, someone tells me the way I love Mia is wrong. I've done bad things for her, but she's happy. That absolves me of my crimes. Despite the odds, we've been reunited in this life. I hope we are together in the next. The Soul Keeper said I've always loved her. I know it in my heart. People have never understood the way I feel about Mia. I don't care anymore. This is how I love her now.

THE END